Stephen Metcalfe's stage plays include *Vikings, Strange Snow, The Incredibly Famous Willy Rivers, Emily and Loves* and *Hours*. Screen credits include *Cousins, Jacknife* and *Beautiful Joe* as well as the production drafts of *Pretty Woman* and *Mr. Holland's opus*. He is the author of two novels, *The Tragic Age* and *The Practical Navigator,* both published by St. Martin's Press.

Stephen Metcalfe

ATTACHMENT PATTERNS

AUSTIN MACAULEY PUBLISHERS™

LONDON • CAMBRIDGE • NEW YORK • SHARJAH

Ordering Information
Quantity sales: Special discounts are available on quantity purchases by corporations, associations, and others. For details, contact the publisher at the address below.

Publisher's Cataloging-in-Publication data
Metcalfe, Stephen
Attachment Patterns

ISBN 9798886931815 (Paperback)
ISBN 9798886931822 (Hardback)
ISBN 9798886931839 (ePub e-book)

Library of Congress Control Number: 2023901598

www.austinmacauley.com/us

First Published 2023
Austin Macauley Publishers LLC
40 Wall Street, 33rd Floor, Suite 3302
New York, NY 10005
USA

mail-usa@austinmacauley.com
+1 (646) 5125767

Week 1

Day 1 – Crazy

If there was one good thing that the artist, Robert Boone, brought away from his first day of cognitive behavioral therapy, it was the thought that if he was crazy, he certainly wasn't as crazy as a lot of people. That he was attending an outpatient clinic at a hospital in New Haven, Connecticut, that was crazy. That he was paying for part of it, yes, that was crazy too. That his health plan was paying for the rest of it, in fact, *most* of it, well, that was crazy on their part. But was he as crazy as the demented looking guy standing in the mid-morning March downpour, puffing morosely on a cigarette?

Not likely.

Was he as crazy as the middle aged, black woman who, standing in the hallway, claimed in a strained, angry voice, that she would be happier if her entire neighborhood of "junkies, pushers, whores and gangbangers" were wiped from the face of the earth, gone, forgotten, had never existed in the space-time continuum at all so she could finally *"get out of my apartment"*?

Hardly.

Was he as crazy as the dark-haired, young man with cerebral palsy who, dragging himself thirty minutes late into the opening lecture, fell into a chair, and then proceeded to interrupt the therapist every five minutes to go off on long, incoherent, monologues.

"...the entire COG model of what is post-Covid normal reflects an Evangelical Christian morality code that should be exorcised from the cultural zeitgeist at all fucking costs and..."

– until he was unequivocally told by the instructor to *save it for discussion group*.

Was Dad as crazy as that?

(Well, maybe.)

No, I can tell you that my father, Robert Boone – *Dad* – didn't consider himself crazy at all. What had brought him to this seventeen-day mental health program (he said) was an aberration, that's all. A glitch. A moment of unexplainable weakness.

Three weeks earlier on a temperate February afternoon, after coming in from a five mile run, Dad was greeting his dogs, Mick and Angela, when he had inadvertently burped. Almost immediately he experienced a bad taste in his mouth followed by a sudden ache in his throat. His chest muscles had begun to feel tight, then his shoulders and neck and it suddenly felt as if there were electricity in his hair and beard. The more he tried to ignore the symptoms the worse they became. Coronary distress? Ridiculous. Dad averaged twenty miles of roadwork a week. He worked out with a trainer on Mondays and Thursdays. He was *in shape*. And then, suddenly, he thought of Jim Fixx, the man who had written the best-selling *The Complete Book of Running*. Dead of a heart attack while jogging at the age of 52 (just four years older than Dad). Panic set in and, dripping with cold sweat, my father called 911. It was in the ambulance on the way to the emergency room in New Haven, his hands numb, his heart tightly beating in his chest, that he realized he was experiencing something totally unexpected.

Blessed relief.

It was over. At last. No more pretending. No more ruminating. No more staring at the walls while silently railing against the storm. A few things unfinished, some people to be dearly missed (me!) but he could live – *die* – with that. Dad went into the emergency room as relaxed as he had ever been in his life and when, after a complete inspection of engine, chassis and tires, he was told he had suffered heartburn followed by a panic attack, nothing more, he began to weep. The weeping gave way to deep racking sobs and after any number of increasingly violent statements, all along the lines of – Oh, Lord, I want to die, I'm going to kill myself, give me a knife and let me kill myself! Robert Boone, ever the creative artist, made a sudden lunge for a nurse's ballpoint pen, fortunately grabbing nothing but the woman's ample boob. He later said he felt as if he were standing outside himself quietly watching as he was sedated and sent on a stretcher to the hospital's in-patient psychiatric ward where he finally slept.

Twenty four hours later he was himself again. Which means (according to him) he was stoic, practical and eminently self-possessed. Only the in-patient staff, the brainless *doctors*, refused to believe it. They wanted to know if he was depressed. Did he feel hopelessness? Anxious? Did he sleep well? Had he ever experienced suicidal thoughts in the past?

"No, no, no, yes and hasn't everybody at some time or another in the last several years wanted to *shoot themselves*? Now may I go home?"

"Not yet," said the *doctors.*

"Let's put it another way," said Dad. "I'm leaving."

Only he couldn't.

The not-so-brainless *doctors* proceeded to explain to him that if they thought he was in any way a threat to himself and others, they could detain or *section* him for up to fifteen days of observation.

"Do I at least get a phone call?" asked Dad. He did and he immediately called his best friend, agent and art dealer, Carter Hurley, in New York.

"Carter, this is Bob. I need you to get me a lawyer."

"Why?"

"Ah, I'm stuck in the hospital and they won't let me out."

"What?"

"They think I'm planning to kill myself."

"Why would they think that?"

"Because I said I was."

"Bob!"

Dad rationalized, poo-poohed and underplayed and Carter, once slightly assuaged, called a lawyer he knew who immediately called the hospital and proceeded in no uncertain terms to tell them *who the artist, Robert Boone, was.* To which the hospital replied they didn't give a slimy booger if Robert Boone was the President of the United States, they were not going to let him go anywhere until they were convinced he wasn't going to go home and grab the nearest ball point pen.

(Good for them.)

For the next three days, my father lay in bed and stared at the ceiling. He ate in the ward's cafeteria where he found the food inedible. He watched bad television with any number of people in hospital masks and bathrobes, all of whom seemed to be comatose with fatigue. Twice a day he was pulled into a cluttered, untidy office to answer questions. Dr. Giancarlo, a small, elfin looking man in his sixties with a head of abundant hair and a toothy smile, was (naturally) a psychiatrist.

"What do you do, Bob?" said Dr. Giancarlo, staring at the clipboard in his hand. For some reason the man was wearing a ski jacket.

"I'm a painter." Dad sighed. "An artist."

"Oh, really. You any good?"

"I make a living."

"Mmm," murmured Dr. Giancarlo. "You like being an artist?"

"It's not bad. Do you like being a shrink?"

"We're not here to talk about me, Bob, we're here to talk about you. You married?"

"No."

"Divorced?"

"No."

"Gay?"

"Hardly."

"Are you offended when I ask you that?"

"My answer was a statement of fact, not a moral judgement."

"You've never been married."

"I would suggest that's why I'm sane."

"Are you?" Dr. Giancarlo's eyes twinkled. "No children then."

My father hesitated. "A daughter," he finally said.

(That would be *me*!)

"Oh." Dr. Giancarlo waited. He waited some more. Dr. Giancarlo finally stopped waiting. "How'd you make it through the pandemic, Bob? Any lingering fears or anxieties?"

"I work alone and live alone. It wasn't that big a deal."

"Mmm. There are scars on your hand, where did they come from?"

Dad glanced down. The scars were small, white whispers on the top of his right hand and fingers. "I had a fight with a truck radiator, the radiator won."

Dr. Giancarlo made a quick note on his clipboard. "So… all told, you're just one happy guy then."

"I'm not unhappy," said Dad with a shrug.

"Things are good."

"They're not bad."

Dr. Giancarlo smiled, his eyes no longer twinkling. "Then why is it you think you wanted to die, Bob?"

"I have no idea," said my father, suddenly feeling tricked, trapped and decidedly resentful. "I never wanted to before, I have no desire to now and I have no intention of ever considering it again. Now may I go home?"

"Mmm. No, I don't think so. We'll talk again tomorrow."

And so, they did. And the next day and the day after that. Dr. Giancarlo asked about Dad's childhood. He asked about his relationships, about his overall sense of self. Was my father an optimist or a pessimist? Did he use sex, drugs or money to make himself feel good? Before the pandemic and now after, did he socialize much? (Hah!) "What are you, Bob, feeling at this exact moment?" Dad bobbed, weaved, fabricated and outright lied until *finally*, at the end of the third day, a compromise was reached. He would be released from the hospital *if* he promised to see a therapist and *if* he agreed to enroll in the hospital's out-patient cognitive behavioral therapy program, which was, explained Dr. Giancarlo, "A practical approach to mental health issues. By changing a patient's pattern of thinking, we can change the way he feels about himself and others."

"And why should I do this?" asked Dad. (It sounded like gobble-de-gook to him.)

"Because," said Dr. Giancarlo, not smiling and not twinkling, "it is my opinion, Bob, that you *are* depressed, *are* anxious, are *not* happy and unless you do something about it, you're going to wind up in the hospital again. Or worse."

Dad quickly agreed, signed some papers, walked out the door and went home. When asked what he was going to do by his long time housekeeper, Marisol, who, having been there, was aware of the situation, he replied, "Nada. Nothing at all."

Only I – *me*, Isolde Boone, Robert Boone's sophisticated, stunning daughter – wouldn't let him. Having heard what happened from Carter who was concerned my father wasn't returning his phone calls and having gotten the details from Marisol who said he was acting like everything was completely normal, I jumped on the next train out of New York, insisting that he meet me at the New Haven train station. There, my father quickly hugged me, kissed me on the cheek, took my bag, muttered, "Let's get out of here," and hightailed it towards the door. I waited until we were in his pick-up, driving out to Branford to voice my concern. As always I was compassionate and caring.

"You are such an asshole, Dad! You really are such a self-involved creep!"

"Oh? And why is that?"

I was happy to tell him. *"Da-add!* You were threatening suicide! You were saying you wanted to be *dead!* And then, you didn't even tell me that it happened! How do you think that makes me feel? Huh? How?"

"You've wished me dead a lot of times," said Dad, ignoring the second part of my monologue.

"That's when I was pissed at you! That was just talking!"

"Oh. Does that mean you're just talking now?"

"No! I'm yelling! This is not talking, this is yelling!"

"I think you're making a big deal out of nothing."

"Da-add! This is not nothing!"

My volume and intensity – my *yelling* – didn't bother my father in the least. Twenty-six years old and an aspiring writer living in New York, I had excelled at righteous indignation from an early age. I also knew that there were only a small number of people in the world who could get La-de-dah Robert Boone to even consider doing something he didn't want to do and I was at the very top of the list. Better believe I took full advantage of it. That night when I said to him that if he didn't do the cognitive behavioral program, I wouldn't be seeing him again any time soon, "Because you have to, *okay?* I want you around for a long time!" Dad knew the lamb shoulder with a mint chimichurri sauce he'd prepared for dinner was toast.

With no choice now, the following Monday morning, my very grumpy father got up early, drank some French press coffee, ate an English muffin, took a last threatening phone call from me down in New York – "I'll be checking on you, better believe it!" – got in his old, red pick-up truck and reluctantly drove in. At the hospital he was directed to the inpatient office where he filled out paperwork and answered questions. Had he been vaccinated recently? Vaccinated any number of times, replied Dad with a sigh. (His arm still ached.) He was then given a thin, bound text, a notebook, a ball point pen (dramatic irony?) and a small plastic badge with his name on it – Robert B. A masked nurse arrived to escort him out and down the hall, then through a door into a courtyard where, as if an omen of what was ahead, it had begun to rain.

They continued inside through yet another door to finally come into a small lecture hall, where Dad took off his jacket, sat down in an uncomfortable, hard back chair with attached tablet arm and watched as what he assumed were his fellow patients/inmates filed in and took their seats.

The lecture, when it started, was given by a young woman in her late twenties and was on, of all things, the subjects of Guilt and Shame.

Guilt, intoned the young woman, is a *strong emotion.*

(And one best to be avoided, thought Dad, as all around him people nodded and scribbled in their notebooks.)

Guilt is linked to the feeling that something is or has been *expected of you.*

(My father felt that as an artist, it was important to *defy expectations* so obviously this didn't apply to him.)

Guilt is often linked to *should have* statements.

(Dad was of the opinion that *should haves* applied to things in the past that couldn't be changed and because they couldn't, weren't worth worrying about. Hopefully this was going to get better. He had things to do.)

Shame then, said the young woman, is the painful feeling brought on by an overly acute sense of *guilt.* It is often associated with *secrecy* and *avoidance.*

(No, it wasn't getting better. In Dad's opinion (and mine), too many people spent too much time either asking for permission or begging for forgiveness. Dad (and *me*) circumvented both options by unequivocally speaking our minds up front, not after the fact. (It was Dad's opinion this was why I didn't have a steady boyfriend.) As for secrets, my father had no intention of discussing any he might have had. That's why they were called secrets.)

At this point an interruption was called for and so a buzz headed thirty year old with garish tattoos and gauge earrings raised his hand as if he were in grade school and when called upon (did Dad detect a wince in the face of the young lecturer?) proceeded with some relish to embark upon a long, drawn out list of dark actions, all of them sexually explicit, that made him feel ashamed and worthless. He went on until a middle-aged woman pulled down her hospital mask and loudly protested – "And so they damn well should!" A small uproar ensued.

(Was it going to be three weeks of this, thought my father? He'd never make it.)

Guilt, continued the lecturer, after she had suggested the young man with the gauge earrings take a bathroom break, was short term, while *shame* was long term. Guilt had the potential to be good as it kept one's *behaviors* in line.

Shame, however, if unresolved, could easily evolve into *depression*. It was, therefore, important…

And this is when the dark haired, young man with cerebral palsy entered the room, disrupting the lecture for the next five minutes, "…to *evaluate* a given situation and using *facts*, assign the appropriate responsibility to the appropriate parties, one's self included."

Okay, this was not uninteresting. My father liked facts. Facts were good. But as for appropriate parties, (I mean, really?) there were none. It was an every man for himself world out there. Best to keep other parties at a distance so as avoid those given situations as much as possible. (Easily said, not easily done.)

The young woman then went onto discuss how one could determine if one was holding oneself to a higher standard than others and if he'd been listening my father would have said that yes, he did do that and proudly so but he wasn't listening. He had opened his notebook and taking his ballpoint, was doing sketches of the faces he'd seen in the course of the morning, breaking them up and reassembling them in abstract, multiple of points of view. He didn't stop until the lecturer called for five minutes of mindfulness which Dad also ignored completely.

"Group," which took place in a small, claustrophobic room, was thankfully short lived. Introductions were made by the group's resident therapist, another woman in her late 20s. For my father's benefit, basic rules were gone over. What happened in COG stayed in COG, any mention of politics was *not* permitted, group members were asked *not* to communicate with one another outside of group and no physical intimacies, however innocent, were permitted – no hugs, no pats on the back, no handholding. Face masks were optional and – "Lunch tickets are available if you wish to go the hospital cafeteria after group."

(I can tell you that at this point Dad had no intention of talking to or touching anybody and it goes without saying the thought of another hospital cafeteria was about as appetizing as Campbell's soup.)

They then went around the circle making introductions that went in one ear and out the other. Other than the strained looking, black woman who had said she wanted her entire neighborhood extinguished from the face of the earth so she could get out of the house, my father's fellow group members consisted of a very large, dour looking man in his mid-to-late thirties, a balding, cheerful man in his forties, an unshaven, vacant eyed man around thirty, the crazed, young man (whoa, boy!) with cerebral palsy and – she arrived late and between shy smiles, apologized profusely for it – a plump, pleasant looking woman with a mop of Shirley Temple curly hair and a prominently displayed silver cross hanging from a chain around her neck.

After listening to how depressed and/or anxious the others were (there was a checklist for it) and then, how they planned to spend the rest of their day, Dad was given his own break down sheet on depression and anxiety. A quick glance told him that except for a mildly upset stomach, due no doubt to a rushed bowel movement on this less than typical morning, he was at a steady one for both.

(Liar, liar, pants on…)

Several minutes later, to his vast relief, Dad was pulled from the group by an attractive, dark skinned woman in a sari. She led him to a small examination room where she took his vital signs and asked about pre-existing conditions, finally releasing him.

Finished for the day, my father left the examination room, walked down the corridor to the men's room and entered, only to find the two small urinals occupied. As one man finished and turned to the sink to wash his hands, an unshaven, zombie eyed guy in filthy clothes and a ragged, short brimmed cowboy hat, entered and not waiting his turn, pushed past, went straight to the free urinal, unzipped, emptied his bladder, turned and with zipper still down and dangling, exited out the door. Dad stood a moment, then moved to the urinal and careful not to let anything touch anything (men have that advantage), took his own pleasant pee. He then moved to the small sink and using hot water and soap, diligently washed then dried his hands. Crazy? Maybe so. But not as lonesome cowboy, zipper down crazy as that.

With this final reassuring thought in mind, the ever enduring artist, Robert Boone, went outside, got into his pick-up and drove home, contemplating what he would make for dinner.

So

So. It goes without saying that everything I've told you so far, and will tell you from this moment on, was disclosed to me, confided in me, remembered by me, surmised by me and in some cases (okay, more than some;) is totally and completely made up.

(By me.)

Still, all of it is the God's honest truth.

Day 2 – Difficult People

It was Tuesday, the second morning of Cog, and in group, my father had shared his depression and anxiety levels. He'd decided to raise them both to a six, which was the high end of mild, so as to avoid questions from his fellow group members, all of whom seemed to be in their forties, fifties and in the case of the despondent, unshaven man, the nineties. This meant that they all thought that the future was hopeless, they were expecting to be punished or infected, were blaming themselves for their faults (and infections), had lost interest in people, were terrified with the state of the world, weren't sleeping well and were suffering from various levels of constipation.

The only things Dad had identified with was a nervous stomach and a loss of interest in people, but since he had never had any real interest in people (other than the chosen few) and because, once again, he hadn't had time for his usual leisurely morning sit on the toilet, these didn't count.

He had also been forced to share his "Grapes." This was an acronym for Gentle with Self, Relaxation, Accomplishment, Pleasure, Exercise and Social. Grapes, Dad was told, were a very useful tool in maintaining emotional regulation and planning one's day. Three out of the six had him flummoxed.

Accomplishment? He would work, of course. (Whether he accomplished anything or not, well, that had been debatable for a while now.)

Exercise? He did that most every day as well. He ran, he lifted, he rowed on machines. It kept him – (Oops, dare we use this word?) – *sane*. More important, it also allowed him to eat pretty much whatever he pleased. Case in point. For dinner, that night, he was already contemplating a roast chicken Provencal accompanied by a fresh green salad and a nice Cotes de Rhone. But relax. Who could relax?

(Relax does not run in this family.)

Oh, but then Dad consulted the list on the back of the sheet and saw that *reminding* himself to relax would suffice. Fine, he could do that. Four down.

17

As to Gentle With Self, the list suggested things like self-forgiveness, self-encouragement and self-help books. (If all else fails, I plan on writing one someday.) No, Dad went further into the list and settled for drinking enough water daily. Good for him, one to go.

Social. That was the tough nut to crack. By habit and inclination, he was not social. Attend a www.meetup.com group? What was that? (I could have told him.) Whatever it was, it was not going to happen.

Go to a social event through church? To my father, religion had always seemed like a bad business agreement with an unseen employer. Work hard and toe the company line and in return, receive not a salary but a retirement bonus that was quite possibly a scam as the payout was given once the employee had stepped off the mortal coil into the hereafter. No, he didn't think he'd like a church social. (And I doubt a church social would have liked him.)

Talking to another group member on break seemed the best idea. It would have to be tomorrow after the lecture and hopefully he'd forget about it by then. If he came back at all.

Dad sighed.

The subject of the morning lecture had been Coping With Difficult People and it hadn't been helpful. The lecturer, Gwyneth, yet another young woman, this one wearing librarian glasses, had explained that there were any number of kinds of difficult people, a fact he already knew. It amounted to this.

The *passive* person is the person who avoids conflict but won't forget about it.

(One of my first boyfriends.)

The *aggressive* person is the person who seeks to control the situation with volume, passion and intensity.

(Hello!)

The *passive-aggressive* person is a person who won't engage in conflict but leaves you no doubt you're going to *pay for it*.

(My *last* boyfriend).

The *thwarter* is the person who has the uncanny ability to frustrate or upset you even when you know you're right.

(Mom).

The *stubborn* person is the individual so obstinate, they won't be swayed by a tsunami.

(Dad, unless the tsunami is me).

And finally – the *judgmental* person, the *complainer* and the *victim*. These are people who will admit you're right but add that it isn't fair and they're helpless to do anything about it.

(My college roommates freshman year and good riddance.)

This was all old information as Dad had long ago come to the conclusion that people were argumentative, incoherent and best to be avoided, which was why he was having a problem filling in the social block on his Grapes sheet.

Regardless, here he was now in a bare, claustrophobic room, now being asked to explain himself to a small herd of strangers sitting in hard backed chairs. This was not how he wished to spend the morning.

"You want to fill the group in on why you're here, Bob?"

"Uh…no, I'd rather not," said my father.

He now knew the group therapist's name was Heidi. When he had mentioned the chicken and Cotes de Rhone as part of his grape's pleasure package she had quietly pointed out that "people, while in the COG program, are asked not to drink."

(This was another reason why he might not be coming back tomorrow.)

Heidi looked down at her notes. "You were in the hospital saying you wanted to kill yourself, Bob. Why don't you tell us about that."

(Holy…!)

The young man with cerebral palsy looked up, intrigued. The Shirley Temple haired, pleasant faced woman's expression went to one of immediate consternation. The other members of the group seemed on high alert. Dad cringed inside. Still…

"I'd really rather not."

"Mmm. Well then, in that case why don't we do some thought records for later in the week."

"Which are?" asked Dad, knowing they weren't anything good.

Which are, explained Heidi, a way to look truthfully and rationally at your life. "Several times a day write down your thoughts and feelings, especially when you have an emotional reaction to something. What we'll do then is try and see how much you really believe it to be true. And if it isn't, we'll try to find a balanced replacement."

"Sounds good," said my father, having already made up his mind not to do it. No need as he now was *definitly* not coming back tomorrow.

"Can anyone talk about their own issues," said Heidi, "so Bob can better relate to what he's feeling?"

Of course they could!

Apocalypse hungry Megan J. furiously asked, "Just what am I s'posed to tell people about this *"agoraphobic"* thing these doctors say I have? That after being stuck in my apartment for like, *forever*, I been terrified to leave it the last year and a half? And when I do, I just want to go running back! What do I tell my husband and kids? Sorry baby, I can't go shopping for groceries no more, what you see now is what you get? What do I tell *you* people? I didn't ask for this to happen! Let some other girl have it!"

(My father wasn't completely sure what an "agoraphobic thing" was but by the sound of it, yes, he was happy to let somebody else have it.)

After suggesting to Megan J. that she quietly *discuss* these feelings and fears with her husband and children so they better understood what she was dealing with, the group turned their attention to vacant eyed and scraggily bearded William G. who proceeded to explain in a monotone voice that he was still dealing with severe depression due to his now two year old divorce. He was unable to work, unable to socialize and unable to think clearly. He was living with his parents and he wasn't allowed to see his kids which was okay because he didn't want them to *"see me like this."*

"Have you been working with the pleasurable activitiies inventory and the activity planning form?" asked Heidi, gently.

"No," said William G.

"Why not?"

"I'm too depressed."

Hmmm. My father's immediate reaction was that he wanted to kick stolid, scraggily William G. in the ass and tell him to stop feeling sorry for himself. Obviously he was alone in his opinion. After encouraging William G. to recognize his negative thoughts and substitute them with balanced, *realistic* ones (Huh?), the group moved on to the young man with cerebral palsy, Colin L., who, as in the lecture hall, spoke with such bitter, manic intensity, Dad could barely understand him.

"...And I know the whole object of COG is to make me feel better and in order to feel better I need to change the way I think but if I change the way I think, I'll be changing who I am, which pisses me off so fucking much—"

"I think we're getting a little off topic," said Heidi.

Acknowledging that he was:

"…because I have to leave early today because I'm stuck *again* with public transportation which totally sucks because I'm still not convinced it's even *safe* and…"

Colin S. went on for another red-faced three minutes and then left to go catch the bus.

(Dad's feeling about all this was that he too would have been profoundly pissed off if he had to take public transportation.)

The group then turned to the seemingly cheerful man, Walt O., who, during the Covid epidemic, he said, had fallen prey to such severe panic attacks he'd been hospitalized. He'd had no choice but to leave his job as a high school history teacher and now was uncertain as to whether he wanted to return to it. His wife of fourteen years—"a real go-getter"—was less than sympathetic and had been *on edge* for awhile now because of *"the loss of income."* She was talking about a trial separation, furthering Walt O's fear and anxiety. Still, Walt O. was all smiles. "The new meds are starting to kick in. Oh – and I'm working on my Deesc script."

"Death script?" Dad unwittingly blurted out the words, for that's what he'd thought he'd heard. The group collectively chuckled.

"Deesc scripts," said Heidi, making it sound like *desk*, "are a communication tool. Describe the situation. Express what we feel. Empathize with the other person. Specify what we want. Discuss the positive consequences."

(Another anocronym! COG is full of them.)

"I'm going to try it out on my wife tonight," said Walt O., all smiles.

(Good luck, thought Dad. If the man's wife was already on edge, reciting from a script certainly wasn't going to elicit any kind of standing ovation. Unless his talented daughter – *me* – wrote it.)

"Beverly," said Heidi in a soothing voice. "Would you like to tell us how you've been doing?"

Beverly. So that was the plump, Shirley Temple haired woman's name. "Well…" Her mouth crinkled pleasantly and her brown eyes widened. "I've been working on the forgiveness letter to myself."

"A forgiveness letter," Heidi explained to my father, "is a way of showing compassion for ourselves for something that happened in the past. We try to acknowledge that we did the best we could with what we had at the time."

(Great, thought Dad, also thinking that along with the evening's roast chicken he might make a simple rice pilaf.)

"Do you feel up to sharing your letter with us?" asked Heidi.

"Oh, yes, I'd really like that," said Beverly, exuding heartfelt gratitude. And with that, she reached down into the bag at her feet, took out a small notebook, opened it and settled back. To Dad's horror, her brown eyes began to pool with tears. "I want to forgive myself for not – not being there…" The voice broke down into a soft, keening moan. "…for my daughter, when she needed me the most…"

Beverly sagged in her chair. It was as if her arms were trying to a clutch a child close to her body but the weight was too much and she didn't have the strength.

"You were eighteen. You didn't know what postpartum depression even was. You just knew something terrible was going to happen."

(You always know.)

"And then it did," moaned Beverly. "You broke down. You had to leave your daughter and go to the hospital. You thought your husband would be there for her but he wasn't. Neighbors heard your daughter crying. No one had fed her… or changed her diapers. She was all alone."

Tears washed down Beverly cheeks and slid off her chin. Heidi handed Beverly a box of tissue. Beverly wiped her eyes. Her flushed faced beamed with gratitude. "Do you want to continue?" Heidi asked quietly. Beverly took a breath and then nodded her head. The focus from the group was palpable.

"You and your husband divorced. Four years later you met another man, a wonderful man, and the two of you got married."

"And you two had your own children," said Heidi.

Beverly nodded. "A boy and a girl. God's blessed me so much."

(God again. How was it God always gets the gratitude but never the blame? Sorry to interrupt.)

"You tried to be a good mother. You tried to be there for your daughter… but it was like she hated you. She'd go to her father's, who'd let her do anything she wanted. Then in high school she started hanging with horrible people, stealing and using drugs. Pills. Opioids. And when she couldn't afford those, heroin. I don't know why but she was in *pain*."

(Stop. Dad wanted Beverly to stop but he knew she wouldn't. There were times when it's impossible to stop. Not even pain killers killed pain.)

22

Beverly hummed a chord deep in her throat and forced herself to continue. "When she was nineteen, she took her things and moved out. You wouldn't see her for months at a time. And then, out of nowhere, she got pregnant and came home. She didn't know who the father was but it didn't matter. She cleaned up. She stopped using drugs. She seemed so happy. *You* were so happy. But she started using again right after the baby was born. You begged her to stop but she wouldn't. She left the house again… and you couldn't find her. And then one afternoon, out of nowhere, you got a call… your daughter had OD'd in a room in some ugly neighborhood… she was dead." Dropping the notebook, Beverly sagged in her chair and wept.

Click.

The involuntary camera that was my father's brain saw diamonds cascading from tortured eyes.

Click.

Beverly's face was breaking into rough, jagged pieces.

(Women, the artist and male, chauvinist pig, Pablo Picasso, once said, are suffering machines. Who's fault is *that*?)

"Beverly?" Heidi asked softly.

"Yes."

"How old was she when she died?"

"She was twenty-two."

"And her child – your grandchild – is with you."

"Yes. She's five years old now. She's beautiful."

"And what is your relationship with her like?"

"She calls me Mommy."

(Of course she does, thought Dad.)

"I think," said Heidi, "we can all agree that you tried to do all you could for your daughter and that it's time to take yourself off the hook."

"I know. It's just…" Beverly, wiped at her eyes and runny nose. "I was supposed to *be there* for her."

"You were, baby, you were," angry Megan J. said softly. "Shit happens. Sometimes nothin' you can do."

The others in the circle all nodded and murmured their agreement as Beverly closed her eyes and shook with emotion.

(Talk about difficult people!*)*

My father's pick-up truck hit 90 mph as he fled home.

Wiki-Notes

Did I mention that my father, the artist, Robert Boone, has a Wikipedia page? He totally does and guess what? He's never so much as looked at it. He's *aware* of it, he would *love* to know the person who set it up (it couldn't have been *me*) but he's never seen it. Total misanthrope that he is, my father doesn't use social media, doesn't own a cell phone or hates the very idea of a computer. This can make it difficult to look yourself up on line. Not that he would even if he could. No, I had to tell him about it. In detail, with relish, pride even. To which he replied, "Who writes this crap?" (Ouch.)

To start, Wikipedia will tell you that Robert Boone is an American Artist known for his range and versatility. His early work is rooted in both classical and modernist traditions and uses highly theatrical contrasts of light in modelling starkly realistic images while his later work shows the fierce influence of both fauvism and abstract expressionism.

Okay, reality check. If he ever *were* to read this, Dad would tell you that when it comes to art, he *hates* words and phrases like classical, modernist, starkly realistic and fierce influences. A painting is a painting is a painting. A steak is a steak. You like it or you don't. You respond to it or you don't. In his opinion, anything else is just gild on the lily that certain people use when attempting to prove to other people how smart they are. Prehistoric man was not thinking of classic tradition and starkly realistic when he etched his drawings on cave walls. In a candid moment, Dad might admit that he *does* have his influences but to refer to them as stark or fierce does them a disservice.

Wikipedia now goes on to say that Robert Boone was born in New Haven, Connecticut July 3rd, 1974. His father, Benjamin, was a sucessful lawyer and his mother, Mary, an illustrator of children's books. The family resided in Brandord, Connecticut where Robert first attended public school and began drawing and painting at an early age.

Yes, Dad was born in in New Haven, Connecticut and yes, his father, Benjamin, was a successful lawyer and yes, his mother, Mary, was an illustrator of children's books, but if you were to ask him, Dad would tell you that where he was born is irrelevant, that success is not necessarily synonymous with a family man working 60 hours a week and that to say his mother was just an illustrator of children's books is the equivalent of saying Shakespeare wrote some plays.

(Which ain't that easy. I've tried.)

From early he wouldn't know when, my father was enthralled with what his mother put on the page. I've seen the books. It's alternate worlds. It's child carrying bears chasing cloud-carrying zephyrs. It's doting fairy godmothers, magic pencils and talking flowers. It's innocence and faith.

In her own private time, Mary Boone worked in water colors, painting beach scenes of The Thimble Islands, Guilford marshes and Long Island Sound and from early on, my father would accompany her to play and listen as she worked. "Look, Bobby. Really look. Being an artist means seeing it, taking it in and letting it be a part of you. And then, when you begin, remember. There are no mistakes." Mary would smile, Dad would smile back and stick in hand, he'd continue carving swirls, curling lines and figures in the sand.

(So much for the influence of fauvism and abstract expressionism.)

Because of his mother and with her encouragement, my father began putting pen to paper when he was six and paint to canvas when he was ten. And now, the hard part.

In 1986 (says Wikipedia), Boone's mother, Mary and his two sisters, Melissa, 16 and Karen, 10, were killed in a car accident, victims of a drunk driver.

To simply state that Mary and my father's two sisters, Melissa and Karen, were killed in a car accident, victims of a drunk driver, is like saying the end of the world happened on an alternate Tuesday. Dad was focused on his drawing the morning his mother took the girls shopping and so he didn't go along. Coming back, driving east on Route 1, a pick-up came across the meridian doing at least 70 and impacted the car head on. It was whispered at the funeral that firemen had to use the jaws of life to pry apart the wreckage in order to free the mangled bodies inside. I'm not sure my father has ever been good enough with words to understand the irony. (But I am.)

What's the impact of sudden death on a thirteen year old boy? My father has never talked at length about it, not even to me who, when I was a eight years old, first asked. All we can do is move on, said Ben, his father. Which is what my grandfather did. He turned sixty hour work weeks into seventy and his single evening cocktail became a full blown martini habit. Four years later he'd marry a junior law associate, a woman Dad despised three minutes after meeting her. (It took me two).

Dad remembers his older sister, Melissa, as being outgoing and funny and popular with her peers. He remembers his younger sister, Karen, as angelic looking, quiet and shy, happiest when on the couch, curled up in her mother's arms.

(I think they all were.)

From 1989 to 1991 (continues Wikipedia), Robert Boone attended the Choate School in Wallingford, Connecticut where was considered a problem student. In 1991, he was accepted at the Rhode Island School of Design. He left after one year citing "an apathy for academia." For the next three years, he commuted on a semi-weekly basis from the family home in Connecticut to New York City where he attended classes at The Art Students League.

(Reality check. School. What is school? Education. What is true education? *Life.*)

In 1993, Robert Boone was introduced to Carter Hurly who, upon seeing Boone's work, insisted on showing him at The Hurley Gallery in New York. The now celebrated *Angels in the Darkness* are a series of paintings, all of which picture vividly realistic images of women and children, singularly and together, sometimes suggesting the idealic and the divine, but most often in a physical state of agitation. The figures are set against a vast, fugue-like blackness. In contrast, *The Sound* series are depictions of the shorelines and islands of Eastern Connecticut, featuring rich colour, masterful brushwork and bold contrasts of light and dark. Both series of paintings were embraced by critics and collectors alike. Five years later, the Aura paintings showed a complete change of technique. Influenced by the work of Jackson Pollack, Mark Rothko and Franz Kline, they were "action-paintings" in which Boone created the visual symptoms associated with pre-migraine auras.

(Influence. That word again. Finally, what really Wiki-matters:)

Robert Boone is known for his reclusive nature. He does not attend public showings, does not grant interviews, does not use e-mail or social media and he does not write about or comment on his work. His releases, for the last decade, have been minimal. His work continues to be highly sought-after by museums and collectors.

Okay, it's true. Dad doesn't get out much. And he doesn't talk much, at least not about himself and what he does. I think my father decided early on that the death of his mother and sisters was an event that people would use to define both him and his work and from the very beginning it was imperative that the work, *minimal* as it might be, stand on its own. A lame excuse to seek shelter from the storm? Maybe. All I can tell you is that when Robert Boone's daughter (me) looks at her father's paintings, what she sees is this. She sees unspoken memories. She sees loss and longing. She sees the faces and hears the voices he's kept hidden in the empty rooms of his heart.

(And even though I tried to gild the lily and now so wish I hadn't, let Wikepedia try and tell you that.)

Day 3 – Emotional Regulation

The subject of Wednesday's lecture was emotional regulation and my father, who was suffering from a slight hangover having drunk two bottles of red wine the evening before (think of it as a personal statement), thought of emotional regulation as a good thing, especially when it meant other people keeping their feelings to themselves. The lecturer today was not a young woman in librarian glasses but rather a handsome Hispanic man named Julio who started the lecture by saying, "Men! Are not big on *emotions!* Why? Anyone? Ladies?"

"Because they're jerks," said an older woman, drawing titters and head nods from every other woman in the room.

"Because they're cowards!" called a woman sitting two seats away from her.

"Hah! Goes without saying!" Julio was all grins. "We'd rather play golf or go fishing than talk about our feelings!"

(Everyone laughed except for Dad who groaned inside. He didn't need a stand-up comedian telling him what to feel. Three days in the lecture hall had made him realize that the majority of the participants in the COG program were ordinary looking folks who had come through a difficult time. Most of them were neatly, if casually dressed. The women, some of them still masked, sat clustered in the middle of the room, chatting amiably till the lecture began. Most of the men (like Dad, mostly unmasked) sat by themselves in the back or on the outskirts as if hesitant to admit they were even there. The exceptions, of course, were Colin L. and the man with the shaved head and gauge earrings. They both sat front row center, the better to interrupt the proceedings.)

"What," Julio continued, "is the difference between *thoughts* and *emotions*?" Not waiting for an answer, Julio turned to the whiteboard behind him and began to scribble. "*Thoughts*…are *ideas*…we tell ourselves…"

(Hmm. As often as possible Dad thought in pictures so obviously this didn't apply to him.)

"…while *emotions* are patterned *reactions*… that signal us *something is happening!*"

(Hah! This was not news to my father. In life, something was always happening. In fact, things happened *far too much* and when they inevitably did, people didn't handle it well. The result was helpless people, hopeless people, desperate people. Okay, yes, even *crazy* people. It was so annoying that in response, Dad often felt compelled to write anonymous checks which he sent off to organizations hoping that the organizations would make the annoyances go away. The organizations rarely did. Which was so doubly annoying that Dad occasionally felt compelled to get personally involved himself.

Just that morning, coming into New Haven off the I-95 with his head aching and his stomach upset, he had seen an unkempt, obese woman bundled in a worn, shapeless overcoat, sitting on the sidewalk. As he got closer he saw that that there were soiled blankets covering her legs and that she was holding a small sign – *I may be fat but I'm still hungry.* (Gah!) He'd had no choice but to swing the truck towards the sidewalk, stop, get out, reach into his pocket, take out his folded wad of cash, strip off the top three twenties and head averted, thrust them in the woman's general direction. "God bless you, sir," mewed the woman as she half-rose, trembling and reaching. Which increased Dad's level of annoyance to such a level of intensity he had no choice but to hand her two more twenties. Once she was safely back down, cash stashed in her coat and blankets back in place, he returned to his truck and motored on, already resolving that if he returned to the clinic tomorrow he'd take a different route.)

"This, then, is the COG model of emotional regulation," said Julio, still scribbling. "Our thoughts inspire *feelings*… and our feelings lead us to *actions* and *behaviors*. When *anxious*, we *avoid*… when *afraid*, we fight or run… when we are *sad*, we *isolate*… and when we feel *joy or love*… we feel the urge to *connect* with others."

Julio turned from the whiteboard. Was he looking straight at Dad? My father had the uncomfortable feeling he was. Thankfully the young man with the buzz cut and gauge earrings raised his hand. "When I feel sexual desire, I often feel the urge to demand subjugation from my—"

"Talk to me after the lecture," said Julio, cutting him off completely.

"I don't trust joy or affection," said Colin. "I think connecting with other people is pure fucking—"

"Colin. Put a lid on it."

(Hmmm. Dad suddenly sort of liked this guy.)

Julio tossed the marker aside. "By honestly identifying our thoughts and feelings, we can learn to act in ways that don't hurt us and don't hurt those we care about. *That* is emotional regulation."

(Well said.)

"I'm getting a cup of coffee," said Dad. "Can I buy you one?"

It was the break between lecture and group and cheerful, Walt O. was standing by himself in the hallway. It seemed a good opportunity to get the social block of his Grapes out of the way, nothing more. "Why, sure!" blurbled Walt O., smiling as if this was the most generous surprise anyone could have ever sprung on him. Off they went.

The coffee, served at an outdoor kiosk, was horrible. "This is horrible," said Dad. (It was an Italian roast, so tepid it wouldn't have stained a porcelain sink.)

"Oh," said Walt O. "Take mine." It was a mocha java and he quickly offered his paper cup.

"No, I can live with it." (Meaning the Italian roast.)

"Hah! What other choice is there," said Walt O, smiling again. (For someone afraid and anxious, Walt O. exuded the positive, good will of a Mormon missionary.)

"I was, uhm… moved by what you said yesterday," murmured Dad. (Moved was as good a word as any as it suggested a desire to go someplace else.) "Must have been difficult. Leaving your job." (Simple conversation with a fellow human being. It wasn't so hard.)

"No. I was, well… tired of it. The thing about teaching history is you come to realize history just keeps repeating itself. We never learn. Try teaching that to kids."

"And you and your wife are doing better?" (Best to change the subject. This was getting serious.)

Walt O. nodded. "She's a great girl. I'm lucky to have her. It's been tough though. She's still working from home half the time. Me, I'm just hanging around, always in the way."

(Yet another can of worms. Best to change the subject again.) "Any children?"

Walt O. suddenly seemed to be quivering. "Fraid not. She didn't want'm."

(Boy, oh, boy, this was the problem with talking to people. They *told* you things.) "Sorry if I'm being too personal."

"No, I appreciate it." Walt O. lowered his voice. "Between you and me, Bob, I was exactly where you are at one point. Gun to my head, didn't want to live. I'm better now."

"I think we better get going if we don't want to be late," said Dad, dumping his paper cup of bad coffee. He suddenly wondered if he should skip group, go home and walk the dogs. Oh, and Marisol was feeling under the weather today and it would be good to check in on her. He could do that as well.

(Sadly, he didn't.)

In group, the first person up was big, dour Paul F., whose apparent problem was that he felt persecuted by people at work constantly ordering him around and telling him what to do. Paul F. felt the solution to the problem was becoming the boss which meant *he'd* be the one ordering people around, telling everybody else what to do. "S*ee if they like it."*

"Where is it you work again?" asked pleasant Walt O.

"Home Depot."

"And how are you doing communicating with your husband?" asked Heidi.

(*Husband?* To Dad, Paul F. looked and sounded like an out of shape, NFL lineman. Perhaps he'd met his husband at a storm-the-capitol confrontation.)

"There's no communicating with him. All he wants to do is talk."

Heidi suggested that both these situations, job and home, showed a lack of *empathy*, meaning the ability to acknowledge the feelings of others.

(Which made Dad wonder if *he* was feeling empathy because he totally understood resenting someone telling him what to do.)

Empathy, continued Heidi, involved achnowledging another's point of view and making a concerted attempt to sympathize with their feelings, without negating your own. Paul F. nodded as if this made sense.

(Which made no sense to my father who decided he must have been feeling something else. Regardless, Paul F. seemed like a real dork.)

"When you criticize me for having given up my teaching position, it makes me feel frightened and ashamed."

It was Walt O.'s turn and he was reading from his Deesc script, the one that had been *encouragingly received* by his wife the evening before. "I get that my ongoing anxiety and lack of steady income has you on edge and that you expect more of me. But I'd really like it if you could try to be optimistic and encouraging about our future. If you can do that, I think I can move forward with a more positive attitude and help you do the same." Walt C. looked up, a hopeful expression on his face.

"Thoughts? Anyone?" asked Heidi , looking around the circle.

"I think it's wonderful," cooed curly-haired Beverly. She and Walt beamed at one another.

"Like I said, I deal with job and relationship issues too," said dour Paul F. "I know where you're coming from." Walt. C nodded gratefully.

"Any one else?" asked Heidi.

"I think you should tell your wife to go fuck herself!" snarled Colin.

(Like a stifled laugh coming out the wrong pipe, Dad farted into the seat of his chair.)

"You're dealing with mind blowing anxiety and your wife is concerned about your loss of fucking income!"

"Colin, is there another way you could express what you're feeling?" Heidi was looking alarmed.

"No! She's probably the reason he got all anxious to begin with!" Colin turned furiously back to Walt O. "You're the one who had to leave your job. You're the one who's on medication. How are you supposed to have empathy for someone who has no empathy for you? How do you empathize with a shithead?"

"I think I need to go," said Walt O.

"Ohhhh," moaned Beverly. "Don't."

"I agree with Colin," said neighborhood hating Megan J. "Lose the bitch and move on."

"Do not call my wife *a bitch*," said Walt O., his voice rising.

"Then tell her not to act like one,"replied Megan J., glaring. "Write a death script on *that*."

"I hate people," whispered depressed William G. "I hate the world."

Beverly moaned dolefully and as if in answer, William G. put his head into his hands and began to cry.

"Let's all take a moment," murmured Heidi, looking overwhelmed.

Dad sighed inside. It really was time to go home, walk the dogs and check on Marisol. The dogs had already been walked and Marisol wasn't feeling remotely under the weather but perhaps she could pretend to be. (For him.)

Marisol

If you were to ask him, my father, Robert Boone, would tell you that there has hardly been a time in his life when there wasn't Marisol.

He remembers a short, dark haired woman showing up at the house three times a week when he was a little boy, perhaps seven years old. Unlike Mrs. Rosa, the recently fired housekeeper, who apparently drank (what that meant, he wasn't sure) this woman's English was next to uncertain and she seemed mostly to communicate with nods and single word questions and answers.

"Where does she come from?" Dad asked my grandmother.

"From somewhere in East Haven," said Mary. "And she's highly recommended."

As if my father could think otherwise. The woman – Mrs. Arriola – was a cleaning dervish. Accompanied by an AM radio that played brassy music, she moved from room to room with mop, broom, cloth and pail, stripping and making beds, sweeping, polishing furniture, washing, drying and ironing clothes, and emptying the over flowing ashtrays left by Dad's chain-smoking father, Ben. In short, she took over the house, doing everything imaginable, so much so that Mary again began going out on painting excursions leaving Bob and his sisters at home.

"Make them lunch, Marisol, if you don't mind. I'll be back in a couple of hours."

"Si, senora. Su almuerzo, Meester Bob. What is you like?"

My father had no idea what almuerzo was but since his mother had mentioned lunch, he made a lucky guess. "Tuna fish?"

"Sandwich de atún. Bueno."

The sandwich, when it came to the table was tuna made with mayo, chopped green peppers, topped with melted cheese and it was much better than anything Mrs. Rosa had ever made him. (My father was impressed.)

"Why is she calling me, mister?"

It was later that evening and my grandfather, Ben, just home from work, was preparing himself his first evening cocktail.

"Why is who calling you Mister?"

"Mrs. Arriola," said Dad.

"It's a sign of respect. And you should be calling her Marisol."

"Why?"

"Because that's her name."

(Dad was confused now. There seemed to be a number missing from this equation.)

"I like your name," said Dad. It was the following day and Mrs. Arriola was vacuuming the living room. The radio was blaring. "Marisol. I like it."

Marisol said nothing. She nodded her head and pushed the vacuum into another corner.

"Bob is a stupid name. It's short for Robert."

"No," said Marisol. "Eez good name. Eez American name."

"My mom says you're from East Haven." (Dad was under the impression it was a foreign planet, hence Marisol's accented English.) "Do you have children?"

Marisol pushed the vacuum in Dad's direction and then stopped. "Mr. Bob. You in my way. I get nothing done. Go now." Marisol pointed out the living room window. "Jugar. Play."

"There's no one to play with."

(This wasn't quite true but it was true enough.)

"Hmph," said Marisol. She wiped her hands on her apron and pushed the vacuum aside. "*Carne asada* for su almuerzo," she said and radio in hand, she left the room.

Marisol liked Dad's name.

Marisol, he learned, had four children.

Marisol didn't have a driver's license and was dropped off and picked up by various family members.

Marisol made carne asada.

At age eight, my father began doing sketches of Marisol. At least he tried to. Marisol made it clear that she didn't like it. She'd frown, turn way and scuttle from the room. Finally she spoke her mind. "Mr. Bob, no, I am not for the drawing. Find someone pretty." Which meant he had to sketch on the sly, pretending that he was drawing something else.

When my father was ten years old, Mary took it upon herself to get Marisol U.S. citizenship. Marisol, seven months pregnant, had come with her husband to the United States at the age of nineteen. She and her husband, whose name was Jorge, lived for almost two years in Los Angeles with family during which time Marisol had a second child. They had then moved to Connecticut where there was yet more extended family and where Jorge found steady work as a stone mason. The process of getting a permanent resident card had proved so confusing to Marisol that unlike her husband, she never applied to become a naturalized citizen. Mary went to Ben who got them an immigration lawyer. Petitions were filed, Mary helped Marisol fill out forms and applications and she scheduled the appointments and interviews. On a warm, sunny Wednesday in October, Mary, my father and his two sisters all accompanied the entire Arriola family to a federal court where a beaming Marisol turned in her green card, took the oath of allegiance and was given a Certificate of Naturalization and a U.S. Citizenship Welcome Packet. They then adjourned to a small house in East Haven. It was packed elbow to elbow with people, was decorated with tissue paper flower garlands and there was enough food on the colorful dining room table to feed a raucous army. In the backyard, beer and tequila flowed and men in white suits, armed with jumbo guitars and trumpets and violins, played the same brassy music that Marisol listened to on her little radio. Mary, Dad and his sisters were toasted at least half a dozen times and best of all, Marisol, splendid in a blue dress and stubby heels, hugged each one of them, happily weeping. It was a great day and ultimately the only one who was less than thrilled was my grandfather. Marisol now refused to work under the table and he had to submit W-2s.

"You must come with me, Mr. Bob. Something has happened."

It was midafternoon and my father was in Mary's attic studio when Marisol came up the stairs and entered. Her voice was quiet and her expression was somber. Marisol's oldest son, Emiliano, was outside waiting in his car.

"Shouldn't we wait till Mom comes home?"

"No. We must go now."

They drove to the hospital where my grandfather was waiting to tell my father that Mary and his sister, Melissa, were dead and that Karen was still alive but in critical condition. By one in the morning, Karen was gone as well. Marisol never left my father's side the entire time. "Is good to cry, Mr. Bob.

The heart is full of tears and they must go." Dad shook his head. He never cried once.

What is grief? Having been protected from it up till then, my father didn't really know. It felt like a hole through which everything you were just drained out and away. He didn't know how to patch it. There were family photographs in the house. My grandfather took them all and locked them away in some old bureau drawers in the attic. Dad felt like he'd never be able to open those drawers again.

Not knowing what else to do, my grandfather decided to take Marisol on five days a week. Dad would make his own breakfast, go to school and Marisol would be waiting to make an early dinner for him when he came home. She gave him three months of leniency and then she stepped to the plate.

"Mr. Bob. You must stop the sorry making. You must do the homework. Su madre would want this."

Because it was Marisol, Dad stopped moping and did his homework.

"Mr. Bob. Lonely is no *bueno*. You must go out with the school people. Your sisters, they would want this."

Even though he didn't want to, Dad went out with the "school people."

"Mr. Bob. The pictures. It is time to do them again."

Dad sketched again. He began painting in earnest.

"Mister Ben," said Marisol, talking to Dad's father. "Your son, he need you and you must talk to him." My grandfather frowned at Marisol's obvious disapproval and made himself a third cocktail.

My father was in his bedroom that night, putting on pajamas when Ben stuck his head in. "How you doing, son, you okay?"

"I guess."

"School's good?"

"It's okay."

"I was thinking we might consider a private school, Bob. Would you like that?"

"I don't know."

"It was something your mom and I talked about."

Because it was something Mary had talked about, my father said he'd do it.

When the day came to head off to Choate, Marisol helped Dad pack. She bought him a portfolio for his art supplies, the first one he ever had. Before he left, she took him aside. She put her hand on his cheek. It was rough from all the work she did but it felt so wonderful. "Mr. Bob. You are not far. I am here. You will be as a son to me." She hugged Dad and he hugged her back and then he turned for the car where Ben was waiting so she wouldn't see that he was crying.

Finally crying.

Already missing the only person left in the world who seemed to care about him.

Day 4 – Attachment Patterns

"It kills me!" said Colin, trying to keep his voice down and by doing so, half choking on the words. "When I tell my doctors the world is just this global disaster that makes me want to *kill myself*, they tell me I'm crazy! And then, when I tell them, okay, the world is just fine and isn't under the thumb of dictators and asshole billionaires, they admit that, okay, yes, the world is messed up but hey, no one should want to kill themselves over it, right? I mean, *huh?* Who's the one who's crazy here?"

My father groaned inside.

It was only five minutes into group and he was already finding the plight of Colin far too much for one day. The poor kid had checked in at a ninety for anxiety and a sixty for depression and you had to wonder if it wasn't cerebral palsy he suffered from but rather a body crushing overdose of stress and self-loathing.

"Either the world is crazy and you want *to leave* and *that's* crazy! Or the world is crazy and you *don't* want to leave and *that's* crazy. Or the world isn't crazy at all. It's *you* who are crazy! What's the fucking truth?"

(All of the above?)

The morning's lecture, given by a tall young man wearing a hideous tie and sporting a hipster beard, had been Introduction to Core Beliefs. The tall, young man's name was Ron.

"Personal experiences shape our view of ourselves, of others and of the world. They shape our *core beliefs.*"

Hmm. Dad was of the simple belief that those that didn't believe what he did were out of their minds. Oh, but maybe that was the point. He decided not to waste any more time listening to this and he reached for his notebook.

"Ideally the experiences that shape our sense of the world, and our place is in it, are positive," intoned Ron.

Dad reached for his pen. Good lord and butter, he was sick of speeches.

"Unfortunately, a lot of our beliefs are shaped by negative events and can result in behaviors that confirm that belief."

The room suddenly shifted uncomfortably. Several people audibly groaned. Dad looked up to see that the guy with the buzz cut and gauge earrings had raised his hand.

"Yes, question, John?" said Ron

(John, yes. We'll call him *Wacko* John.)

"It's my experience that events that result in sexual domination often lead to feelings of me hating myself," said Wacko John.

"How so?" Ron looked puzzled.

Before Wacko John could answer a large woman with a short, man's haircut loudly interrupted. "Ron? Hey, Ron? My feeling right now is there's someone in the room who just can't keep his mouth shut. My *urge* is to tell that someone to zip it and let people who actually know something do the talking. You want to confirm that for me?" The room tittered. Ron glanced towards the door as if hoping for help.

"I feel a lack of respect when this bull dyke talks to me like that," said Wacko John.

"I don't think she was referring to you."

"Yes, I was," said the large woman with the man's haircut. Turning, she glared at Wacko John. "Now shut up or I'm going to shut you up. Or am I not empathazing with you enough?"

(Dad certainly thought she was.)

"How about we step outside and you *try* to shut me up," said Wacko John.

"You and me, Buster Brown," said the woman, murderously rising to her feet.

My father put down his pen and exhaled.

(There was a lot of exhaling going on in his part of the room where he was sitting all by himself.)

"I don't want to do this anymore," said Dad.

Dr. Giancarlo, who was again wearing a ski jacket and who was seated in his office chair with a book in hand, peered up over his reading glasses. He didn't seem remotely surprised that my father had barged into his office without knocking.

"Do what, Bob?"

"This. The people here are all out of their minds. They're depressed and angry and it's contagious."

Instead of answering, Dr. Giancarlo put down his book and began puttering through a pile of folders on his desk. "According to Heidi, you're not engaging in group, Bob. Why is that?"

"I just told you. Unlike most people here, I don't have this passionate need to talk about myself."

"Mmm, I got that impression. You're a stand-alone guy."

"Are you being sarcastic?"

"Yes."

"Well, then I'm leaving."

Dr. Giancarlo calmly looked up at Dad, obviously not intimidated by the threat of imminent departure. "You know anything about attachment patterns, Bob?"

Oh hell, thought Dad, instinctively knowing that attachment was an active noun to be avoided at all costs. "No, why would I?"

"It's how people connect with one another. Most adults fall into one of four categories. Secure, anxious, disordered and avoidant. What do you think you are?"

"I have no idea. I just want to go home."

"Secure adults find it easy to get emotionally close to others. They have a positive view of people. Is that you?"

"No. And it doesn't bother me in the least."

"Which is a problem. Now, anxious people *do* want to be close with others, but they feel others don't want to be close with them. Is *that* you?"

"You tell me," said Dad, with growing impatience.

"No, but only because your ego is such, you assume others would happily want to have a meaningful relationship with you if you allowed them to."

"It's eighty degrees in here. Why are you wearing a ski jacket?" asked Dad.

"Disorganized patterns," said Dr. Giancarlo, ignoring the question, "means a person is afraid they'll be hurt if they get close to anybody. Ring any bells?"

"What's the forth category," said Dad, ignoring the third.

"The forth category are people who dismiss relationships entirely. They hide their feelings and they distance themselves from others completely."

Silence. (Which can be an answer unto itself.)

Dr. Giancarlo sighed. "Here's the truth, Bob. We are, at different times in our lives, *all* of these things. We are insecure, we are anxious, we avoid, we are afraid. *However*... it is when these negatives take over and effect our well-being that we have to worry. And *do something* about it."

"If the point of all this is to make me feel better, it sure isn't."

"Feeling good, Bob, is seeing and agreeing with the truth."

"That's your truth," said Dad, "not mine."

No, the truth today was Colin. The poor kid was a mess, no doubt about it. "...And now I have to go to the social *services* office today to apply for disability benefits because my therapist is telling me I'm both self-destructive *and* emotionally unstable which is why—" Colin scowled across the circle at Paul F. "I can't even *get* a stupid job!" Colin took a deep breath, as if trying to calm himself. "I want a job. I want a girl. I want to feel like I'm doing okay. I want to feel like *I'm* okay."

The small room was stifling. Looking up and beyond the circle, my father noticed for the first time that there were metal framed prints on the grey papered walls. Prints of what? Pansies? Lilacs? Whatever they were, they were as escetically pleasing as the front page of a newspaper trumpeting stories of a holocaust.

(Or was it just him?)

"Does anyone," asked Heidi, "have any insight into what Colin is feeling?"

"Your problem is you have cerebral palsy."

Was it my father's imagination or was the room suddenly freezing cold. (No wonder Dr. Giancarlo wore a ski jacket.) He couldn't believe what had just come out of his mouth. And now, to his own dismay, he couldn't stop talking. What was *wrong* with him? "You're angry about it. You have every right to be. It's a bad deal. But it's the elephant in the room and you need to face it and deal with it."

The room was deathly silent.

"Colin?" Heidi's voice was a whisper. "How do you feel about what Bob just said?"

Colin was statue still. His eyes were stones.

Click.

Robert Boone saw a face of broken lines and tilted angles.

Click.

Behind the face was a blurred, distorted landscape.

"He's right. You're right, Bob." Turning his head, Colin regarded the group. "I'm a freak. Spastic man. People look at me and all they see is a pathetic, crippled thing. They always have and they always will. 'Cause that's what I am."

(What have I done, thought Dad, feeling very tired.)

"Colin?"

It was Beverly. Her eyes were filling with tears. (Would they never stop?) "I don't see a crippled thing. I see a sensitive young man who God truly loves."

"Me too," murmured Megan J. "I'd just lose the profanity."

"Sometimes you get going too fast," said big, dour Paul F. not looking quite so dour. "But what you say can make a lot of sense."

"I like you," said world hating William G., not looking up from the floor.

"I think we all do," said Heidi.

"Here, here," said cheerful Walt O.

"Okay, fine," said Colin, eyes wet but now breaking into a wicked grin. "But the thing is, who really cares who you guys think? You're all as completely screwed up as I am."

Colin began to laugh and everyone laughed with him. Dad laughed too. Not because he had to but because it was funny.

(Still. He felt awful.)

Social Service

Feeling awful meant that when Robert Boone came driving out of the hospital parking garage forty minutes later and saw an underdressed Colin shivering at a bus stop, he felt he had no choice but to pull to the curb and roll down the window.

"What the hell do you want?" said Colin, pulling down his face scarf and clutching his backpack.

"I thought I'd offer you a ride."

"We're not supposed to socialize outside out of group," said Colin.

"And we're not supposed to shake hands or pat one another on the butt because someone might have a nervous breakdown. You want a ride or not?"

"In that?" Colin stared contemptuously at the old pick-up.

"Would you rather wait for the bus? Now are we going or not?"

It took Colin a good two minutes to get from the sidewalk into the front seat of the pick-up but they went.

"Where exactly are we going?" asked Dad, as they slowed at the first light. (He hoped it wasn't too far. The kid needed a shower and a decent deodorant. Even the scarf he was wearing gave off fumes.)

"Social services."

"Which is where?"

"Bassett Street."

"Which is where?"

"Take a left."

Ten minutes later they were lost.

"It's not my fault," snarled Colin, "that you don't have a cell phone with a decent navigation app."

"Why don't you?" asked my father.

"I do but they turned off my phone."

"Why?"

43

"Because they're assholes."

"I'm sure it had nothing to do with not paying your bill."

"Are you just *trying* to make me feel bad?"

They searched for a while. They looked at street signs. They asked several Yale students, all whom regarded them warily. They stopped the search and pulled up next to a parked police car.

"We're looking for social services."

"Field Office is on Humphrey Street, Development Services is on James Street," said the cop.

"Humphrey or James?" Dad asked Colin.

"How the fuck do I know, I thought it was fucking *Bassett!*"

"Careful," said the cop.

They went to James Street. "No, that's not it," said Colin.

They went to Humphrey Street which was. "You're welcome," said Dad as Colin slid carefully out of the truck.

"Aren't you going to wait for me?" replied Colin, implying Dad would be a total asshole if he didn't.

After a good thirty minutes of waiting, my father got out of the pick-up, went into the building, saw that social services was on the third floor and took the elevator up. He found Colin sitting in a waiting area, red faced and on the verge of tears.

"They're saying I might not be disabled *enough!*"

(This was getting ridiculous.)

"Wait here," said Dad and he went back downstairs, out the door and around the corner to a Verizon store they'd passed, where, after calling Marisol to give him his credit card number, he bought a phone and signed up for a plan. (Dad never carries a credit card because he's always afraid he'll lose it.)

Out on the sidewalk, he called Carter in New York. "Carter, I need you to call that lawyer for me."

"Oh, Bob. You're not in the hospital again, are you?"

"No. Jesus, Carter. I'm with some crippled kid, who's getting the run around from social services. He needs some help."

"And you're helping him?"

(Carter sounded incredulous which Dad found annoying.)

"Are you going to call the guy or not."

"No. That would be *enabling* you, Bob. What I'm going to do is give you the number and *you* can call him."

They argued awhile and finally, vowing vengeance and threatening to take all his future work somewhere else (which they both knew was *not* going to happen), Dad took the number and called.

"Mr. Jorgensen will have to call you back, Mr. Boone," said a woman on the other end of the Verizon network.

"When?"

"As soon as he can."

"Tell him to ask for Colin."

Dad hung up, walked back to the social services building and took the elevator to the third floor where he found Colin completing the crossword puzzle in a discarded New York Times. "Here," he said handing the new cell phone to Colin. "Keep it."

"What do you mean?"

(Colin looked not so much as surprised as suspicious.)

"I mean, keep it. I don't want the damn thing. When my lawyer calls, tell him what the problem here is. Tell him to fix it and put it on my bill."

"You have your own lawyer?"

(Again, Colin looked suspicious.)

"Lately, yes."

Thirty minutes later they pulled up in front of a non-descript looking apartment house in Westville. Again, rejecting help, Colin carefully got out of the pick-up, grabbed his backpack and stood a moment, looking more suspicious than ever. "Okay, why are you doing this? 'Cause I don't trust it."

"Emotional regulation," said Dad. "Guilt and shame. And apologies. Not for what I said but for the way I said it. See you tomorrow and listen, we won't talk about this to anyone." Putting the truck in gear, my father drove to the I-95 and motored on home.

(Correction. Feeling that the afternoon had turned oddly *positive,* my father put the truck in gear, drove to the I-95 and motored on home.)

The Congress of the Crow

The place Robert Boone was packed off to, Choate-Rosemary Hall, was – *is* – a private, boarding school for the privileged few and those who aspire to be, in Wallingford, Connecticut. It was a total waste of his time.

(I have my own experiences there but we'll get to that later)

Dad did just enough schoolwork to get by, played no sports, engaged in no meaningful friendships, went on no dates, did no drugs (errr…), drank no alcohol (uhhh…) and spent the vast majority of his four years in the library studying artists and their work, creating a historical timeline that started with Greek idealism and ended with post-modernism and deconstructivism. Freshman year, on a book shelf in the school library, he discovered *Hereward Lester Cooke's Painting Techniques of the Masters*. This was a large, illustrated book in which a renowned art scholar and curator broke the work of artists like Da Vinci, Botticelli, El Greco, Vermeer, Cezanne, Degas and Picasso down into lessons on form, line, color and space. It became my father's bible, so much so that he stole it and took it home that first summer.

(Note. Up to this point in his life, my father had always sketched and painted for the sheer joy of it. Was this sudden and obsessive course of study an act of joy or was he now using "art" to hide from other things. You'd have to ask him.)

As to Choate's art department, my father found it less than inspiring and he avoided it, taking no classes and keeping totally under the radar. It was a *"problem"* then, at least to the department, when he was not just accepted into the Rhode Island School of Design his senior year but given a full scholarship based on the diverse portfolio of work he had created over four summers at home in Branford.

"Why the hell would you want to go there?" growled Ben, his father.

"What do you care? You're not paying for it," retorted Bob, his son.

(Needless to say, father and son had been distant for quite some time now.)

At the Rhode Island School of Design my father was considered a bit of a wunderkind and under different circumstances, he might have learned and accomplished quite a lot. The problem, call it fate or circumstance, was that he almost immediately entered into a torrid affair with a visiting professor in textile design, Ellen Horvath. Ellen was an attractive, outgoing woman with a passion for life and art. Married, she was in her late-thirties and as an artist, felt unbound by the rules of conventional society. (Totally get it. Can't quite act upon it.) Her marriage was an open one, she adored the attention and company of men and to say that Dad, who had spent his adolescence living under a rock with his dick in his hands, was gratefully seduced would be an understatement. (Penis. When talking about your father's dick you should use the word penis.)

"You. Handsome boy," said Ellen. "Come over tonight. We'll tip a glass of something and discuss the incorporation of art into woven, knitted and manufactured fabrics."

"I'm not interested in carpets."

"And I'm not interested in oil paintings on lavatory walls. But come over anyway. You can paint me. Nude."

Dad did and they did.

In the coming months Ellen introduced my father to passionate sex, good food and fine wine (she had Master's degrees in all three subjects) and took him on any number of over night trips down to New York where they stayed in hotels and went to restaurants and museums; things my father had heard, read and fantacized about but never experienced. He missed countless classes, did minimal drawing, got no painting done, and other than a number of positions in the Kama Sutra (Ellen's favorite was the Congress of the Crow – think sixes and nines) and how to make a stunning béchamel sauce, he didn't accomplish much of anything the entire year. Still, for the first time in forever, life felt intoxicating. And so, in May, when Ellen abruptly announced that she wouldn't be coming back in the fall, that her faculty position and husband were waiting for her in New Mexico, a disconsolate Robert Boone decided he wouldn't be coming back either. Call it academic apathy but the Rhode Island School of Design wasn't going to be the same without Ellen Horvath. Having said that, my father had learned an important lesson. One could be an artist or one could be a lover. One could not be both.

(At least not at the same time.)

Day 5 – Depression

It was Friday, the final day of the first week (thank goodness), the subject of the morning's lecture was the COG model of depression and dad, with time on his hands the previous evening, had spent a half hour reading about it in his workbook.

It had depressed him.

Depressed people didn't feel pleasure or happiness. They were irritable, aggressive and they kept to themselves. Whereas unhappy people could feel *sad* about something but could bounce back, depressed people felt sad about *everything* and bounced as much as a delated beach ball. Dad had quickly concluded that he wouldn't want to hang around people like this and since there were days when he experienced a decided lack of bounce, he could only conclude he didn't want to hang out with himself. It was an alarming thought.

The workbook suggested *monitoring* the problem but that would mean *thinking about it* and he didn't want to do that. The book also suggested making a list of pleasurable activities that could help foster a *positive attitude.* This seemed like another version of Grapes, and he didn't want to do that either.

And so, putting all positive attitude aside, my father reluctantly took his seat in the lecture hall and nodded at Beverly and Walt O. who were respectively beaming and smiling in his direction. He looked at dour Paul F. who lifted a heavy hand in greeting. He glanced at Colin who was talking manically to Wacko John and at William G. who was staring into space and at Megan J. who was violently tearing pages out of her workbook. Taking out the heavy lead pencil he'd brought from home, he opened his own workbook with the intention of drawing rather than listening. Two minutes later, the day's lecturer walked in, and he nearly broke the pencil.

It was Annie.

Unlike the other female therapists, she did not wear librarian glasses, slim fitting slacks, stylish shoes and a fashionable blouse but rather was attired in a loose turtleneck, a drab, denim jacket and a long, shapeless skirt. There were flat Espadrilles on her feet and her blonde hair was pulled back in a severe French braid. Her eyes and her lips were make-up free.

Oh, but Dad knew those eyes and lips.

It had been eight months ago, and it had started with a phone call from Carter. "Bob, I need a favor."

"I don't do favors."

"Whenever I ask for a favor, you say that and then you do it."

"And what have you done for *me* lately?"

"The list is far too long to go over, now will you just listen?"

Dad listened. Carter had a new client, an up-and-coming painter, talented, he said. Carter was doing an exhibition at the Hurley Gallery—"the first in quite some time"—which is what Carter did.

"I would like you to come."

"Why?"

"Because even though you don't like to think about it, in the world of art, you are still something of a *name*, Bob. Your presence at an opening *means* something. It will mean something to the artist, it will mean something to the other patrons, it will mean something to the art press, and it would mean something to me."

"No."

Of course, Dad went. Bitching and moaning to himself the entire way, he got in the pick-up and motored down the Wilbur Cross to the Cross County Expressway and then down the West Side Highway into lower Manhattan. Parking the truck at a garage, he walked across Canal Street and then up Wooster to the Hurley Gallery. He was late and in his leather jacket, black T-shirt, Aussie boots and jeans, underdressed as usual. He walked in and went straight to the bar.

"You made it," said Carter, looking dapper as usual in blazer and bow tie.

"Mmm," said Dad, sipping his vodka on ice, something he rarely touched.

"Bob, this is Eugene Rothenberg," said Carter, introducing a young man in a dark suit and an untucked shirt.

"You, sir, are one of my heroes," said Eugene Rothenberg.

Dad nodded and sipped.

"Enjoy," said Carter.

"Mmm," said Dad.

He proceeded to have a wonderful time. No one recognized him and if they did, they didn't say a word. The work, mostly figure paintings done in separated, thickly applied colors, was better than good. Eugene Rothenberg was talented and after a couple of more vodkas, my father, having already forgotten the young man's name, told him so.

"You're talented. I'm going to buy some of your work."

"I'm honored," said Eugene Rothenberg. "Any advice you can give me, anything at all..."

"Never listen to anyone. Especially me."

Thrilled with such profound advice, Eugene Rothenberg invited my father to an after-show party. With friends.

"Is that one of your friends?" Dad's gaze drifted to a stylishly dressed, high-heeled, blond woman on the other side of the gallery. Her perfectly shadowed eyes had been bouncing off him all evening and because of the vodka, he hadn't felt like rolling up into a ball and hiding.

Dad felt intrigued.

Dad felt confident.

(So much so, he'd been eye bouncing back.)

"I'd like to meet her."

"Happy to," said Eugene with a smile and he waved her over. Up close, the woman seemed older, perhaps in her late thirties.

"Annie, this is the *esteemed* artist, Robert Boone. Mr. Boone—"

"Bob."

"...*Bob*...this is Annie...uh..."

"Gilmore," said the woman, wine glass in hand and a smile on her lips.

"Hi," replied Dad, sipping vodka, the liquor of confidence.

"Esteemed?" asked blonde Annie, eyes a twinkle.

"*Eminently* esteemed."

"I like the leather jacket. Are you as tough as you look?"

"Tougher," said Dad who considered himself about as tough and esteemed as tapioca pudding.

"I'll get out of the way and let you two get to know one another," said Eugene Rothenberg.

They did.

"Good! So good! Oh, so sweet!"

After any number of seductive looks, shared observations and sexual innuendoes later, Dad and Annie had escaped the gallery, jumped in a cab, motored up town, jumped out of the cab, hurried through revolving doors, crossed a hotel lobby, got in an elevator, kissed and groped all the way up to the eighth floor, got out of the elevator, rushed down the hall and hurried into Annie's modest hotel room where they'd torn off their clothes, fallen onto the bed and gone to town. Dad's manhood (a much better term than penis), usually a nervous tenor with a tendency to pout in the dressing room (great metaphor), was in full voice as Annie rolled over on top of him and proceeded to rub her pudendum (a literary term) up and down against his pelvic bone. "Harder! Oh, God, harder! Much harder!" She orgasmed with such a shriek, he worried the residents in the next room might call 911.

"Are you always like this?" he asked as they cuddled after.

Dad felt sated and replete. He felt virile, spent and relaxed. *Life was good.*

Annie giggled and kissed his shoulder. "Glad you liked it."

"I did. I like *you*."

"I like you too."

"What are we going to do about that?"

"We'll have to see, won't we," smiled Annie.

Her hand caressed Dad's tenor which, much to his amazement, took a deep breath and prepared to sing again. When he woke up in the morning, Annie was packed and gone.

"No number or address," said the clerk at the front desk. "She booked online. Not that I could give it to you anyway."

"Contact info? No." said Eugene Rothenberg when my father, called. "I mean, it's not like I knew her *that* well." Eugene sounded apologetic. "Listen, I'll ask around. I'm sure someone knows how to get in touch with her."

"No. Don't bother."

"You sure?"

"You asked for advice. Here it is. You can be an artist, or you can be a lover. You can't be both. Not at the same time."

Dad hung up the phone, got into his truck and forcing himself not to look back, went home to Connecticut.

And now, here she was again. Dressed down and seemingly trying to hide in plain sight but still – obviously – Annie.

"Let's talk about…" Annie, wrote the word on the whiteboard in large, capital letters. "DEPRESSION!"

Dad was all ears. (Depression now sounded like a hell of a lot of fun.)

"Globally more than 350 million people suffer from depression each year." Annie's sunny smile filled the lecture hall. "You are not alone!"

(Dad wasn't sure how a depressed person would find that comforting. Maybe it was a strength in numbers kind of thing.)

"Depression can be caused by chemical imbalances in the brain and by stress or loss in our daily lives. Depression can affect how we feel about—" Annie drew a triangle on the whiteboard—"ourselves, other people and the future!"

(In my father's opinion, stress and loss and imbalance summed up much of modern life. He blamed it on human nature. I blame it on politics and social media not to mention viral pandemics and the fact that people don't read books anymore.)

"Example," said Annie. "You're at a party. You meet someone. You like them. They seem to like you. They give you their phone number. The next day you call them up. You leave a message. They do not call back. If we are thinking in a negative manner, what do we think about that?"

"They didn't really like you," said a woman in the second row.

"They didn't really like you," repeated Annie, writing it down. "What else?"

"No one likes you," said a man on the outskirts of the third row.

"No one likes you. Good, what else?"

"No one will ever like you!" barked Colin, in the first row.

"Past, present and future," said Annie, seemingly brimming with enthusiasm. "Now! If we are thinking in a *positive* manner, how would we react to someone not calling us back?"

Dad quickly raised his hand and Annie turned towards him. He watched her eyes widen. She gaped a moment, her mouth open, and then she recovered. "Yes?"

"Yes." Dad pointed at his name tag. "*Robert B.?* Uh-hum… (He cleared his throat.) …maybe… just *maybe… they're* the ones who are screwed up. Maybe *they* are manipulative egomaniacs who like to hurt people…. which means, if you were in a *positive* frame of mind, that you're better off without them. But which also means, if you were in a *negative* frame of mind, you'd wonder what you ever did, what offense did you possibly commit, that they would abandon you so."

Annie's lips smiled again, her eyes didn't. "Excellent. Both sides of the coin, just like that." Turning, she gazed out at the quiet lecture hall. "So! Identifying and changing the negative thoughts that lead to depression! Let's do this!"

Perhaps it was my father's critical state of mind, but the rest of her lecture seemed decidedly halfhearted.

Botteghe

It was in the Fall of 1993 that my father went to New York City. In his mind, he has likened this journey to that of a young painter beginning his apprenticeship in a Renaissance art room or *botteghe* under a master, and in preparing for the move, he spent the first part of the summer at the family home in Branford where despite my grandfather's disapproval and fear for his Chrysler, Dad turned half of the double car garage into an art studio. He sketched, he painted. He made up for lost time. In August, not wishing to ask my grandfather for money, Dad took half a dozen of his mother's water colors down from the attic, and transported them to a well-established, local shoreline gallery that immediately offered to show them. The response was positive, and they sold quickly.

"I think you could have damn well asked me first," said Ben, when told of the transactions. "They were mine just as much if not more than yours."

As much as it bothered Dad to admit it, his father was right. "Fine. I'll go buy them back."

"Don't bother," grunted Ben. "We both know it's what she would have wanted you to do. Though if you ask me, you'd be better off driving a truck." (It was as close as Ben ever came to giving his blessing.)

With the money from the sales, Dad was able to afford the first year's rent on a small studio apartment in the east village. He had hardly unpacked from Providence and after buying a used mattress and some sheets from a shop on East 4th Street, he moved in.

Yes, my father enrolled at the Arts Students League on 57th Street in Manhattan, but to suggest he studied there is like suggesting a juvenile delinquent studies in high school detention. He considered the place a study space, a place to work on technique, brushwork, line, perspective and pigment, nothing more. The vast majority of his work took place on the weekends when he returned to the house in Branford to paint in solitude. Dad's apprenticeship in New York, his *botteghe*, consisted mostly of day long trips to the city's museums where he spent hours staring at, analyzing and sketching those painters he considered masters. It was an endless and intimidating list. On any given day it might be Caravaggio and Vermeer at the Met, Matisse, Van Gogh and Picasso at the Museum of Modern Art, Jean-Simeon Chardin at The Frick, Vasily Kandinsky at the Guggenheim or Degas at The Brooklyn Museum. He did occasionally try to explore the work of his contemporaries but most often he came away unimpressed. The neo-conceptualism of Peter Halley, work that seemed to consist of colored squares, seemed simplistic to him. Damian Hirst's dead, fourteen-foot shark, preserved in formaldehyde, seemed something that belonged in a biology class and Keith Haring's Street art felt like art made for a child's tea party. And speaking of children's parties, what was it with Jeff Koons and his giant balloon dogs and what did it say about the state of modern art that a lot of people obviously liked all this?

"Most people have the taste of tepid tap water," groused my grandfather.

(Okay, I don't disagree with him.)

After his daily sojourns, Dad would return to his chair and easel at the Arts Students League to try and figure out, in bits and pieces and in exacting detail, how it had been done. He rarely spoke to other students, never engaged with the instructors and the only class he attended with any kind of consistency was the one that focused on the female nude.

From the very beginning, Dad was oblivious to other aspects of New York City's cultural life. The closest he ever got to Carnegie Hall, which was within walking distance of the Art Students League, was the pan handler who screamed arias at the top of his lungs on 57th and 7th Avenue. (People gave him money to stop.)

One night on a whim and to get out of the rain, he wandered into a club called CBGB's in the East Village, had a conversation at the bar with a stoned Englishman named Keith Richards, was offered a cocaine by a stranger, refused it, and finally, ears ringing and bored to pieces, left.

Walking uptown towards Zabar's one morning to partake of the free samples – he particularly like the smoked fish and cheese bits – Dad couldn't help but notice the attractive, duck-footed young women with their hair in tight buns, toting their packs down Amsterdam Avenue. It never occurred to him they were ballet dancers going to Lincoln Center. Nor did it occur to him that the young people toting instrument cases might be classical musicians studying at Julliard.

(Fellow artists, oh oblivious one!)

At the beginning of his second year, my father began bussing tables in a restaurant five days a week for food and rent money. He got the position one evening when hungry and penniless, he went into DeVeaux's, a newly opened bistro on Bleecker Street. After a meal of steak pomme frites followed by expresso and a blueberry tart (yum!), Dad sought out the café's owner and chef, Francois DeVeaux, and informed him that though he had no money, he had done a detailed sketch of the dining room and was willing to trade it for dinner.

"Are you kidding me?" said Francois whose daytime name was Sayid Bashir and who was the son of French-Algerian immigrants living in New Jersey.

"Picasso did. Trade art for food."

"If you're Picasso, I'm Paul Bocuse."

"Who is...?"

"Never mind. Lemme see." Francois/Sayid, reached for the sketch. It was of the room and its seated patrons, done in the style of the French modernist painter, Eduard Manet, and Francois/Sayid, who was a graduate of Le Cordon Bleu in Paris, was actually impressed. "What are you, some kind of starving artist?"

"Weekdays I starve, weekends I'm an artist," said Dad.

"Okay. You want to eat here, you work here. You get meals, five bucks an hour and a percentage of the tips to bus tables."

"Are you serious?"

"I'm always serious except when I'm not."

"Thank you," said Dad.

"Someday you do the same thing for somebody else. Now grab an apron and get to work. And I'm keeping the drawing."

Although my father didn't realize it at the time, he had made his first real friend.

Healing Winds

Annie's lecture ended with a mindfulness exercise where everyone in the lecture hall, pretended to be deeply rooted trees. Unlike people, trees didn't judge, trees drew energy from the earth and trees bent with the wind.

(It's unlikely trees ever pretend to be people.)

As everyone cast their leaves aside and filed off to fill the time until group, my father lingered by the lecture room door. He watched as Annie turned from the white board, satchel over her shoulder, arms filled with books. Seeing him, she stopped, hesitated and then approached.

"I was hoping we might talk for a moment."

"Sure," said Dad. "About what?"

"You said some rather forceful things at the start of the lecture, and I thought it might be helpful to clarify them."

"Clarify away."

"Perhaps we should go to my office."

They did. They went outside, went down the walk, went inside and down a busy hallway. They silently took a right and went down a less busy hallway where Annie unlocked a door. They entered a small, meticulous office. There was a desk, bookcases and two comfortable looking chairs near the closed window blinds. Annie closed the door behind her, dropped her books and bag to the floor, turned and tried not to scream.

"*What*…are you *doing* here?"

(So much for emotional regulation.)

"Funny, I was going to ask you the same thing."

"I *work* here."

"You told me you were in advertising. You told me you lived in New York. I guess you lied."

"This is impossible," moaned Annie, holding her head. "This can't be happening. This is crazy."

"That's why *I'm* here," said Dad. (Given the circumstances, he was happy to admit it.) "Does that make two of us?"

"Oh, be quiet! Do you realize how ethically compromised I am? I'm going to have to go to my supervisors and tell them that under no circumstances can I be working anywhere near you. I'm going to have to tell them why. And I am going to have to ask you, please, not to tell anyone in the program we know each other."

"You mean Biblically or on a first name basis?"

"This is *not funny*."

"You left. We laughed, we talked, we made love and then you left. That wasn't funny either."

Annie said nothing.

(It's tough being taken to task with the truth.)

"You know, I tried to get in touch with you."

"You did?" Annie looked surprised. "Why? Why would you do that?"

"I told you that night. I liked you."

"Oh, come on."

"I don't sleep with people I don't think are terrific," said Dad.

"I do."

(I'm not going to say a word.)

Closing her eyes, Annie took a deep breath in through the nose. She held it a moment and then let it out through the mouth. Mindful breathing. Rooted trees. Healing winds in safe places. (Good luck.) "On a personal level," said Annie, opening her eyes, "I'm not sure what we're going to do about this."

"I do. We're going out to dinner."

"No, absolutely not."

"Why not?"

"Because I can't," said Annie.

"Why not?"

"Because I don't *want* to," said Annie, not nearly so calm.

"You're married, aren't you," said Dad, suddenly convinced she was.

"What? No."

"You live with someone. You're in a committed and meaningful relationship."

"*No.*"

"Then what's the problem?"

"I… I don't like getting involved."

"Are you seeing anyone about this? A therapist?"

"Oh, *shut up!*" Both Annie's expression and voice softened a bit. "Really. You can't tell people, all right? In fact… I don't think you're the kind of man that would."

"Oh, I am," Dad replied. "You better believe I am. But I won't on one condition."

"I am *not* going out to dinner with you."

"That's not it," said Dad.

"What is it, Dad?" I asked when he called that evening to say he had something to tell me.

"I wanted you to know I've found a therapist."

"Oh! Well, that is good news."

"Yeah, her name is Anne Gilmore. She works in the Cog program. We have to be careful though. She's ethically compromised."

"What's that mean?"

"We slept together in a past life."

"What!"

"Slept together. Then, without a word of explanation, she abandoned me."

"And now she wants you as a patient?" (I couldn't believe my ears.)

"Sweetheart, no, she'd lose her license if she ever took me on as a patient. She's taking me on as a friend. We're going to meet a couple of afternoons a week for coffee and friendly conversation is all. Therapy will have nothing to do with it. I told her I'd tell everybody here that she's lousy in bed, if she didn't."

"*Daa*-ad! That's blackmail!"

"Don't worry, she knows what she's doing."

"I sure hope *you* do."

"Oh, I can handle it. Hey, you know, I'm feeling pretty good here? Maybe some of this crazy COG stuff is working after all."

Click.

(Meaning the phone, not my father's camera brain.)

Week 2

Day 6 – Anger Management

The Monday morning lecture, given by Julio, was on anger management and my father, who had been feeling angry all weekend long, wasn't really in the mood to listen to it.

"When you're experiencing anger, most likely you've felt hurt by someone, and you are now afraid something terrible is happening."

Meaning, thought my father, that since people were *always* getting hurt and something terrible was *always* happening, everybody was *always* pissed off.

He had no one to blame but himself. Early Saturday morning over coffee, Dad had come to the conclusion that the only thing he really knew about psychotherapy was that he was being forced to take it. This was like being given a shovel and ordered to start digging, the problem being you had no idea what you were digging for, no idea how deep you were supposed to dig and no idea if you'd like what you'd find, if and when you found it. It put one at a disadvantage which was not a position Dad liked to be in *ever*. And so, after his coffee, he got in his pick-up and went down to the Blackstone Memorial Library with the intention of reading up on the subject.

The domed library was one of his favorite buildings. Usually quiet and most of the time, nearly deserted, it was a fine place to browse, sit and read. Only today there was a children's book fair going on which meant tented stalls selling cupcakes and hot dogs, face painting and amusement rides. (Books being secondary to fun.) After purchasing a half-cooked hot dog and leaving a substantial tip, Dad went home and stewed for a while. The need to know was increasingly overwhelming and because it was, he came to a ghastly conclusion.

It was time for him to buy a computer.

"Every person has their own way of coping with anger," said Julio. "The internalizer *stuffs* their anger while the externalizer *directs* that anger towards a target. Our goal is to change both responses."

A computer was something my father had avoided for years. As mentioned, the thought of interacting on social media was loathsome. The thought of apps and search engines and online shopping was even worse. Finally, and most unsettling, computers, Carter had told him, could now be programed to generate original works of art every bit as accomplished as that of the Masters. It was heresy and the artist, Robert Boone, wanted no part of it.

But now… he needed to *know*.

"Where can I buy a computer?" Dad asked Marisol who now collected wages on Saturdays for contentedly sitting in the yard or house, listening to a Spanish station on her radio and hand sewing clothes for her granddaughters.

"You must go to the Apples stores," replied Marisol, as if she'd been expecting Dad to ask this question forever.

"I don't want apples, I want a computer."

"The apples *is* the computers."

(Oh.)

Marisol put down her sewing, rose from the couch, went into the kitchen, pulled an old, local yellow pages out from under the kitchen sink where it was gathering mold and showed Dad that the Apples Store was a store selling electronic devices in New Haven.

"Some people," said Julio, "feel that their anger goes from cold to hot in microsecond. More likely that anger was slowly escalating without them being aware of it."

"I want a computer," Dad said to the bored looking, young man at the Apple Store.

"Look around, what do you see," said the bored, young man.

Dad looked around. He saw people (mostly bored, young ones) gathered intently around mounted screens, keyboards and cell phones of various sizes, all of which, he thought, had the aesthetic appeal of ceramic tile.

"What kind of computer are you looking for?"

"How do I know?" said Dad.

"What are you going to *use* it for?"

"I want to look up the history of psychotherapy."

"I would say the fifteen-inch MacBook Pro is your best bet. Over five million pixels, force touch keypad, OS-X operating system and it's just under two grand."

"That seems kind of expensive."

"You get what you pay for," said the bored, young man.

(Rarely.)

After being assured that a MacBook Pro couldn't *paint*, Dad bought it and took it home.

"Anger," said Julio, "comes out of our *unrealistic expectations* of how we feel things are supposed to work."

"MARISOL? IT DOESN'T WORK! MARISOL!"

"*Que pasa?* What is no working, Mister Bob?" cried Marisol, hurrying into the kitchen.

"This computer! It's turned on, it's all lit up but it's not *doing* anything!"

"That is because, Mister Bob," clucked Marisol, "you no have no *internet*."

"Huh?"

"Eez how computers talk to each other."

"How was I to know that?"

"You would know but you don't never *listen*, Mister Bob."

"Anger," intoned Julio, "can come out of our unrealistic expectations of how we feel things are supposed to work."

"Shit," murmured Dad.

It was quickly decided that Marisol would call her nephew Juan Carlos, who knew everything about computers and the internet and "for a small fee," would come over and make things perfect.

"Anger can be a good thing," said Julio. "It protects us from harm, and it motivates us to *change*."

(Since when?)

Sunday morning, with the expectation that things were going to work out just fine, my father logged onto the internet for the very first time in his life. He had already decided that before studying the history of psychotherapy he'd like to know a little bit more about Annie and her dating issues and so, using his two index fingers, he carefully typed, *women who sleep with strangers* into what Juan Carlos had called the "search engine." Two clicks later he found himself on a pornographic website. There wasn't a whole lot to learn. (At least I never have.) Trying to remember exactly what Juan Carlos had shown him,

Dad pressed the touch pad and was immediately diverted to *another* pornographic website, this one seemingly focused on anal intercourse. (Ouch.)

"Often," said Julio, "when we are experiencing anger, we are experiencing what we feel is a *loss of control*.

Dad took a deep breath. He pressed the pad again. And found himself staring at a heavy breathing, young woman in a negligee who stared back as if looking into a camera. What was *this*? It seemed to be a club of some kind, certainly one that he had no intention of joining. He poked the pad—hard. *Warning, warning!* The screen had now turned to a page that stated his computer had been infected with a virus and he was now at mortal risk.

Poke.

Poke.

Poke.

The page would *not* go away. (Sort of like men and the subject of anal intercourse.)

"Anger is an *emotion*, not a *behavior*. It only becomes a problem when it is *acted out*."

Roaring in frustration, Dad rose from his chair, picked the MacBook Pro up off the table and heaved it across the kitchen, where it banged into a cabinet and fell to the floor. The dogs cowered as pulling on a jacket he went out the door, slamming it behind him. Getting into his pick-up, he drove down to the library. The children's book fair was thankfully now history and my father parked, went inside, and spent the rest of Sunday afternoon sitting quietly in a comfortable chair, reading.

"Here," said Dad, handing the reboxed MacBook Pro to Colin as they transitioned from the anger lecture to group. (It hadn't broken on its flight across the kitchen which meant that maybe it was worth the money.)

"You're *giving* it to me?" Colin looked dubious.

"I don't want it.

"*I* do," said Colin, and he eagerly grabbed for it.

"*Positive interactions*," Julio had summarized "help us deal with our anger and achieve what we want."

(My father had no idea what he wanted but Colin looked like a kid who had discovered his first candy shop and again, he found himself quietly pleased.)

In group, Megan J., who wanted to wipe her entire neighborhood from the face of the earth, *wasn't* internalizing her anger.

"Basketball," said Megan J. through clenched teeth.

(Huh? The woman didn't look like much of an athlete but then, what did Dad know?)

"My sons spent the weekend at the local community center playing basketball on a busted up, broken down court with no nets."

"And how is that bad?" asked Heidi.

"I am five foot five. Their *father* is possibly five foot eight. And yet he has our boys convinced that basketball is going to get them a college scholarship. I tell them to study their books and do their homework. That's what's gonna get them to college. Guess who they listen to?"

"That must be tough on you," said Heidi.

"Not as tough as it's gonna be on him," scowled Megan J.

After suggesting to Megan J. that she write down *other* reasons her husband might be doing what he did and then evaluate if any of those reasons were *good ones*, and if not, how to calmly *discuss* them with him, Heidi moved on to Colin who announced that his anxiety level was at a 25 and his depression was at a 12 – "the lowest it's been in forever!" The reason for this, added Colin (glancing at Dad as he said it), was that he now had a lawyer looking into – "everything I'm eligible for at social services" – which was a huge relief.

(Which was a huge relief to Dad. Now if he could only figure out where to buy a basketball court.)

Next up was scraggily bearded, desolate William G. who in a vacant monotone described how – "Sometimes I drink too much. I don't know why. I think it will make me feel better, but it never does. Still, I do."

(Hmmm, thought Dad. Did he drink too much? A couple of glasses of wine in the evening often turned into a bottle which occasionally turned into two. He knew that every year Carter gave up all alcohol for the forty days of Lent and he now decided to do so as well. Lent, thankfully, was nine-odd months away which gave him plenty of time to reconsider.)

"I worry about the world we're leaving to the next generation," said cheerful Walt O., looking very serious. "People are marching and I'm thinking of marching with them."

(Dad had once read that dinosaur had marched the earth for two hundred million years. So far, humankind had held sway for a mere two hundred thousand. It was his opinion that marching wasn't going to close the gap any time soon though it might be a way to fill in the social box on one's Grapes list.)

On they dinosaur walked to the finish line. Beverly and her family had attended a picnic with her church group, and she had felt *grateful to* be around other people, Paul F. had gone through a bitch of a conversation with his ex-wife, the one he had married before he finally admitted he was gay and Walt O., jumping in again, said his wife was going away on a two-day business trip and he was feeling anxious about being alone.

Done.

"Bob, how was your weekend?"

(Not done.) "Uhh... pretty uneventful," said Dad. (*Sure,* it was.) "I did some reading, learned a few things. Nothing special."

"Would you care to share?"

"Maybe later."

(He was, in fact, already planning on it.)

Blue State Coffee

"Did you know that the Ancient Egyptians thought hysteria in women was caused by a wandering uterus?"

It was the first thing out of my father's mouth as Annie dropped her satchel to the floor and sat down across from him, a steaming cup of tea in hand. They were at Blue State Coffee on York Street and in anticipation of the event, Dad had arrived thirty minutes early to make sure he procured a table. Annie, again in a drab skirt, thick sweater and shapeless denim jacket, looked startled at the question. (Or maybe it was the thought of a uterus wandering.)

"*What?*"

"They also thought fumigating the woman's vagina would return it to the correct position."

Annie glanced around the room as if other people might be eavesdropping. Even in the middle of the afternoon the comfortably retro coffee house with its wood floors and couches and chairs was busy. Students sat at tables with laptops open. A group of uniformed nurses on break chatted in the corner. Two businessmen in suits sat on stools near the window. There was a line of people at the counter with its humming expresso machines and well-stocked food cases. When, Dad wondered, had society became so addicted to caffeine? Not that he judged. He was on his second café latte. The steamed milk on top of the expresso was shaped like a pine tree. He approved.

"What are you *talking* about?" asked Annie.

"I spent Sunday afternoon reading about the history of psychotherapy. Did you know that women were also given laxatives for weird behavior?" (Hmm. Maybe I should try that.)

"I am *not* weird."

"They were also given clitoridectomies." (I wouldn't try that.)

"Mr. Boone."

"We're friends here. Call me Bob."

69

"All right… *Bob*. One more stupid, insulting comment and you can drink your coffee alone."

Dad blinked in surprise. "I thought I was being funny." (Men so often do.)

"No, you're being a misogynistic creep." (Men so often are.) "Now, listen." Reaching down, Annie pulled a folder up out of her satchel. Putting it on the table, she opened it. "I asked the administration office for your file. I know what happened to you."

"I thought you weren't supposed to."

"Well, now I do and the only reason I'm meeting like this is I'd like to help you if I can."

"You hurt me." Dad tried to sound matter of fact. "It would help me if you could explain why."

"I really can't do that."

"Why not?"

"Because I'm already finding it hard to be objective here and without objectivity, which comes with a degree of distance, I cannot effectively give you a *friend's* good advice."

"Yeah, well, with *friends*, it doesn't work that way. You know about me; I need to know about you."

"All I really know about you is you're *esteemed*."

(Did my father detect sarcasm? It gave him courage.) "You talk, I talk, we both talk, or I leave. By the way, can I get you a muffin or something?"

"I don't eat sweets." Annie closed the folder and pushed it aside. "All right. But if at any time, I feel these get togethers are crossing any kind of personal line—"

"They won't."

"Or that you're saying stupid, insensitive things."

"I won't."

"…I'll terminate them."

"Deal," said my saintly father.

Annie sighed. She took a sip of tea. "Now then. To address your question. There are certain women—"

"You?"

"…Women who are most comfortable engaging in uncommitted relationships. There could be any number of valid reasons for this…"

She started slowly and hesitantly but with Dad's undivided attention, Annie went on to explain in detail what those reasons might be.

A Brief History of Crazy

The awareness and treatment of mental illness (my father had read on Sunday) dated back to five thousand years before the birth of Christ. At the time, the population of the world was around seven million people. In Mesopotamia they were inventing the wheel and in China, they were busy inventing rice and domesticating water buffalo. Still, they weren't too busy to drill holes in the heads of people they considered spiritually possessed.

(That's one way of getting the crazies out.)

When exorcism, threats, bribery and torture didn't work, an ancient psychiatrist's go-to treatment was homicide.

(Oh, well. Next patient.)

In ancient Persia they thought mental illness was caused by demons, but there they practiced precautionary measures such as personal hygiene and purity of the mind and body.

(Dad wondered if this was why drinking, sex, women driving cars and shaking with the left hand seemed to be frowned upon in the Middle East.)

Around the fourth century BC the Greek physician, Hippocrates, suggested that *unique personalities* (now there's a good name for crazy) were caused by imbalances in the blood, the phlegm, the bile and the black bile.

(Okay. But what color was non-black bile? As an artist, Dad felt it important to know these things.)

In order to restore the body's balance, the Greeks recommended bloodletting, purging, and special diets. Hippocrates also encouraged changing the occupation and living circumstances of the patient.

(Dad now wondered if the ancient Greeks had some form of universal health care. All this seemed expensive.)

Throughout history, mental illness had a social stigma attached to it. Crazy threatened the family's identity as an *honorable unit*.

(Really? When it comes to human history, honor seems a moot point.)

Even though the first psychiatric hospital was built by Muslim Arabs in the eighth century, the middles ages was pretty much one big catastrophe when it came to mental health. Crazies were isolated, excommunicated, burnt at the stake and housed with lepers, vagrants, the handicapped and criminals. They were chained to walls and kept in dungeons without heat or bathrooms.

(Out of sight, out of mind!)

Big sigh. Rising from his chair, my father went to the stacks and found another book. Returning, he opened it somewhere in the middle.

The 19th century, Dad now read, was fertile ground for the treatment of crazy. An Austrian physician, Franz Mesmer, believed that human beings contained a magnetic fluid that was *affected by the planets*. If the planets were out of orbit, so was the person. Oh, but wait! There were certain people, particularly Mesmer, who could use their own personalities to affect the magnetic fluid in others(!). Patients were seated around a tub filled with chemicals. Iron rods attached to the tub were applied to parts of their body. Mesmer would then enter wearing a turban and purple robe and proceed to touch the patients with his hand or with a wand. Voila! Cured!

(Dad closed his eyes. He felt a headache coming on. Obviously, his planets were preparing to jettison orbit. He went back to the stacks and got another book.)

The first significant advance in psychology, Dad now read, was the development of psychoanalysis by Sigmund Freud in the late eighteen and early nineteen hundreds. Freud broke the mind down into three parts – the id, the ego, and the superego. The unconscious *id* was all about sex and aggression. The unconscious *superego* existed to tell the id to get its shit together and calm down. The *ego* was there to try and keep peace between the other two.

(Why Freud should have come to this conclusion, Dad had no idea. Maybe this whole subject was beyond him. He was, however, getting tired of searching through the stacks and so, turning the page, he continued reading.)

Freud believed that mental illness occurred when the three parts of the human mind started arguing with each other. Apparently if a person could figure out what the argument was about, the illness would be put to rest. Hence, *talking cures* – free association that dredged up repressed trauma, thoughts and feelings from the past. This took *time and professional supervision.*

(Well, of course it did. If Freud was the father of modern psychiatry, one has to assume he was also the father of ongoing and expensive psychiatric medical bills.)

Dad skipped several pages ahead. Jungian Analysis, he now read, was psychotherapy where *imagination, fantasy, dreams and the unconscious* are used to discover meaning, provide relief to psychological suffering and further the development of the individual into what they truly are intended to be – a conscious and fulfilled human being.

(Wow. This sounded like a lot of work. And as with Freud, why all the emphasis on the unconscious? Weren't there already enough things to think about without opening up an undiscovered can of worms? As for dreams, most of my father's dreams consisted of trains stuck between stations and airplanes flying to the wrong destination. He wasn't sure he wanted to know what this said about him and wasn't even sure he cared. Again, he skipped ahead.)

The first lobotomy was performed in 1935 and entailed the destruction and/or removal of the prefrontal lobes of the brain. Later advancements included the "ice pick" lobotomy in which a spike was driven up beneath the eyelids of both eyes and swirled around in a circular motion. The procedures had *mixed results* and often gave way to patients being electro-convulsified, tranquilized, and when all else failed, thrown into padded rooms.

(Hmmm. Not for the first time in this afternoon's endeavor, Dad found himself wondering just who the crazies were – the patients or the doctors. Bored now, he began to skim.)

Psycopharmaceuticals were introduced in the 1950s. This led to many patients being deinstitutionalized.

In 1982 it was announced that homosexuality was unrelated to psychological disturbance or maladjustment. (Dad couldn't wait to tell Carter this. He'd be relieved to know.)

In 1999, Prozac became the third best-selling prescription drug in America. (Dad disliked even taking aspirin. He also had no doubt that the sales of illegal drugs and alcohol put prescriptions drugs to shame. He flipped towards the end.)

To read that fifty percent of all Americans would undergo some form of psychotherapy in their lifetimes.

To read that nearly one in 12 Americans reported having depression issues.

To read that anxiety issues affected 40 million people in the United States alone, that eight percent of all adults would develop post-traumatic stress disorder, that for every reported suicide there were 25 unsuccessful attempts and that over 200 billion dollars a year was spent on mental health making it the costliest medical condition in the country.

Dad closed the book. Who would have thought there could be so many different kinds of crazy? Who would have thought that so many people could have mental health problems and that they'd cost so much? Did *he* really have such problems? Artists often did. "Let me go quietly on with my work," Vincent Van Gogh had written his brother. "If it is that of a madman, well, so much the worse, I can't help it." Dad also knew that Michelangelo, of Sistine Chapel fame, had suffered from obsessive compulsive disorder and refused to go anywhere without wearing boots, that Francisco de Goya had such severe anger issues he was impossible to talk to, that Picasso, Pollack and Goya were rumored to have had clinical depression and that Edward Munch was, to put it mildly, The Scream. And that, Dad was sure, was just the tip of the iceberg. Crazy was part of the artistic landscape. Was COG therapy helping him in any way, shape or form? At least no one had drilled a hole in his head or chained him to a wall or performed an exorcism or a frontal lobotomy.

Yet.

Finished, the artist, Robert Boone, returned the books to the stacks, went outside, got into his truck and drove home. As always, the best cure for crazy was a good dinner.

(But then, everyone knows that.)

Carter

"Rembrandt's eye."

It was the first thing Carter Hurley ever said to Robert Boone, and it took him completely by surprise because that's exactly what it was.

It was August of 1995 and my father had just returned from an underfinanced pilgrimage to Washington D.C. where he had spent two days wandering the National Gallery of Art and the night between them sleeping under a bush in the Enid A. Haupt Garden. (Without getting arrested!) The famous self-portrait by the Dutch painter, Rembrandt van Rindj, the point of the whole trip, had occupied him for hours and now, having returned to New York and his small space at the Art Students League, he was attempting to replicate the artist's left eye and its surrounding wrinkles and folds.

(Fun!)

The man, standing behind him was perhaps thirty, was slight of build and balding and in his tweed jacket, collared shirt, kakis and penny loafers, effete looking in a calculatedly Ivy League sort of way. Dad hadn't heard him approach and because he hadn't, felt as if caught in a questionable act.

"Painting Techniques of the Masters?" asked the man, smiling pleasantly. "Page 222? Keep your nose out of my painting, the smell of paint is bad for you?"

Dad now felt annoyed that his cherished book on artists should be evoked so easily by a stranger. Still, it was obvious the intruder knew a little something. Perhaps this was why he wouldn't shut up.

"Rembrandt was bankrupt at the time he did that particular self-portrait, you know. He lived rich and died poor. A mistake for any artist."

"How did you get in here?" Dad growled.

Unperturbed, the balding man stepped forward and peered over Dad's shoulder for a closer look as the canvas. "What's interesting is Rembrandt was right-handed. In most of his self-portraits, he's facing left, to free up his painting hand. In this case it's thought he was referencing Raphael's Portrait of Baldassare Castiglione. Making himself out to be the rich gentleman. You familiar with it?"

Okay, maybe the guy knew more than a little something. "Are you a painter?" asked Dad.

"No. I'm a dealer." He held out a soft looking hand. "Carter Hurley. The Hurley Gallery. And I'd like to see some of your work."

"No."

"No, you don't have any?"

"No, you can't see it."

"What can I do then?"

"You can buy me a glass of wine."

Carter did. Over two glasses of Chateau Franc Mayne at the Plaza Hotel (old fashioned but plush), he explained that he was the son of Nathaniel Hurley.

"Dad was a less than-prominent painter in the eighties. Neo-expressionism. Lot of sound and fury signifying. Fortunately, there was some family money."

He had attended Harvard where he had majored in Art History and Criticism.

"Pretty good program. Koerner was fabulous."

He loved art but had no talent for it.

"I couldn't paint my way onto a paper bag let alone a stretched canvas."

But he had an eye.

"I'm a homosexual, Bob, I know good when I see it."

He and his partner, Theo, had a gallery space.

"We can afford the rent on it for another six months."

And he was looking for paintings and photographs to show.

"And I have a gut feeling, and I trust my gut, that you, my friend, *you*, have things worth seeing. Another glass of wine?" Carter raised a hand, signaling a waiter.

Two glasses later, a skeptical Robert Boone told Carter Hurley that though he wouldn't promise anything, if Carter was willing to get there on his own, he could come up to Branford some weekend and look at some work.

"How about this weekend," said Carter. "I'll bring a picnic."

Admiring Carter's taste in wine and thinking it might extend to foodstuffs as well, my father said yes.

"Oh, my goodness," said Carter softly.

Dad, having pulled the first of the Angel in the Darkness paintings out from behind a stack of blank, stretched canvases, had placed it on an easel and was now staring uncomfortably at the floor.

"Oh, goodness, goodness me."

"What."

"It's Biblical. It's fabulous."

"Gimme a break, it is not.

"Gimme a break, it sure is. You have more?"

My father had twenty-one more to be exact.

The first exhibition of Robert Boone's paintings took place in November 1995, and I know for a fact that it was a less than enthralling experience for him. This was mostly because his father showed up with his former law associate, now second wife. Dad had made the mistake of mentioning the show to him, even though Ben, much to his distress, had recently announced he was selling the Branford house and at the behest of said wife, was moving to Fairfield, Connecticut so as to be closer to her parents.

"But I live here on the weekends," protested Dad.

"That's not my problem," said dear, old Ben. "Besides, you're too old to be living at home. It's time to move on."

And to think Dad had considered not attending the opening at all. "I can't, I'm busing tables for Sayid that night."

"Sayid's catering the opening so no, you're not," said Carter. (Dad had introduced him to Francois/Sayid and they had become immediate friends.)

"The thought of strangers talking about my work drives me crazy," said Dad.

"No excuses," replied Carter. "They're going to love them." His partner, Theo, who was an interior designer, had framed them simply and beautifully. Their friend, Erik, a theatrical lighting designer, had lit them just so. Another friend, Brian, a pianist, had been recruited to play Chopin in a corner of the gallery. As Carter had said, homosexuals knew good.

"Oh, for goodness sakes, it's your dead wife and children," said the former law associate and second wife, glaring at Angels in the Void #4. "I thought that was behind us."

Dead. Behind us.

The words, coming from the woman's mouth, felt like an abscessed tooth in my father's mouth. She went ahead to wander the show, my grandfather in tow, intimating to anybody within earshot that "we always knew Bob was special" and "I think this particular talent comes from Ben's side of the family."

"Pay no attention to her. She's drunk," said Ben who, having made any number of visits to the bar, was drunk.

"Your father doesn't know anything about what you do," said Carter, totally dumfounded.

"My father doesn't know anything about anything," Dad replied. He left soon thereafter and went home to his comfortable hovel.

(But! Some people do. Know something, that is.)

Carter called him the next morning with news. "We have healthy five figure bids on every painting."

"You're kidding me."

"I kid you not. And we're holding out for more."

"That's crazy."

"Bob?" said Carter.

"What?" said Dad.

"Please tell your father you're buying the house in Connecticut."

It was a great source of pride to Carter and quite a surprise to Ben Boone when Dad qualified for the mortgage.

My Father's House

My father's house sits back off the road on an acre and a half of land. Purchased by Benjamin and Mary Boone in 1968 for one hundred and thirty-five thousand dollars, the house is two stories with a wood shingled, gabled roof that holds a large, third floor attic. It has a living room, dining room, book filled study, family room and four bedrooms and three bathrooms. It has a small basement that has been converted into a utility room. It has grey clapboard siding, dormered windows, hard wood floors, high ceilings, two stone fireplaces and a farmhouse kitchen. Rear French doors lead out on to a stone patio beyond which is a lawn with surrounding seasonal flower beds. There is a small white gazebo towards the rear of the property. The interior of the house has a comfortable, historic feel. My grandmother, Mary, was fond of woven, naturally dyed fabrics, hooked rugs and pillows, wall sconces and early American antiques. Adjacent to the house is a separate, A-framed, two car garage and storage room, half of which my father converted to a studio in 1991, adding the other half in 1994 after purchasing the house from his father. The property is separated from the road by a white picket fence and the house is hidden from adjacent properties by stands of trees. The back of the property abuts a 30-acre tidal march beyond which can be seen the Branford River. It is a 15-minute walk from the house down to Branford Point and Long Island Sound. If put on the current market the house would now sell for about 1.6 million dollars.

That's the house.

This is why I think my dad bought it.

The house and grounds encapsulate the only times in his life when he was at peace. It is filled with the memories of the people he loved, and it creates pictures in his head. In the empty family room, my father can still see his younger sister, Karen, playing with her dolls. Alone in the kitchen, he still sees his older sister, Melissa, spilling lemonade on her homework and laughing about it. When he looks into the vacant back yard, my father can see his father, Ben, raking leaves. In the unoccupied dining room, he can see the entire family sitting and eating together at the table. He can look at a closed bedroom door and remember that same closed door on a Saturday morning and the sound of a man and a woman making love. He can be in bed at night, unable to sleep, staring at the ceiling and suddenly, his mother is there, bending down to kiss him goodnight, just as she did when he was a child.

And then there's this.

When my father was in his late teens and early twenties, he would sit by himself in front of the fireplace on winter nights, staring at the flames. Perhaps it was his imagination but if he listened hard enough it was as if he could hear his mother and sisters talking. These were not the voices of ghosts. They were the voices of the angels that he would eventually transfer to canvas and if he had known that once painted, the voices would leave the house and move on – no longer needed? – somewhere else to go? – lost? – he would never have picked up the brush.

There are still times that my father sits at night, in front of the fire or stands outside looking up at the stars, hoping that those voices, and others, will return. He knows it's unlikely, but he feels that if he were somewhere else, there would be no chance they'd ever find him, no chance he could ever fill the house – any house – with voices again.

And so, in safety, he waits.

Day 7 – Boundaries

"You, dude, are the bomb!" said Colin.

It was just after 9 am on Tuesday, the seventh day of COG, and the artist, Robert Boone, was already in a precarious state. Coming in from the parking lot, he had taken a wrong turn and had found himself walking past a crowd of disheveled, boisterous people gathered in front of a wall of snack machines. These were the participants in the Dual Recovery Program, people dealing with both mental health issues *and* drug and alcohol problems, and they seemed to love standing in the hall, sharing personal horror stories and substituting their various addictions with vast quantities of junk food. They scared the willies out of him but at least they made the people in the COG program seem somewhat normal. Passing them, my father had continued down the hall only to encounter two of the DRP's, a man and a woman, engaged in an angry argument which seemed to consist mostly of F-bombs. The woman was middle-aged and slovenly, and the man was the lonesome cowpoke who hadn't wash his hands in the men's room after urinating. As Dad passed, the man suddenly roared and put his hands around the woman's neck. Taking two steps, Dad knocked him back into the wall and proceeded to thumped him into the hard white surface.

"You don't – (thump!) – take your shit – (thump!) – out on a *woman*!"

Five minutes later, he found himself in Dr. Giancarlo's office being (there was nothing else to call it) reprimanded.

"You got a little out of line there, Bob."

"The guy was beating up on a woman and I was out of line?"

"You could have stopped it without being aggressive. Or you could have called for a hospital orderly."

"I'll remember that the next time I see someone getting choked to death."

Dr. Giancarlo stared a moment. "You're upset, aren't you."

"Damn right."

"About what exactly?"

"I told you, I don't like seeing people getting pushed around."

"People pushed around, or women pushed around?"

(We cut to the chase!)

"I don't feel I need to defend myself on this," said Dad.

Dr. Giancarlo stared a moment. "Normally this would be a reason to terminate your participation in the COG program—"

"Great! Thank you!"

"But in your case, I'm not going to do that. You need this program, Bob. It's already helping you."

Abruptly, all the air went out of my father. He suddenly felt (yes, he had to admit it) ashamed of what he'd done. Beating up on a semi-comatose lame brain in a cowboy hat who could hardly push back. What had he been thinking? (The woman probably could have beaten the lonesome cowpoke up by herself.) And now it suddenly hit him. Maybe his daughter (me!) was right as well. If he didn't like seeing women pushed around, why is it he'd had no trouble demanding Annie engage in the coffee klatches? Maybe it *was* blackmail. It was a troubling thought.

"You're going to be late for the morning's lecture," said Dr. Giancarlo, his eyes going back to the papers on his desk. Feeling like a chastened little boy, Dad left the room.

And now, here he was in the courtyard having to deal with an overly excited Colin. "You're an artist! You're in museums!"

"Will you *please*—" Dad looked around to see if people were looking—"keep your voice down?"

"Bullshit!" said Colin, not keeping his voice down. "I hacked into Verizon to see who's name the phone was under—"

"Hacked? You hacked...?"

"On the computer you gave me and then I looked you up. You're on Wikipedia, dude! (Ouch.) By the way, you never set up a password for your account, I did it for you."

"Oh, thanks so much."

As if to seal the deal, Colin now gave my father a light punch on the arm. "Okay, I want to see your stuff."

"Then go see it." Dad turned and started towards the lecture hall.

Colin followed at a fast shuffle. "I checked. The closest place is New York."

"Then go to New York," said Dad feeling increasingly unsettled. (Or was he still upset about assaulting the bum in the pickled cowboy hat?)

"I can't fucking *afford* to do that."

Colin suddenly stumbled and turning, my father quickly caught him. Jesus. What was he thinking, making the poor kid move too fast. "Okay, tell me something, why do you want to see my work?"

"I want to show you my support."

"I'm in museums and collections. Why do I need your support?"

"My *personal* support," said Colin, as if that made all the difference.

It did. Dad, much to his surprise, felt oddly touched by the stupid kid. (Who's the one who's stupid?) "All right, look…. we'll drive down to New York sometime. We'll look at… *something.*"

"I'll need to eat."

"I'll buy you lunch."

"*Really?*" Colin seemed more excited at the prospect of food than he did of art. "Where?"

"Don't worry. I know places, okay? But you won't say a word about any of this."

"You got it," said Colin with a grin.

The subject of the day's lecture was on boundaries and because of the morning, my father felt he no longer had any. Annie was conducting the lecture and she seemed be directing every other sentence to him.

"Boundaries," said Annie, "refers to the line between *I* and *you.*" This suddenly seemed like an accusation. Had he truly blackmailed Annie into meeting with him? The thought now wouldn't go away.

At yesterday afternoon's coffee, after assuring him that as a practicing psychologist she had gone through years of professional psychoanalysis, Annie had talked nonstop. Dad now knew that at the age of four, Annie had been adopted out of a Russian orphanage, brought to the United States and raised by Daniel and Elizabeth Gilmore. As parents they were warm, supportive and nurturing and Annie deeply loved and respected them with all her heart. They were also socially conservative, evangelical Christians and as Annie had grown older, she had begun to secretly question their strict beliefs. Which, yes, had made her feel guilty and ashamed. She had also felt ashamed and guilty that upon hitting adolescence, she had been attracted to boys, clothes, make-up and Cosmopolitan magazine (hello to all four!), so much so, that out of respect for her parents, she had avoided them completely.

"By setting *limits*," said Annie, staring directly at my father from the front of the lecture hall, "we *protect* ourselves and increase our ability to deal with *difficult situations* and *intense emotions*."

It wasn't until halfway through college, Wellesley, near Boston, Massachusetts, that Annie felt brave enough to explore the taboos of her adolescence. She bought clothes and shoes, used but stylish. She bought make-up. Wearing the clothes and make-up, she looked at herself in the mirror and saw a stranger. She saw a masked superhero, enticing, brave and invulnerable. (Wonder Annie!)

"Intact *boundaries* mean we have a *balance* between taking care of *ourselves* and being open to the needs of *others*."

Wonder Annie took the bus into Cambridge, went to a club, had her first ever drink ever, and allowed herself to be picked up by a super-villain, in this case, handsome, young Harvard-Man who took her back to his dormitory room where, as Annie put it, *we were intimate.* Exhilarated, she left him fast asleep at around 3 in the morning, hailed a cab and went back out to Wellesley where she stripped, showered and went to bed. When she woke in the morning it all seemed like a dream.

"*Partial* boundaries are when we have *intact boundaries* in certain situations and *nonexistent boundaries* in others."

Sans the clothes and make-up, Annie then tried sleeping with a pleasant Babson College senior, as just plain, unadorned "Annie." It was a disaster. She felt unattractive, clumsy and ashamed and she felt terrified that others would know she had *done it* and was *bad at it*.

"Rigid boundaries are when we are closed off to others. We are *afraid* of our feelings. We are *isolated* even in a crowd."

Thus began Annie's double life. A modest, soft spoken, psych major by day and a mysterious, wanton heroine, beautifully dressed and painted by night. The routine followed her to graduate school at New York University where she received her master's and on through post graduate training at Columbia.

Annie knew her double life was outside the curve. She knew it was both physically and emotionally unhealthy. But she couldn't help it. As she said in the coffee shop, "Committed relationships don't work for me. I'm more comfortable with one-night stands." Annie hesitated. "If I hurt you, I'm sorry. It wasn't intentional. It's just what it was. And is."

Somehow that hadn't made my father feel any better.

"In cognitive therapy," said Annie, her gaze now sweeping the lecture hall, "we deal with the thoughts, feelings and actions that have created unhealthy boundaries in our lives. We identify them and we look to change them. But first, we must *want to*." The last sentence was almost like an unscripted afterthought. Annie turned back to the whiteboard and in a flat voice, continued the lecture to its end. When it was over, she quickly left the room.

My father arrived in group to find all his fellow members glancing sideways at him as if he was standing naked on the other side of a mirror (a boundary?) and they didn't want to mention it. And then the dam broke (another boundary?) and within moments, it became clear that Colin had not said a word about him being a "famous" artist, he had said paragraphs. Beverly quivered in Dad's direction and depressed William G. look confused.

"You didn't say you did stuff," frowned dour Paul F.

I don't, thought Dad.

"I knew your name rang a bell," said cheerful Walt O.

As his name tag said he was Robert B., my father doubted that.

"You better not be painting *us*," warned Megan J.

Sending poison dart frogs in Colin's direction, Dad assured her he was not.

Heidi entered and things came to a semblance of order. Everyone was feeling a bit more relaxed than usual, and Dad wondered if they'd be dismissed early. He hoped so. After the morning lecture, he had sought out the semi-comatose lamebrain in the cowboy hat and apologized. His apology had been readily accepted – "no problem, y' did a' right thing" – but he was still feeling out of sorts. He wanted to go home.

"Does anyone have anything they wish to discuss?" asked Heidi. Half the circle raised their hands and Dad groaned inside. What was it going to be about today? Gender pronouns, emotional avoidance, faltering relationships and giant squid? Uh-uh. No way he was opening his mouth this morning, not even if he was water boarded.

"I'm ashamed I'm a damn queer," big, dour Paul F. said softly. His was head down and he was staring at the floor. "I want to stop being ashamed. I want to be proud I'm queer."

Click.

My father saw Michelangelo's The Last Judgement with its group of idealized, naked men embracing as they entered heaven.

Click.

He saw the heavy, desolate man in the lower corner of the fresco, one eye covered as if in shame, unable to join them.

"But it's hard, you know? I mean, my parents and ex-wife and brothers, they look at me weird when I go to visit. Old friends, they hardly talk to me anymore and they won't even meet Bill. And my kids, geez… I don't *know* what they think. Even if I could ask, I'd be afraid to."

Kids. It had never occurred to Dad that dour Paul F. might have children, that there had been a woman who once loved and desired him. How uncertain he must have been to leave that life behind and resurrect himself as something completely different.

"Uh… Paul?"

(Oh, no, it couldn't be. Was my father talking? Oh, help and double help, yes, he was.)

"I have this friend. Actually, he's my best friend and even though he doesn't use the term, he's, uhm… queer. And I can tell you he's proud being queer. He says being queer makes him both sensitive and strong because he has to be. He says it makes him part of an extended, supportive family and that it helps him appreciate the differences in people. He says homosexuals know good when they see it and he's right. He's one of the finest, most generous people I've ever known."

There. Dad had said it. What now? What now was hearing a murmur of appreciation ripple around the circle and Paul F. giving him a quick, grateful nod. It made my father wish that Carter had been in the room to share it.

"Two weeks ago," said Beverly, "my husband decided he wanted to paint our bedroom. He moved all the furniture out into the living room." Starting to grow teary, Beverly reached for Kleenex. "And he hasn't even *started* yet. Whenever I say anything about it, he says he's busy at work and he'll get to it. And we're still sleeping in the living room." Beverly looked like a helpless child. "I don't know what to do about it."

Dad's instinct was to ask Beverly where she lived, hire a painter and send him over. "Why don't you give me your address and I'll hire a painter and send him over," the white knight said before he could stop himself.

"Ohhhh!" said Beverly, looking ecstatic.

"That would *not* be solving the problem, Bob," said Heidi, sternly. "The issue isn't getting the bedroom painted, the issue is Beverly being able to tell her husband what her needs are."

"Oh," said Dad.

"Ohhhh…" murmured Beverly, looking disappointed.

Heidi turned to her. "Would you like to try a Deesc script here in group?"

Oh, not again. Dad had already decided that if someone ever sprung one on him, he would acquiesce to whatever was asked for and then do as he pleased. (Right.)

"Who," said Heidi, addressing the circle, "would like to play the part of Beverly's husband? I think we should have one of the men do it."

(No, thought my father, knowing what was coming, please, no.)

"Bob? Would you like to try?"

"Me?"

"Yes. Why don't you."

Heidi was now smiling at him. Megan J. was smirking, Walt O. was exuding generosity of spirit and Colin, Paul F. and even William G. looked as if they were trying not to fart into their chairs. Beverly was looking hopeful. So much for silence.

"What's your husband like?"

"Oh, he's so sweet. Though sometimes he can get sort of impatient."

"What's he do?"

"He's a barge master at the Gateway Terminal in New Haven Harbor."

Obviously, the only thing Dad had in common with Beverly's husband was impatience. "Okay, I'll try."

Heidi beamed her approval. "Remember, Beverly, first we describe the situation. When you…"

"When you say you're going to paint the bedroom…" began Beverly.

"What!" barked Dad. "Huh?"

Beverly looked startled. "…when you say you're going to paint the bedroom—"

"I will. Didn't I say I would? What's the rush? Gimme a break, I'll get to it!"

"But…but you haven't…"

"I've been working! Don't you know busy when you see it?"

"I…I understand you've been busy," said Beverly.

"I drive barges for a living! I bring home the terminal bacon, baby!"

(I think Dad was starting to enjoy himself.)

"I know you do but—"

"Complain, complain. It's all you do. It'd be nice to be appreciated around here every now and then."

"But…I do…!"

"Hah! You want the bedroom painted so bad, maybe you should go do it yourself!"

"*Shut up!*" screamed Beverly. "Shut up and listen to me! It was *your* idea to paint the bedroom! It was *your* idea to move the furniture into the living room! It was all *your* idea! Now paint the bedroom and move the furniture back or you're going to be sleeping in the garage by yourself!"

"Okay," said Dad. "Consider it done."

There was a beat of silence in the room.

"Yeah!" said Megan J., breaking into applause.

"Love it!" grinned Walt O.

"Awesome!" said Colin.

"My husband leaves the house when I talk like that," said Paul F., seemingly thrilled.

William G. smiled softly at the floor.

Beverly pulled her arms close to her body as if hugging herself in surprise and delight.

"How did that make you feel?" asked Heidi.

"So good," said Beverly, quivering.

"That's might not be the best way to talk to your husband but now you know you can do it if you have to."

Beverly nodded vigorously. She was radiating happiness.

"Nice job," said Heidi, turning to Dad.

"*De nada.*" (It was nothing.)

Only it was.

Paul F. had made him share something of himself. Beverly had asked things of him and perhaps because he was pretending to be someone else, he had responded. What was happening to him? My father wasn't sure. What he did know is that the morning's worries had inexplicably drained away.

When Colin asked for a ride home after group, Dad didn't say no.

Performance Art

"So, you're you."

It was several days after the opening at the Carter Gallery and my father turned from where he was bent over, squinting at the bottom right corner of Angels in the Darkness #18. Was that a thumbprint? Had someone touched the painting that was no longer Dad's painting having been sold to persons unknown for sixty-three thousand dollars? (He still couldn't believe it.) The young woman staring at him was…. *unusual* was what came to mind. She was certainly the first Caucasian woman he had ever seen who wore her hair in a mass of Medusa-like dreadlocks. They framed her sharp, expressive face and Dad had the immediate desire to draw that face. His next thought was that it was eleven in the morning and the only reason he was there was so he could be alone.

"How did you get in here?"

"Well, that's rude of you," said the young woman. "The door was open, and I walked in. I wanted to see what the big deal was all about."

The way the young woman said "big deal" made it sound as if it wasn't much of a big deal at all. Dad couldn't have cared less. What he didn't like was being called rude by an attractive woman with uncombed hair.

"I don't think I know you."

"Cecilia von Schoop," said the young woman, offering her hand. The tone of voice and the look on her face seemed to say that Dad should know that name and much to his surprise, he did. A week earlier he'd been leafing through Art Forum magazine when he noted a positive review about a New York artist who's subject of choice was toilets. (Yes, toilets.) The artist's name was Cecilia von Schoop. He had assumed it was a joke.

"Do you want to give me the first-class tour or not?" said Cecilia von Schoop, smirking ever so slightly. (Note: A smirk is a smile evoking insolence, scorn, or offensive smugness.)

The first-class tour consisted of the two of them walking from painting to painting, my father fidgeting while Cecilia hummed and hooed. "Not uninteresting," she finally said, turning from the last painting. "Old fashioned but compelling in a visceral sort of way." (Note: Visceral is the response of the *body* as opposed to the *intellect*. Think of it as a sex sort of thing.)

"Thanks for coming," said Dad and he escorted Cecilia to the front door, locked it behind her, then hurried into the gallery office and called Carter at home.

"Cecilia von Schoop."

"Yes?" said Carter.

"She's an artist."

"You might call her that. Her real name is Cecilia Hackett, and she does installations and performance art."

Hmmm. There had been a young woman at the Rhode Island School of Design, a performance artist, who had videotaped herself naked, pushing paint-filled eggs out of her vagina onto a canvas. Ellen Horvath had loved it. Dad had thought it was idiocy. Still, it was important to be open minded and so the following Monday night, with Carter alongside for support, he went to a gallery space on Lafayette Street to see the work of Cecilia von Schoop. It was around seven in the evening, the gallery was crowded with people and yes, the installation featured toilets. There was a gold gilded toilet, a spiked, barbed toilet, a toilet with a halo and angel wings, a toilet painted like a world globe that overflowed with realistic, plaster clumps of shit, a toilet giving watery birth to smaller toilets and a toilet with belts and manacles that suggested a torture rack. There was a stained, broken toilet surrounded by gravestones, and a toilet mounted on another toilet in a way that suggested two people engaged in sexual intercourse. At exactly 8 pm, the lights dimmed, and Cecilia von Schoop came out, took off the robe she was wearing and stark, sexy naked, sat down on the toilet that looked like a torture rack. She proceeded to buckle herself in and sitting as if she was the unfeeling figurehead of a ship, began to stick tiny pins into her forearms and thighs as she stared straight ahead.

"It evokes such longing and sadness," murmured the man behind him to his stylish companion.

"Sacred and regenerative," whispered an older woman in a jeweled turban.

"Ephemeral. Deeply profound," said another young man, his dark, shaved head glistening under the lights.

My father thought it was complete bullshit and once Cecilia had wiped away the blood, disembarked from her toilet and the lights had come back up, he said so to Carter.

"This is complete bullshit."

"It's different," said Carter. "And certainly controversial."

They stood and watched as Cecilia made a grand entrance in a floor-length, African dashiki, her dreadlocks cascading down her back. To continuing applause, she smiled, greeted, shook outstretched hands, curtsied, listened attentively, laughed gaily, put her hand over her heart and lowered her head modestly. Dad had never seen anyone play a crowd like this in his life. (*This,* obviously, was the performance art part of the show.)

Cecilia von Schoop found him alone on the outskirts of the gallery some forty minutes later. "*You.* You've come." She put her hands on my father's shoulder and kissed both his cheeks. "Tell me that you liked it."

"It's different. And certainly controversial."

"I knew you'd understand," Cecilia said solemnly, and after quickly excusing herself to her friends and patrons, she escorted my father out the door and across town to her loft apartment on Mott Street where she took him into her bed and where, except for forays out for food and wine, they spent the next three days making like screwing commodes.

When they weren't otherwise engaged Cecilia talked.

"…And what is so really meaningful to me about an installation is that the impact of it is so much more important than the quality of the work itself…"

– and talked –

"…I mean, the moment Chris Burden stood against the wall and had his friend shoot him through the arm, *that* was the opening salvo of true modern art…"

– And talked –

"…Do we really need landscapes or portraiture anymore when we have photography? To me, and no offense, *you,* because I know it's your métier, but realistic depictions are suited for not much more than comic books. Which is what Lichtenstein was saying with his proto-pop imagery…"

Cecilia talked so much and said so little that by the end of the second day, my father was having a hard time staying infatuated and by the end of the third day, impatient and disappointed, he'd totally had enough.

"May I say something?"

"I'm sorry, what?"

"I said, may I finally say something?"

"Oh, *you*. Of course. Anything."

"Technique combined with talent is art. Technique without talent is craft. No technique and no talent is modern art." (Meaning toilet installations.)

"I think you should leave," said Cecilia von Schoop.

"I do too," said Dad and he did.

A week later, Cecilia unexpectedly accosted him while he was setting tables at DeVeaux's. "I'm sorry, *you*, but I have horrible news. I've come to say that I will not marry you."

"What are you talking about?" said my father, glancing over at Francoise/Sayid who was behind the bar polishing wine glasses, trying to eavesdrop.

"I thought ours was to be a union of body, art and soul. Obviously, that is not and can never be the case. I'm sorry to hurt you like this."

"What are you talking about? I never planned on marrying you."

Cecilia looked shocked at the news. "You don't love me?"

"No. Nothing personal."

Cecilia suddenly looked grim. "Oh, it's personal, *you*. It's very personal."

"Wait a minute, you're the one who's breaking up with me."

"Yes, and I thought it would bother you just a little bit."

"You mean, you have no trouble blowing me off but now that it doesn't hurt me, you're upset?"

Cecilia was now beginning to look distraught. "I'm an artist, damn you! You hit me where I live!" (Good excuse.)

My father thought a moment. He had spent three days listening to Cecilia talk about nothing but herself and he thought he knew what to say. "Listen, Cecilia... I'm pretending, that's all. I can't lie to you, my heart is breaking."

"Do you really mean that?"

"I really do. I can't believe you're doing this to me."

Cecelia looked relieved. "Oh, *you*. Thank you, I can leave you now. And please don't worry, someday there will be somebody like me in your life again."

"I can only hope."

"Goodbye, *you*."

"Goodbye."

Fourteen months later, Cecilia showed up on the doorstep of Robert Boone's recently acquired house in Branford. She had a baby in her arms.

The Personal Bill of Rights

Annie was twenty minutes late.

"You're late," Dad said, as Annie dropped breathlessly into a chair at the table where he had a hot Earl Grey tea, and a raisin swirl pastry was waiting for her.

"Something came up. I would have called but you don't *have a phone*." She seemed aggravated about it. (I often am.)

"I do now but it's being used by somebody else."

"Well, that's silly." Settling back in her chair, Annie noticed the plate in front of her. "I told you, I don't eat sweets."

"Yeah, why is that?" Dad sipped his latte. "In my experience a pleasant desert makes most people happy."

"That's only because deserts remind us of happy times. Holidays, birthdays, wedding celebrations. In truth, sugar is nothing but empty calories. In heavy amounts it can cause anxiety."

"You don't eat anything sweet at all?"

"Not really. I'll occasionally eat some chocolate."

"Ah-hah," said Dad.

"What is that supposed to mean."

"You're a chocoholic."

"What?"

"It's obvious."

"It *isn't* because I'm *not*. And you can stop grinning." Dad stopped grinning and grew serious. "Okay, okay, listen, I want to apologize. I never should have implied I'd spill the beans about us if you didn't meet me for coffee and if you want to end this right now, I completely understand."

Annie looked thoughtfully down at the tabletop, then looked back up. "Bob, if I didn't want to do this, I wouldn't have. Nothing you could have done or said would change my mind. Having said that, I do appreciate the apology."

"Hey, I'm not a total asshole."

"No, not quite." Raising her cup of Earl Grey, Annie sniffed, sipped, murmured her satisfaction, and then settled back in her chair with a relaxed sigh. "Now then. Did you have a chance to take a look at the help sheets that are outside the lecture hall?"

"Sure did." At her suggestion, my father had grabbed a couple post group that morning and read them over a quiet lunch.

"Excellent. Which ones?"

"Let's see." Dad unfolded a sheet of paper and glanced at it "This one is about ways to relieve stress."

"Are you ever stressed, Bob?"

"Lately between the hours of nine and one." (Ha-ha.)

"Mmm. Did any of the stress relieving methods talk to you?"

"Dance a jig."

"Sorry?" Annie looked taken aback.

"That's one of the options that talked to me. But I don't think I'm going to talk back."

"It's merely an option. What else?"

Dad looked down the list. "Make time for solitude."

"That can be helpful."

"I spend 95 percent of my time alone already." (This is true.)

"You're right, that might not be helpful." Annie picked up her fork and cautiously poked at the pastry in front of her.

"Play pickleball," read Dad.

Annie's eyes narrowed. "Is that on the list?"

"You'd know better than I do."

"Let's let that one go. Anything else?"

"Doodle in the margins."

"Of what?"

"I don't know. This paper? But if you ask me, too many people spend too much time doodling in margins."

"Mmm." A single raisin made its way up from the plate to Annie's mouth.

"Blow bubbles," read Bob. "I think that's doubtful. But I could make a funny face and hold it for ten seconds.

"These are all on the list?"

"Yes."

"In that case, we should take them in the spirit that they're given."

"Or we could revise the list."

"Let's just move on, shall we?" A small forkful of pastry went surreptitiously into her mouth. "What else have you looked at?

Dad unfolded another sheet of paper. "This one is… the Personal Bill of Rights."

"Oh, and did anything ring a bell?"

"I have the right to ask for what I want."

"A person does, Bob, they really do." A second, small forkful of pastry went into Annie's mouth.

"Yeah, well, personally, I think if you want something you should just get it yourself."

Annie chewed, swallowed, then brandished her fork at my father. "And *I* think you're taking this a bit too literally. For example, what if we're not asking for a physical object? Let's say it's a significant other and they're asking that you not get upset when they're inadvertently running late."

"Like you were?"

"I don't think you're getting the point."

"Maybe you can explain it to me over dinner tonight."

"*No.* The list." Annie ate another bite of raisin swirl.

Dad glanced back down at the sheet of paper. "I have the right to express my feelings." He snorted as if amused.

"Is there something wrong with that?"

"What if other people assume they have the same right? And then, what happens if I express my right not to listen? Do we cancel one another out?"

"I don't think it works that way."

"If I don't have to listen to their feelings, they don't have to listen to mine. That way everyone's happy."

"Let's move on," said Annie, coldly. Her fork moved back towards the plate.

"I have the right to say no to requests I cannot meet."

"Of course, you do. What are the alternatives?"

"I think it'd be easier to ignore the requests and if reminded of them, feign memory loss."

"Oh, that is so like a man," said Annie. She put down her fork with a bang.

"I have the right to say I don't know."

"Hah!" said Annie. She picked the pastry up off the plate with her hand and took a bite. "For most men, *I don't know* is a state of being. Not only that..." Annie took another bite of pastry. "Most men don't *know* that they don't know, and they have absolutely no desire to *find out*!" Annie pushed the last of the pastry into her mouth and chewed.

Dad smiled. "I thought you didn't like sweets."

Annie frowned, trembled slightly, chewed, swallowed, then swallowed again. Reaching for a napkin, she wiped her mouth and sticky hand. "I seem to be allowing personal feelings to intrude on our conversation today."

"I think you might be dealing with hidden anger."

"*What?* That is such bull—"

Dad held up a third sheet. "Checklist for Hidden Anger? Number 3 on the list. Facial tics, fist clenching and spasmodic foot movements."

"I do not have hidden anger," said Annie, rapidly blinking, the heels of her Espadrilles tapping like castanets on the floor.

"Course not." Dad took a quiet sip of his latte. "But if you did, what would you do about it?"

"I.... I would take a warm bath. I might meditate. I could do yoga."

"Yoga?"

"Yoga has been shown to center the nervous system and increase over-all body awareness." Annie now spoke with quiet confidence. She seemed back on solid ground. "It clears the mind and calms the senses. It can relieve both depression and post-traumatic stress."

Dad put his cup down and leaned forward. "Okay, but here's the big one. Besides dressing up and going out to seduce strangers on weekends—"

"...I *so* resent it when you put it like that—"

"...what do you do to be social?"

"I am not a social person and I'm warning you, if you bring this up again."

"...see? Angry."

"I take it back, Bob. You *are* a complete asshole."

"And *you* are *angry*. What are you going to do about it?"

"Yoga!" Annie cried shrilly and rising from the table and picking up her bag, she crossed the room and went directly to the service counter where she bought herself a chocolate éclair and a vanilla-fudge muffin.

When she returned to the table, she did not share.

(I wouldn't have either.)

Isolde

"Hello, *you*, this is your daughter," said Cecilia von Schoop and without a moment's hesitation, she handed the artist, Robert Boone, a small, swaddled, dark-haired baby. (Me.)

"What?" My father stood there at a frozen loss for words.

"She is four and a half months old, *you*. She was delivered by midwife at the Mount Sinai West Birthing Center in New York City on December third, exactly nine months and twelve days after our final assignation." Cecilia seemed pleased that she had the numbers down pat.

"I think you should come in so we can talk about this," Dad said, covertly trying to hand the baby (me) back.

"No time. I'm on a flight to Brussels in seven hours."

"Brussels." It was like a food stuff Dad had never heard of before.

"I have a commission," said Cecilia, smiling smugly. "An installation. Surprised? Some people *respect* my talent, you." Cecilia glanced down at the baby (me) who had stopped its caterwauling the moment it hit her (my) father's arms. "She's yours till I get back."

"You can't be serious," said Dad, a sudden panic welling in him.

"We're artists, *you*. We sacrifice." Holding out a hand, Cecilia dropped a large diaper bag on the steps. "I'll see you and my little sweetheart in six months." And with that, she turned and walked down the brick path to her waiting town car, pausing exactly three times to call back over her shoulder. "Concrete blocks, you! Steel rods! The foundations of civilization!"

"Wait!" called Dad, also three times. "You can't just – this is – what's her name!"

"Isolde," Cecilia called as she opened the car's rear door. "Isolde Hackett-Boone!" She slipped into the town car, closed the door and as if on slick ball bearings, it glided away.

I gurgled. My father looked down at me. I stared back at him with deep, blue eyes. There was a sudden liquid sound in the vicinity of his right hand. The sound repeated itself. I scrunched my little face into what resembled an overcooked red cabbage. Dad knew what was coming and it did. I began to cry. "Shush, shush, shush," said Dad. I cried harder. Not knowing what else to do, my father turned and went into the house. As he crossed the threshold, he was met by Marisol who, having heard the sound of a wailing infant, was moving down the hall at a fast waddle. The sight of the bundle (me) in my father's stiff arms threw her fragile English right out the window.

"*El bebé. Lo que está mal con el bebé?*" Marisol sniffed the air. "*Ella ha llenado sus pantalones. Dámela. Hay que atender a su. Con rapidez.*"

(Rough translation: "Where'd the kid come from? She's crapped her pants. Hand her over. *Now.*")

"Take her!" cried Dad, understanding nothing but seeing that Marisol's arms were open and beckoning.

Thankfully there were diapers in the bag Cecilia (Mom!) had left as well as bottles, baby formula and several changes of clothes. Seemingly within minutes, Marisol had me cleaned, dried and changed and was humming a soft, Spanish lullaby as she cradled and fed me. Again, my father had no idea what any of the words meant but he had to work hard not to be too enthralled. He watched as I whimpered slightly and stirred in Marisol's arms.

"Hmm. Te quiere usted, Mr. Bob. She want you."

"*What?* No… really?"

"You are her papito. She just like you. I will prepara su came. Make a bed." With that, Marisol handed me to Dad, clucked in disapproval, showed him how to correctly hold me and then turned and left the room. Again, Dad looked down at me and I quietly looked back up at him. He wasn't sure he saw any resemblance at all.

They put me down on the guest room bed, surrounded by pillows, a soft cotton blanket covering me. I was asleep almost at once. Marisol then said she would go home, pack some things and come back and spend the night.

"Maybe you should move in for a while."

"*No seas tonto,*" said Marisol. "Don't be silly."

"For a couple of days anyway. A week or two. A month. I'll pay you."

"*Por supuesto que lo harás,*" said Marisol, finally nodding. "You will." And with that, she left.

Leaving the bedroom door open, Dad hurried to the kitchen and called Carter in New York and asked what he should do.

"It's an issue, isn't it," said Carter.

"Yeah, so what do I do?"

"I'm not sure I've ever encountered a dilemma quite like this," said Carter.

"Well and good. But *what* do I *do*?"

"The first thing you might consider doing is determining paternity."

"What does that mean?"

"You find out if the child is really yours."

My father did just that. He went to a doctor who took swabs from the inside of both our mouths and cheeks and then sent the swabs off to a DNA testing lab. The doctor called back two days later with the news that there was only a 99 percent likelihood that Robert Boone was my father.

"You mean, there's a 1 percent chance I'm not?"

"She's yours, Mr. Boone. There's no doubt about it. Congratulations."

"Thanks so much."

For my father, the next six months was an unending series of sleepless nights and interrupted days. It was foul diapers and hiccups and baby spit up on his shoulders. It was a crib in his bedroom and long walks with me, Holdie (Isolde seemed one syllable too long), snug in a baby carrier on his stomach. It was drool and cold, chamomile-soaked washcloths applied to aching gums when I was teething. It was a frantic race to the emergency room one night when he felt certain that I was burning up with fever. (Not even close.)

At what Dad calculated was seven months of age, I began scooting around the house on my bottom, slithering on my stomach, or rolling across the room. Keeping me safe was like trying to corral a cat. Putting me in my crib unleashed desolate, angry wailing. Even worse, I quickly learned how to climb out, unafraid and unintimidated, even though more than once I fell and landed on my head.

My father got no work done.

He went nowhere.

He lived on cold cut sandwiches.

He wondered if he was losing his mind.

At the very end of sixth months when my mother, Cecilia Hackett von Schoop, reappeared on his doorstep, he got right to the point.

"I want joint custody. I want visitation. I want weekends, summers and some holidays. When she isn't with you, I want her with me."

Mom smiled to herself as if she'd been expecting this all along. "And what do I get out of it?"

"I'll pay for schooling. I'll pay for food, clothes and rent. I'll pay for whatever you want."

"I think we can work something out," said Mom.

(She had already decided that there were few things better than a responsible babysitter who was not only on call 24/7 but was willing to pay for the right to sit.)

Day 8 – Problem Solving

On Wednesday, the eighth COG session – (only nine more to go, thought Dad!) – the lecture was on, of all things, problem solving. "Problem solving," the assembly was informed by a studious looking, Black woman named Whitney, is about "*achieving a goal when the path to the goal is not obvious*." Everyone in the room, obviously keen to learn this process, started to furiously scribble in their notebooks.

My father didn't. His handwriting of late seemed to have degenerated into an illegible scrawl. It was a problem.

"How can we tell if we are *stuck* in our problem-solving process?" Whitney turned to the whiteboard and began to write. "We *avoid* the problem, we become *stressed* over the problem, and we feel *depressed* about the problem."

(Dad felt unmoved. His long-favored method of problem solving was not letting problems arise in the first place. Which was a problem of late.)

"Problems become more difficult to solve if our attempts to solve them prove unsuccessful."

(Which was *also* a problem of late.)

The lecture continued but his mind was elsewhere.

Coming in from the parking lot earlier that morning, he had passed scraggily, stolid William G. who, as opposed to his usual hoodie, today was wearing a down vest over a baggy T-shirt. High on the bicep of his pale arm, my father saw the bottom of a tattoo. My father disliked tattoos. As works of art, they were at best rudimentary and at worst they were sloppy, crude and often imbecilic. But he recognized this one. It seemed impossible but there it was and now he was curious. Dad hated being curious. Being curious meant you had to do something to assuage your curiosity. (At least he did.) Which was another problem.

"The Cognitive Triad of Negative Thoughts," said Whitney, "is when we think negatively about *ourselves*, the *world* and the *future*."

Dad glanced across the lecture hall to where scraggily, stolid William G., who did all three, was sitting in his hard back chair, closed notebook in his lap, staring with vacant eyes at nothing.

Click went the mind camera in Dad's brain despite his intense desire for it not to. *Click.*

"Ongoing negative thoughts lead to ever increasing feelings of *hopelessness*. We feel unable to do anything about them."

Dad sighed inside. If a person couldn't do anything to help themselves, and obviously William G couldn't, then somebody else had to do it for them. But did it have to be him? This was a problem that had to be solved quickly so as to be taken off the board.

Dad came to group early to find William G. already there, sitting alone in the circle, staring blankly at the wall. "Hey," he said, sitting down next to him. William G. looked at my father as if not recognizing him. "Interesting tattoo." Dad pointed at it. William G. glanced toward his bicep as if it were an unfamiliar thing. "I know a guy who has the same tattoo. He's a personal trainer, you should meet him."

William G. looked at him. Was there a glimmer of interest? "I don't think so." William G. looked away.

God, this was annoying. Solving problems. Being curious. (Somewhere a cat needed killing.) "You have something better to do or are you going to go home and hang out with your folks some more?" Impatient now, my father plucked William G.'s notebook up off his lap. There was a pen in the spiral binder. "Here's the address of the gym," said Dad, writing it down. "It's called Raiders. I have a workout today at three o'clock. You show up, I'll introduce you."

"We're not supposed to hang out together."

"You're not going to hang out with me. You're going to hang with him."

William G. stared straight ahead. "I doubt I'll make it."

Group began. William G.'s anxiety was at a ninety and his depression level was a one-twenty. His parents, he said, were now threatening to throw him out of the house if he didn't look for a job. He was sleeping days and wandering the house nights. He was following none of the recommendations of the COG program.

There was no way, William G. was coming to the gym.

William G. came to the gym.

My father was on the crunch machine, being insulted and cheered on by the owner of the gym and his personal trainer, Dylan, when William G. entered and looked around as if he'd stumbled onto another planet.

It was.

Feeling bored with running one day, Dad had wandered into Raiders to find a shirtless, Black man, balancing on a large, inflated rubber ball. Dylan's muscles rippled, his rock-hard abs trembled and the cords in his neck stood out like heavy ropes. He flashed a wide grin. "Now this looks like man ready for a workout!"

"I'm not ready for that." Ball-balancing looked dangerous. One mishap and the guy was going to land headfirst in the adjacent Stairmaster.

"You will be," said Dylan and he jumped effortlessly down off the ball to the floor. "You, my man, are having a free work out with me right now and when it's finished, I guarantee you'll be signing up for the special three-week trial package!"

When the work out was over, Dad, who disliked being dictated to, signed up for the special *six-week* trial package. He'd been coming ever since, even during Covid where in a local park Dylan had conducted workouts from ten feet away. And why not? Being cajoled, teased and cheered on by Dylan was the equivalent of surrendering your brain to a higher power.

With unshaven William G. standing in the doorway like a cave dweller squinting at sunlight, Dylan glanced at my father, who nodded. Turning, Dylan pointed. "Hey, you! Soldier! Yeah, you! You here to buff your sorry ass up!" Dylan's voice, which was rarely below an enthusiastic Mach ten, was at a Mach twenty.

"Huh?" William G. looked startled.

"*Huh?* Don't you *huh* me, soldier! Get your pale, white butt over here right now!"

William G. hesitated and then did. Dylan reached out and yanked up his shirt sleeve. The tattoo, as Dad had suspected, was of a bald eagle holding a world pierced by an anchor. At the top, words and letters were seemingly etched in stone. Semper Fidelis. USMC. United States Marine Corp. It was the same tattoo that Dylan had on his muscular, right upper arm.

"What division?" asked Dylan, quietly.

"Eighth," whispered William G.

"Afghanistan?"

"Yes."

"What rank?"

"Private first."

Dylan turned slightly, showing and flexing his left bicep. On the dark skin was the tattoo of a red shield. In the shield was a hand holding a torch. Above the torch was the number two. Under it was a red and gold chevron. "Sergeant, 24th. Operation Iraqi *Freedom*, baby!"

William G. looked down at the floor. Again, he nodded slightly. Dad had often wondered what the shield tattoo meant. Now he knew. Obviously, William G. did too.

Dylan glanced back. "You good?"

"Yeah," said Dad, not sure what good meant. "I'm good."

Dylan regarded William G. for a moment. His usually cheerful features had grown stern with authority. "You listen up, Marine! On the floor and give me ten right now!" It was as if his voice came through a megaphone.

"Huh?" William G. looked frightened.

"Don't you start *huh'n* me again, Private. I said, you get your ass down on this carpet and you give me ten push-ups now!"

"...no."

"No?" Dylan sounded dumfounded. *"NO!"* He sounded apocalyptic. "Private, when I give you order, you will *do* it and you will say thank you, *sir*, may I do it *again*! Now get your ass down or I will put it down!"

William G. hesitated and then not so much knelt as collapsed down onto the floor. His hands were under his chest. His T-shirt had edged its way up and the pale band of flesh at his waist pushed up and over his belt.

"On my count, Marine! You ready? You better be! One!"

William G. grunted and pushed. His upper body came several inches up off the floor, and then he collapsed.

"You call that a push-up? I could do better 'n' that with my limp dick! Again! On my count, Marine! Two!"

"I can't," William G. moaned.

"Can't? You *can't?* There is no can't. There is only *can*! There is only *I will!* Three!"

William G. pushed and strained and started to rise.

"Yes! That is *you*, Marine! That is *you*! You do not give up! You will never give up!"

William G did just that. As Dad watched, he collapsed to the floor and lay there. Dylan quickly knelt down next to him. He leaned towards his ear. My father heard every word.

"It's all right, Marine. It is all right. You are a *man*. You have been through hell, and you have *lived*. You are with friends now. You are with fellow soldiers. I want you to listen to me, because this what you're going to do. You are going to be here at the crack of dawn every day from now on and you and I are going work out together and eat together until you are in the best physical shape of your young life. If you do not show up, even once, I am going to find where you live and I'm gonna drag you here. You are not going down. You hear me? Not on my watch."

William G. said nothing.

"Ooh-rah," said Dylan. (It's a battle cry.)

"Ooh-rah," whispered William G. and with Dylan's help, he climbed to his feet.

The problem wasn't solved, not nearly, thought Dad, but it was a start. And best of all, it wasn't his problem anymore.

The Dust of New York

At the age of twenty-four, fifteen months after leaving, Robert Boone moved from Connecticut back down to the island of Manhattan. To say he was excited about it, would be like saying a worm is excited about a hook. The proximity alone makes for squirming.

My father had long ago concluded that the city had the esthetic appeal of a foundry. He found the towering buildings claustrophobic and the crowded sidewalks and the congested streets, unsettling. He found the people, all of them so intent on their own personal daily missions, to be impersonal and faceless. Yes, there were images and scenarios that put through the prism of an artist's imagination, could certainly express something. The problem was that in a chaotic urban environment, Dad's imagination felt trampled upon. He had always done his best work in Connecticut and armed with the colors and images of New York's museums and galleries, he had consistently retreated to the Branford house on weekends to paint in quiet and solitude. Sixteen months living in the house full time had only increased his apathy for city life, but now I was there and being part of my life superseded any misgivings he had about returning.

Dad went down on a Tuesday and by Thursday had signed a lease with option to buy on a two thousand square foot, rent controlled, loft space in Tribeca. The loft had crumbling bricks walls, stained floor-to-ceiling windows, no kitchen, no wall partitions, no utilities and only overhead florescent lights. Its only real selling points were an elevator and a location that put him five blocks from Cecilia's apartment in SoHo. (I still live here. It's worth I don't know what now.)

By the following week the place was spotless thanks to Manhattan Industrial Cleaners. My father then hired a contractor (a relative of Sayid/Francoise's), who built a large kitchen and living room area, a separate bedroom, bathroom and shower, and a childproof children's bedroom and play area. (For me.)

Carter's interior designer partner, Theo, came over, gave the empty loft one look and shuddered. Theo wrote out a list.

Dad had the floors buffed and polished.

Dad bought a bed. He bought a bureau, a rocking chair and a couch. He got rid of the fluorescents and bought new lights. He installed large ceiling fans.

Dad bought towels. He bought pots, pans, silverware and plates. He bought a number of fake Persian rugs (from a relative of Sayid/Francoise's), a dining room table and chairs and an antique wooden map drawer he found in a secondhand furniture store on lower Broadway.

At Marisol's suggestion, he bought a *cune* – a crib. (For me!)

At Carter's suggestion, "because it might be a good idea not to bequeath your infant daughter black lung disease," Dad bought an industrial strength air purifier to remove dust and particles from the air and had the whole building tested for latent asbestos.

Only in New York.

My father gathered up his brushes and paints and palettes and palette knives and glazes and canvases and his drawing paper and his charcoal and graphite pencils and throwing them in the back of the recently purchased used Ford pick-up, drove down to the isle of Manhattan and moved in.

Dad and Mother-St. Cecilia quickly worked out a loose arrangement where he had me three days a week including overnights. It quickly became clear however, that three overnights a week could morph into four or five because my mother had a busy social life and other than the cooking lessons, he now took twice a week from Sayid, Dad had none. Granted, he had the occasional glass of wine with Carter and Theo, and, at Carter's insistence, he made the infrequent appearance at a gallery opening. And yes, he had the rare date, outing or short affair with one of the aspiring dancer/actress/singer waitresses that Sayid/Francois hired at the restaurant, lovely and intelligent women who most often entered the relationship impressed with the rumor of Dad's success (and semi-good looks) and then quickly left it, dismayed at his emotional distance and his reluctance to *"get out and do anything."*

(Though actually my he did *"get out"* for it was around this time that due to the wine, cooking classes, and subsequent elaborate meals at home, my father became aware of an expanding waistline. Thus began his birth as a runner, working up to and eventually averaging five miles a day along the Hudson River Greenway.)

Dad still prowled the galleries and museums of New York, studying and sketching, but too often now, he felt disconnected from what he was seeing. My mother was right. Message had become more important than formal technique. Artists were entrepreneurs and image was everything. It made it easy for him to put the work aside. Better to push me around in my stroller and tuck me into bed and make me breakfast, lunch and dinner and deal with my very loud objections to eating, sleeping and getting into anything that had a seatbelt.

"Funny. She never gives me any trouble at all," said Mom, picking me up one afternoon. (Which made Dad wonder if divas, regardless of their age, had an innate mutual respect for one another.)

"It's killing me," he complained to Carter one day. "I'm exhausted all the time. I'm getting nothing done."

"Horse pimples," said Carter. "I doubt you've ever been this happy before in your entire life."

To my father's dismay, Carter wasn't in a happy place. Through much of the late eighties and early to mid-nineties, too many of his friends and acquaintances had succumbed to AIDS. Brian, the pianist who had played Dad's first gallery opening was gone and Eric, the lighting designer, was at death's door. My father knew that Carter was more guilty than thankful that he hadn't yet contracted the virus that was killing the people he loved and so he went by the gallery on a daily basis and groused and moaned about totally inconsequential things (like *art*) in order to cheer him up. (It did.)

By the age of three, I was a precocious, demanding child who knew exactly what I wanted and when I wanted it which was right away. It made my father fear for my future significant others. (Rightly so.)

At the age of four, at my mother's insistence, I was enrolled in a private elementary school in the West Village. It was progressive and multicultural, emphasizing critical and creative thinking and had an integrated curriculum that allowed for exploration, learning, failure and growth, not necessarily in that order. Dad thought it was full of itself. However, he didn't complain because almost immediately three and four days a week of taking care of me turned into four, five and sometimes six as he volunteered – and was inevitably called upon – to pick up me at school.

Or ballet class.

Or piano lessons.

Or a friend's get together.

On September 11, 2001, at 8:45 a.m. Dad was walking me to school when a Boeing 767 loaded with 20,000 gallons of jet fuel crashed into the north tower of the World Trade Center.

We both heard it.

We both turned and saw the smoke.

I began to cry.

Dad picked me up and ran. At 14th Street, with the sky turning black behind us, he waylaid a cab. At 9:03 a.m., as the second jet crashed into the South Tower, my father, with me in his arms, was running into Grand Central Station. At 10:03, as a fourth flight crashed near Shanksville, Pennsylvania, the two of us were on a Metro North train passing 125th Street, bound for New Haven. Dad didn't yet know the details, didn't know that the towers had already come crashing down, all he knew was that he had to keep me safe and if that meant running like a scared rabbit, so be it. It took Cecilia a week of phone calls and an in-person visit from Carter before he'd bring me back down to New York. He did so reluctantly. There was still a layer of dust on Greenwich Street near the loft. He took several large handfuls of it, put it in a jar, and not sure what he'd ever do with it, placed it on the back shelf of a supply cabinet.

Yet even with dark clouds hanging, there were wonderful times in New York. There was Halloween where I'd dressed as a princess or a witch or a fairy and Dad, wearing a Lone Ranger mask, would take me around to neighbors. There was Thanksgiving with Carter and Theo and Sayid/Francoise and his entire family at DeVeaux's. My mother got Christmas, invariably taking me to visit her sedate, middle-class parents in Michigan. Dad got New Years and turned New Year's into another Christmas which meant that I got two. (And would insist on and celebrate two for the rest of my life!)

It was the Christmas of 2004, when I was seven, that I came up from New York and while opening gifts, out of nowhere asked Dad about my grandparents. Not the boring ones in the mid-west where I'd spent the last week with my mom, no, I wanted to know about my *other* grandparents. *His* parents.

"You've met Grandpa Ben. He lives in Fairfield."

"Yes, but he's with that woman. What about my grandmother. My *real* grandmother. Where's she?"

Dad hesitated, then decided to tell me the truth. "She died when I was a boy, Holdie."

I was stricken. "How? How did she die?"

"She was killed in a car accident. Along with my two sisters, who would have been your aunts."

"Oh, Daddy!" Beginning to cry, I dropped the gift I'd just opened and threw myself into his arms. "Daddy, *you're* not going to die, are you?"

"Never," said Dad, stroking my head. "Not while you're around."

(I totally believed him. I guess I still do.)

He then went up to the attic, brought down some of Mary's children's books and sitting on the couch, shared them with me. He sat beside me as I turned the pages.

"Oh, Daddy," I finally said. "I miss them."

"Me too, baby. Me too."

(He said no more.)

It should be mentioned that my father did, in fact, paint something of *significance* during these years in New York. It was 2006 and he had recently seen an exhibition at a downtown gallery by an artist whose influences seemed mired in 50s abstract expressionism. He had not been impressed. "It's as if some idiot threw paint across the room in the general direction of a canvas to see if anything would stick," he complained to Carter.

"I saw the exhibition and liked it," Carter replied. "The work has a wonderful inner vibration."

"Vibration, my ass. A three-year-old could do better with a spray can and a box of Crayola's."

"If you think it's so easy, why don't you try it?"

"I could do crap like that with my eyes closed."

"Even with eyes open, I doubt you could."

"Is this a challenge?" Dad asked, feeling challenged.

"Call it what you will if it will get you painting again."

Working off and on, using primary colors, multiple layers of glaze, a house painting brush, assorted palette knives and his thumbs, Dad completed the first painting within two weeks. "Not great," said Carter. "I'm not responding to it."

Frustrated, my father did another one, and then another, this time exploring secondary colors, crisscrossed with thick indiscriminate brush strokes of black and white. "Better, but not quite there," said Carter.

Spoiling for a fight, Dad did two more, this time painting tertiary hues in rough horizontal lines, going from a long color wavelength of reds and oranges in the middle of the canvas that bled into yellows and greens and then into short color wavelengths of blue and violet at the top and bottom of the canvas. The colors were heightened by small swirls of silver and gold. (When your father's a painter, you grow up knowing this stuff.) "Obviously not your milieu," Carter sniffed.

In a frenzy now, my father took a twelve-foot canvas, unrolled it out onto the floor, took several buckets of house paint, a gardening trowel and a yard rake and again, starting at the center, he dripped and dribbled and poured and raked and troweled, swearing passionately at the canvas the entire time. I was there watching when he dropped to his hands and knees, raked his elbows and rubbed the top of his head across the entire mess, the coup de grace. It took three days to get the paint out of his hair and the painting two weeks to dry.

"Screw you if this piece of crap ain't it."

Carter grinned happily. "Bob. It's wonderful. They all are, each and every one. Perfect and unique. I can't wait to show them."

"You tricked me," my father said, feeling a hint of outrage.

"Yes. And I'm so glad I did. What shall we call them?"

"I don't care what you call them. They give me a headache."

"Excellent idea," said Carter. "I'll run them past Theo. The poor thing experiences acute migraines. He'll come up with something."

The Aura paintings were born.

"I still say they're crap," said Dad, the afternoon before the opening. "Worse than that, they're rip offs. Jackson Pollack is turning over in his grave. Nobody is going to give them the time of day."

To his shock, just about everybody did.

Day 9 – Automatic Thoughts

It was Thursday, the ninth day of COG and group was not going well. Everyone had gone through depression and anxiety levels, Heidi was frustrated that my father had forgotten to do his, and Dad was frustrated that he had forgotten to make something up.

"This is a lack of commitment, Bob. You are procrastinating and you are avoiding."

"I'm feeling overwhelmed."

He wasn't, not really, but the Tuesday morning lecture on problem solving had suggested being overwhelmed could *be* a problem when one was trying to *solve* a problem. It seemed like a good excuse.

Everyone had then gone through their Grapes list.

Colin was exploring on-line dating websites. "Gonna hook up with my new computer," he said, glancing wickedly at Dad. ("*Huh?*" thought my imbecile-tech father. Hook *what* up?). Depressed William G. said he was going to the gym, news that brought positive reinforcement from the others in the group which caused William G. to almost smile. (Go Raiders, thought Dad.) Cheerful Walt O. had a job interview. "Not teaching," he said, nervously. Angry Megan J., who seemed especially tense this morning, said she was "still lookin' for ways to get out and about and not go runnin' back." Beverly was going to work on a "food drive" with her church group. (Which made my father, who didn't like thinking of people going hungry, wonder if he should contribute canned goods. He didn't have many, but he was sure he could buy several cases of something somewhere.) Dour Paul F. then announced that he and his partner, Bill, were going dancing after work which elicited more approval from the group. (What kind of dancing, Dad wondered. Ballroom, Flamenco, a Waltz? He couldn't picture dour Paul F. doing any of them, certainly not disco.) And now, Heidi was concerned that Dad's social grape again seemed to consist mostly of bad coffee with other group members at the kiosk.

"Ohhhh… I haven't been invited," said Beverly. She looked rejected and Dad winced inside, feeling now that he really would have to purchase a truckload of canned goods to make up for it. This was getting complicated.

'I'm going to assume, Bob, that you haven't done any work on your thought records either," said Heidi."

"Fraid not."

"And why is that?"

"I never think of anything significant."

"What does the group think about Bob's inability to think?"

Off to the races.

The subject of the morning's lecture, given by a sunny, beautifully dressed Asian woman named Lee, was on Cognitive Distortion and yet again, it had to do with what one was *thinking*.

"*Thoughts,*" said Lee, "are *ideas* we tell ourselves *in our heads*." (Isn't that, well… obvious?)

Truth be known, Dad wasn't really listening all that hard. Since morning coffee he'd been thinking about his daughter (me!). He hadn't heard from me in more than several days, hadn't seen me since I insisted he attend this program, and when he didn't hear from me or see me for a length of time, he worried about me.

"Some thoughts happen so quickly we're *unaware* of them. These *are automatic* thoughts."

(Another way of saying people are oblivious. Should he call me, or should he wait for me to call him?)

"*Automatic thoughts* affect our *moods* and *behaviors*."

(Probably better to wait. Dad didn't want me to think he was needy in any way.)

"*Distorted thoughts* are an *error* in thinking and are not a *conscious* process."

(No wonder no one ever knew what they're doing. No, he'd give it to the weekend and then he'd call. Unless he couldn't wait and called tonight.)

"Distorted thinking means you are *focusing on the negatives* and ignoring all the *positives*."

(If something was annoying you, how could there be positives? What was wrong with his daughter (me!) that she should be ignoring him so?)

"Jumping to conclusions is making *negative assumptions* without *sufficient facts*."

(The assumption Dad usually jumped to was that one should be prepared for the worst. Which is what he felt when I went missing for more than a week.)

"*Mindreading* is assuming someone is thinking negative things about you for *no reason*."

(He had given his daughter (me!) *no reason* not to check in. What could I be thinking? It couldn't be good.)

"*Catastrophizing* is expecting the worst possible outcome."

(Maybe I was sick. Maybe I was hurt or dead. I had *never* gone this long with calling before. Actually, I had. Many times. I was insensitive that way. Another thing I got from my mother.)

"*Emotional reasoning* is making decisions based on *emotions* as opposed to *facts*."

(Dad certainly didn't do that. Never, not ever. Except when his daughter (me!) was pissed off at him because he had done something wrong but what?)

"*Labeling* is assigning negative labels to yourself or others when they make a mistake."

(If it looks like a frog and jumps like frog, it's a frog. Ribbit-ribbit.)

"*All or nothing thinking* is the misconception that if we can't do it *perfectly*, why bother doing it *at all*."

(No. It was my father's opinion that if he hadn't done it perfectly, it was because he hadn't done it perfectly *yet*. Perhaps there was still hope that he could be a perfect father and his perfect daughter (me!) would call him.)

"And last but not least," said Lee with a smile, "is the *tyranny of the shoulds*. I should do this, they should do that. When we don't measure up to our own expectations, we feel *guilty*. When others don't, we feel angry and *upset*."

(No shit, Sherlock!)

And now, here was Dad sitting in group, about to be taken to task, when all he wanted was to find the nearest phone (someone *had* to have one) and call his daughter in New York (me!) and apologize for whatever it was he'd inadvertently done wrong.

"You don't really want to look in the mirror," said big, dour Paul F. "Maybe 'cause you're afraid you're not gonna like what you see."

(Ouch.)

"Something's bothering you," said Beverly, her face beaming with good will. "I think you need to determine what that is. I know Jesus would like to help you try."

(Ouch.)

"I think you're trying to make up for something," said Colin. "You just don't want to admit it."

(Ouch.)

"You work out too hard," said expressionless William G., who was now working out on a daily basis. "It's like you're using it to hide from something."

(Double ouch.)

"You never talk about the people in your life," said cheerful Walt. O. "Are there any?"

(Double and triple ouch.)

"Megan?" It was Heidi. "You look as if you'd like to say something."

Dad saw that Megan J. was staring at him as if he was something on the bottom of her shoes. When she spoke now her voice was thick with contempt. "You ask me, you're just all the time lyin' to yourself 'cause you don't want to face up to your own damn issues."

The circle was silent. Dad bit his tongue.

To his sudden dismay, the usually taciturn Megan J. began to hyper-ventilate, her shoulders began to heave, and she fought back in tears. "And believe me, I know all about that, 'cause I don't want to face my issues either." Trembling, Megan F. bowed her head. "I'm so tired... of letting my people down. My husband, he works so hard. On his hands and knees all day fixing washer and dryers... taking care of me and our boys plus his mama. Droppin' me off here in the morning, taking his lunch time to pick me up and bring me home. An' you want to know something? Last night, 'cause he knew I was feeling so down? He went down to the corner to get me ice cream. He was walking home, and he gets stopped. By the police. *White* police."

Megan J.'s look was solemn as she glanced around the circle at what Dad suddenly realized were all pale faces, his own included. (He suddenly had the suspicion Megan J. didn't want to send her neighborhood into oblivion after all. Her fear and anger had long been focused on something else.)

"They get out of the car. They ask him where he's going. Home, he says. They ask what's in the bag. Ice cream, he says. For my wife. They tell him to empty his pockets. Now my husband's not a fool. He knows what can happen when a Black man goes to his pockets with the police watching. He puts his hands on the car and he says, sirs, I prefer you do it for me. They laughed and told him to get his ice cream on home." Megan J. clenched her fists into tight balls and struck her legs. "He was doing that for me! And what makes me so crazy is I can't do nothing for him. I can't do nothing for nobody no more." Megan F. bowed her head again. "Most times I feel so sad and helpless, I just want to die."

"Are the anxiety medications helping?" Heidi asked, quiet eyes on Megan J.

"Maybe. A little bit. I don't know."

"Sometimes it takes a while to find the right ones and to determine how exactly much to take."

"That's what the doctor says."

"And in the meantime, you've told me your family and neighbors are in your corner."

"I don't deserve it."

"I don't think any of us would agree with that, "said Heidi.

Dad sure didn't. He might have ten minutes ago when he was obsessing about meaningless phone calls with me (who he knew was perfectly safe) but he didn't now. What to do?

"Megan?" It was Beverly. "I know it's against the rules, but I'd really like to give you a hug."

Megan J. and Beverly solemnly regarded one another. "Girl, you can give me a hug anywhere and anytime you want."

Beverly looked to Heidi, as if for permission. "I think this one time that would be more than appropriate," said Heidi.

The women rose from their chairs. They met each other in the center of the circle. Beverly's arms went around Megan J.'s shoulders and Megan J.'s arms encircled Beverly's waist. They stood, belly to belly, breast to breast, cheek to cheek, both swaying slightly.

Click.

Robert Boone saw two contrasting faces surrounded by the transcendent.

Click.

He saw two bodies infused with the nurturing power of the feminine.

Megan and Beverly separated. They gazed into one another's overflowing eyes, both beatific. Still holding each other, they just stood. Suffering machines? No. Picasso was wrong. It was men who fought, lied, crashed and burned.

Women endured.

Quattro Formaggio

Through all the years in New York my father lived for the summer. My mother, Cecilia, inevitably had a commission somewhere and if she didn't, she was off to conferences and institutes, sharing the artistic experience with rabidly admiring performance artists in the making. She was a success, no doubt about it, and Dad was glad for it, for this was the time he could whisk his daughter (me!) off to the house in Connecticut where a clucking Marisol waited to sweep her *pequeña pastilla de goma* – little gumdrop (me!) – into her arms. For lucky yours truly, there were beaches and trees and junior day camps and tennis lessons and cook outs in the back yard. For Dad, there was quiet and solitude. He could breathe there. He could sleep there. He could paint there.

I was thirteen going on fourteen years old when Dad suggested, I might consider attending Choate-Rosemary Hall. This was not so much because he thought of the place as an exalted institution of learning, far from it, but rather because Wallingford, Connecticut was a mere thirty minutes' drive from Branford, and he was eager to return full time to the place he considered home. Much to his surprise, Mother Cecilia didn't oppose the idea, however she insisted it be left up to me to make the final decision. With the promise of Frank Pepe's Pizza in New Haven as a reward (the best), he drove me up from New York for a tour and an interview. It was a beautiful October day, and the leaves were turning.

"If this place is nothing but a bunch of snooty-ass white kids, you can forget it," I said as we got off the Wilbur Cross Parkway. (I was paying no attention to October anything.)

"Why? *You're* a snooty-ass white kid."

"*Da-ad.* You know how important diversity is to me." I glowered out the window. "The history of this school is all Wall Street swindlers and dishonest politicians." (I couldn't have named names. I hadn't done *that much* research.)

"I'm sure they have good lit and drama programs." I could tell Dad painfully hoped they did.

Unlike my parents, I had gravitated towards the written word from early on. I had raced through Middle Reader, leap-frogged Young Adult and gone straight to Virginia Wolf, Jane Austin, Alice Walker and Edna O'Brien. At the age of eleven, after thrilling Dad with my acting debut in a drama club production of Wendy Wasserstein's Uncommon Women and Others ("In the sixth grade!" said Dad.) I announced my intention of becoming a dramatist as well as a novelist. "It's a statement of youthful rebellion," Cecilia had said to him. "It's her way of rejecting us and what we do completely." Mom seemed pleased about it.

"Musicals," I announced. "That's what they probably put on here, so they won't *offend* anyone. Stupid Broadway musicals."

Until the age of ten, I had loved Broadway musicals. Over the years, Dad had been forced to sit with me through A Chorus Line, Les Misérables, Gypsy, The Pirates of Penzance, The Flower Drum Song, Cats and The Sound of Music. He had suffered through The Lion King not once but three times. (I'd been so captivated by it, I'd started referring to myself as The Lion Queen. Dad had no doubt I would be someday.)

"Give it a chance. Edward Albee graduated here."

"Edward Albee is *not* to be commended. Who's Afraid of Virginia Wolf is a pathetic portrait of women."

"How old are you again?"

"Da-ad!"

We arrived.

We parked.

We went to the admissions office.

While I was talking with my student guide (she was African American and I was semi-gratified to find out that the school offered free education for families whose income was a *mere* $75,000 or less), Dad wandered over to the Mellon Arts Center to check out the galleries. Trying to keep an open mind, he found the work to be original but for the most part, poorly rendered. Visual imagination and a sense of composition was most evident in the photography. (Right again, Mom.)

Dad wandered. The campus was indeed beautiful. The older buildings were of Georgian brick and stone and surrounded by quadrangles of green. Cottage dorms were still situated on tree lined streets. Walking, my father realized he hadn't appreciated it when he'd been here. He had been in Mellon Library his nose buried in art books. (Wasn't it Edward Hopper who had said that loneliness is the elephant in the artist's room?) For the very first time, Dad wondered what else he might have missed.

"The theatre department is only okay, but they have a great creative writing program," said *moi*.

We were in the pick-up truck leaving the Choate campus and I was feeling full of myself. I'd spoken to various teachers and my interview had gone well. "I'm totally in if I want it."

"You sound sure of that." Dad tried to sound skeptical. He liked my chances, but he didn't want me to be overconfident. (Or disappointed if it didn't work out)

"Dad, I'm *your* daughter. People would be totally pissed if I went anywhere else."

"I wish you wouldn't swear."

"Thoughtful profanity is a meaningful part of a contemporary vocabulary."

"Where do you learn this crazy stuff?"

"Da-ad!"

At Frank Pepe's I was mollified by a small, white clam pizza all my own and a birch beer. Dad went with his favorite, a Quattro Formaggio with sausage and roasted red peppers. "If you're accepted, you'll consider going?" he asked, his mouth full.

"I'll think about it. But it's not like I don't have other options."

The other options were all in New York and my father ached at the thought. "If you were in Wallingford, we could eat here on weekends."

"I'll *think* about it."

That April, I phoned to tell him that I'd received a letter of acceptance and, trying not to sound *too* excited, said yes, I was willing to, okay, maybe give it a chance. Hanging up, my father called Marisol and told her he'd soon be moving home for good, and she should plan on coming back to work on a full-time basis.

All was right with the world.

(At least momentarily.)

Day 10 – Happiness

It was Friday, the end of the second week of COG, and the day's lecture, given by a young woman who introduced herself as Meredith, was on Assertiveness. My father, who felt he was nothing if not assertive, expected it to be a bore.

And it was.

"*Assertiveness*," said Meredith, "is the ability to *express our feelings* while at the same time *empathize* with the feelings of others."

(Hmm. More empathizing. As opposed to all this empathizing with other people, it now seemed to Dad that it would be easier to ignore them. That's what was wrong with group. He couldn't.)

"The way we assert ourselves can be shaped and effected by many things. For example, in various societies a young person expressing his opinion to an older person would be considered rude. As would a *woman* expressing herself to a *man*."

"I think societies like that are on to something," said Wacko John without raising his hand.

"Don't make me start on you," said the large woman with the man's haircut.

"It can often be hard to draw the line between honest and hurtful," said Meredith, trying to ignore them both.

"I *was* being honest," said Wacko John.

"And I *am* about to hurt you," said the woman with the man's haircut.

"I think it might be a good time to move on to ethnic and religious belief systems," said Meredith, weakly.

(Yes, that always helps.)

The door to the lecture hall opened and everyone stared as a young woman, pale and slim with long brown hair, entered in a wheelchair, her notebook and purse in her lap. She was being pushed by one of the nurses. They moved to the end of the front row and the nurse turned the chair into position. The girl locked the wheels and smiled her thanks. The nurse exited.

"We were talking about assertiveness," said Meredith. "It's on page 116 of the workbook."

"Thank you," the girl said quietly. She opened her notebook and pen in hand, looked up and waited for the lecture to continue.

She maintained eye contact.

She maintained an erect body posture.

Her expression was both calm and intent.

She was lovely, yet it was a beauty marked by sadness. It was in the downward set of her mouth, in the statue-like stiffness of the fragile neck and in the thin legs and dead feet that were twisted to the inside in a limp, clumsy fashion.

The girl in the wheelchair's name tag said Sara D. Dad saw this as she was wheeled into group and a place was made for her in the circle. She took the sheets that Heidi handed her, not looking at anyone, a good thing because Colin was staring her, as close to stupefied as my father had ever seen him.

"Sara, would you like to tell us why you're here?" asked Heidi.

"Depression," said the girl. "I've been depressed for quite a while now."

"Would you like to talk about it?"

"Well, it has everything to do with this obviously." Sara D. looked down at her legs. "Up till a year and a half ago I was a dancer with the Hartford Ballet." The voice was monotone. The expression didn't change. "We were doing a guest performance in Boston. There was a party after, and I drank too much. I was at the top of some stairs, and I lost my balance and fell all the way down. I broke my back in two places. The lower break severed the spine. I'll never walk, let alone dance again. I'm back living with my parents. I think I've lost the ability to feel any kind of happiness."

Happiness.

Perhaps it was the girl's unblinking eyes, but the word shivered, then wandered, searching for somewhere to rest in my father's head. The rest of group went by in a buzz and a blur.

Arriving home that afternoon, Dad hurried into the house to ask Marisol, who was scrubbing toilets, her opinion on the subject of happiness.

"When my family is happy, I am happy," said Marisol. (She didn't have to think twice about it.)

"Okay. But what makes *them* happy, so you know that *you're* happy?"

"Is this part of part of your *therapia* so you no kill yourself no more, Mister Bob?" asked Marisol, flushing the toilet.

"No. It's a research question."

"When they are *seguro*, are safe, they are happy. And then, I am happy. When they are not, I work harder to make them so." (Simple as that.)

She went off to clean another already immaculate bathroom and as she did, it occurred to Dad he had no idea if his daughter (me!) was secure and happy. It suddenly seemed terribly important that I was. Any happiness he might ever have depended on it, and he hurried to the kitchen and called me on the phone. I answered on the second ring.

"Are you happy?" asked Dad.

"What?" Frankly, I was taken aback at the question.

"I said, are you happy?"

I semi-spluttered with laughter. "Dad, is this part of your therapy?"

"Answer the question. You either are or you're not."

"It's not as easy as that." My father actually felt a surge of relief. I was one of the brightest people he knew (except when I'm not) and if I considered happiness a challenge it seemed forgivable that he might too. "I mean, most of the time I feel pretty happy. Sometimes I'm not. I really don't think about it that much." (*Try* not to.)

"Okay, let me put it another way. Are you safe and secure?"

"I'm not as successful as I want to be (yet!) and I wish I had a great guy in my life (to come!) but I'm as safe and secure as anyone can be. A lot of that's because of you. I know you're there for me."

I went on for a moment or two longer about nothing in particular and then Dad said he had things to do and please come visit soon and he hung up the phone. He had tears in his eyes and a lump in his throat. It was possibly happiness he was feeling but if it was, it was acutely painful. For further insight, he decided to give Carter a call.

"Carter, tell me something, are you happy?"

"Bob, are you still in therapy?"

"Why do people keep asking me that just because I want to know if they're happy."

"Honest answer?"

"Please."

"I am content, Bob, which is better than being happy."

"How so?"

"Happiness is not sustainable. Contentment, which is the absence of unhappiness, is. I am not unhappy. Therefore, I am content. And happy to be so."

"Carter, you asshole. What makes you content all the time?"

"You do, Bob. Friends and people do. My sister and her husband and my nephews and nieces do. You are precious works of art. All of you are beautifully flawed masterpieces."

"Oh, you're no help at all."

They chatted a moment or two longer, then Dad said he had things to do and hung up the phone. His heart ached, his bowels felt weak, and he felt near tears again. (Poor guy.) He decided to call Annie on the cell phone number she had semi-reluctantly given him because he had asked for it.

"Annie, it's Bob."

"Bob?" Annie sounded immediately concerned. "What's the matter, are you all right?"

"I think I might be happy," said Dad, his voice cracking.

"Oh. But that's a good thing, isn't it?"

"I don't know. Are you happy?"

"... perhaps we should discuss this over coffee."

"Please answer the question."

"All right. Most of the time I'm happy, yes."

"What makes you that way."

"The belief that I'll continue to evolve and grow as a human being. The thought that I'll keep changing for the better."

"And what makes you unhappy?"

"My impatience. Let's both stay happy, Bob."

"I'll try."

But as he hung up the phone, my father knew he wouldn't. It was terrible feeling happy. It was frightening to care about people and be cared about in return. Why? Because there was always the chance that in the middle of such happiness, you would lose them.

(And then where would you be?)

Frida Kahlo

"I don't know, Mister Bob. I am getting so old. My hip is not so well. I don't move so good and I no bend at all no more. It is hard to do the cleaning."

My father was surprised. It was September of 2013 (I had begun my sophomore year at Choate), and nothing, not snow or rain or illness or a bad hip, had ever stopped Marisol from working before. Over the last year and a half, she had slowed down about as much as a locomotive, frowning and fuming as she scrubbed, sanitized, washed, polished and dusted, repositioning everything that had somehow imperceptibly moved since she'd last been there. And now here she was saying she might have to cut back. Perhaps she *was* getting old. (It was an alarming thought.)

"Maybe we could hire someone to help you."

Marisol brightened immediately. "Oh, Mister Bob, what a good idea. I know just the person."

As Marisol bustled from the room with not so much as a limp, Dad wondered if he'd been played. However, nothing happened right away, and he soon forgot about it.

Two and half weeks later, it did.

It was the first week of October and my father looked up from his morning coffee as Marisol entered the kitchen. A slim, tall woman was behind her. Mick and Angela were sprawled beneath the table and their heads came up and they stared.

"This is Kristina. She is my niece, and she is visiting. She will be to help me, Mister Bob."

Frida Kahlo thought my father, not a little bit awestruck.

The woman's long, black hair was pulled back from a symmetrical face. Heavy eyebrows dominated an unblinking gaze. Even in jeans and sweatshirt, she didn't look like a housekeeper, not even a little bit.

"She will learn to do what I do and then when I go to the hospital, she will do it for me."

The word brought Dad back to the reality of the kitchen. "What hospital?"

"I have decided." said Marisol in a tone that suggested nothing would change her mind. "I am getting the hip replacement. It must be done, and you are paying for it, Mister Bob with the medical plan you give to me."

(Oh. Right. Yes, he'd done that.)

Marisol got to work. The woman, Kristina, trailed behind, nodding and helping as Marisol kept up a running monologue of instruction in Spanish. Not needed, Dad went out to the studio. The thought of it didn't really excite him. It had been happening of late; brush in hand, he felt uninspired. Used to being intimately lost in his work, he felt he was staring at something done by strangers. He looked up as the door to the studio opened and the woman, Kristina, entered carrying a mop and bucket. She stopped, looking around at the bins and storage racks, the stools and easels and chaotic worktable and the paint flecked floor, her expression seeming to ask how one should even begin to address such a mess. Shrugging slightly, she moved across the room and put down the bucket. Water sloshed.

"Wait, no," said Dad, snapping to. "You don't clean in here. No clean. It's the way I like it."

The woman stared at him, clearly not understanding a word he was saying. She looked up at the paintings that hung high on the open second story walls, paintings that my father considered second class citizens but that he held on to anyway. For some reason, he stumbled on. "I make... pinturas? I'm a... wait..." He turned to the canvas that was on the easel next to him and moving his hand up and down and around, pretended to paint.

"*Artiste?*" Kristina's voice was quiet and low.

"Si. Yes. Artist."

"*Bueno.*" Picking up her bucket, Kristina turned for the door.

"Wait," blurted Dad. Kristina turned to look at him. "Would you move back there, please? By the window?" He reached for a sketch pad. The woman didn't move. What was the Spanish word for window? He gestured. "*La window...* there... right there."

Holding the mop in one hand and the pail in the other, Kristina moved back to the window and stood.

"This way." Dad cocked his head down and to the side. Kristina did the same.

"Yes. Great. Now don't move." Picking up charcoal, Dad began to sketch. "Kristina, that's a…pretty name." He usually didn't talk while he worked. Words fled. Was he talking because he knew she couldn't understand him? Was he talking to relax her? She didn't look like she needed relaxing. She stood, quiet and unperturbed. Maybe he was trying to relax himself. "Anybody ever told you, you look like Frida Kahlo?" My father glanced up from the pad. "Frida? Kahlo?" No reaction. He went back to the pad. His right hand flew. "She was a Mexican artist. Very unique looking. Had this crazy unibrow. She was injured in a bus accident when she was eighteen. Almost died. The injuries stayed with her the rest of her life. She walked with a limp, couldn't have children. But she did these remarkable self-portraits. Bright colors. Lot of symbolism. Monkeys which, I guess, are a Mexican symbol for lust." Dad looked up. Had he offended? Seemingly not. He went back to the pad. His left hand smudged. "She was also a communist. Had an affair with Leon Trotsky. She died at age forty-seven. Way too young." He blew softly. Dust flew. "There." He tore the sheet from his sketchbook. He studied it a moment. He turned it, and holding it by the top edge, he presented it. "Woman with mop and bucket…. by the window."

His title said it all but didn't. The beautiful, if severe, face was curved and the neck elongated, the chin was sharp, the lips full and sensual. The single, heavy brow above the downcast, almond eyes was shaped like a bird's spread wings. Against the pale background of the window, the straight dark hair was a surrounding rainfall. Kristina moved towards him and putting down the bucket, she reached for the sketch. Dad pulled it back. "No, no. I'm keeping it, thanks." Kristina looked at him for a moment, then quietly picked up the bucket and turning, left the studio, closing the door behind her. Dad stared at the sketch. Picking up a brush he turned to the empty canvas and began to paint.

At four o'clock, they were all in the kitchen. My father was pouring a glass of white wine, wondering if he was being rude not to offer some. Marisol, having gathered her bags and the leftovers from lunch, was preparing go home.

"She will come and help me again on Thursday, Mister Bob. Is good for her and is good for me."

"That's fine. I'm happy to pay the extra."

"Yes. You will."

Marisol turned and marched to the door where Kristina stood quietly waiting. The door opened and they were on the verge of leaving when Dad turned from the kitchen counter.

"Adios, Kristina."

"It's been a pleasure to meet you, Mr. Boone," said Kristina, in perfect, unaccented English. Her dark eyes twinkled in amusement. "My aunt talks about you. Now I know why. Oh, and I plan on trimming my eyebrows tonight."

Marisol hissed with embarrassment and glared at her niece. *"No se puede decir esas cosas!"* (You can't say such things.)

"Por eso, cuando es la verdad?" (Why not, when it's the truth?)

The door closed behind the two women and my father was left alone, wondering how long it would take for Thursday morning to arrive.

Mick and Angela

It is astounding to the artist, Robert Boone, that at forty-eight years of age, he is a first-time owner of dogs. Like many of the good things in his life, he has his daughter (me!) to thank (*blame*) for this.

It was in early February of 2020' when I'd come up from New York for a weekend and had gone into the village to the farmer's market. When I returned, instead of fruit or vegetables, I had a basket containing two wrinkled bundles of flesh and fur.

"What are those?"

"Da-*ad*. They're puppies. What do you think they are?" I then went on to explain that while walking through the village I'd passed a pet store that was having an adopt a homeless puppy day. "And I've wanted a dog for a while, so I did, you know? I adopted. I mean, really, do you mind?"

"Dog is singular. There are two of them."

"They're brother and sister. I couldn't just take one and leave the other all by itself, could I?" (Dad probably thought I could.) I cooed and began scratching the female pup's droopy ears.

"They have feet the size of dinner plates. They're going to be huge."

"Well, I think they're gorgeous." (I hadn't noticed the feet – yikes!)

"I'm glad *you* do." The male pup was now peeing on the floor. (Yikes again!)

It didn't make my father any happier when I left on Sunday evening *without* my newly acquired pets, telling him – "I can't take them down to New York on the *train*, can I? I'll rent a car this next weekend and come back up for them then, okay?"

(Dad might have pointed out that I could have rented a car on this, a Sunday evening, but I know for a fact that the thought of seeing his beautiful, dutiful daughter (me) again the following weekend made him keep his mouth shut.)

It didn't make him any happier again when Marisol showed up for work the next morning and immediately proclaimed that as much as she liked *perros,* cleaning up *mierda* didn't fall under any of her job categories. That the two *perros* in question had left puddles and piles on various floors throughout the night and that cleaning it up was exactly what Dad had been expecting Marisol to do, didn't seem to matter. He had no choice but to do the clean-up himself. Discovering that I had left no dog food (sorry, I forgot) was yet another source of frustration. The pups were whimpering and staring at him expectantly and so my father had no choice but to go down to the grocery store and buy a ten-pound bag of puppy chow. The dogs gobbled it down and then yipped at him, begging for more. Dad shrugged and gave them the rest of the bag. He then took them into the back yard and continued on into his studio. He was interrupted twenty minutes later by the sound of feeble barking and whining and coming back out, he found both puppies, their bellies swollen to the size of small Hindenburgs, lying semi-comatose in large pools of kibble and vomit. He threw them into the front seat of the pick-up, drove to the vet, the puppy-stomachs were pumped and he was sternly advised it was never a good idea to allow dogs, especially shelter dogs, especially *puppies*, who weren't used to it, to over eat. The pups looked at him with accusing eyes all the way home.

Dad was *carefully* eating a porterhouse steak that evening, contemplating driving the dogs down to New York himself, when the phone rang. It was me calling with ultra-exciting news.

"*Dadd*! Mom's going to Italy! She's doing an installation and she wants me to come with her!"

"Oh. Well, that is news. When are you leaving?" asked Dad.

"The day after tomorrow!" I mean, I was totally, like, gushing.

"Uh-huh. And for how long?"

"Three to four weeks! We're going to travel once she's finished. Go to Spain and France. How can I say no?"

"Uh-huh. And what about your dogs?"

The *puppies*, I insisted, would be *more* than happy to stay in Branford with him until I returned for them.

"You could put them in a pound."

"Da-*aad*! They're *adopted.*"

There was no more talking about it as I was already busy packing and had to go. Not knowing what else to do, Dad went out the next morning and bought a *fifty*-pound bag of puppy chow. Perhaps they'd eat themselves to death. They didn't and continuing to be unreasonable, insisted on staying in his bedroom at night, this despite the fact that he placed piles of old towels and blankets on the kitchen floor. Much to his alarm, Marisol now seemed to be enjoying the pups, petting them, rubbing their bellies, filling their water bowl and calling them "little *soldados*" as they bustled around her feet.

"What are su nombres, Mr. Bob?"

"How do I know? Ask Holdie, they're hers."

"No." Marisol was adamant. "Miss Isolde is no here now and they must have names. Is your *responsabilidad*."

"Fine."

With no desire to think any more about it, Dad named them Mick and Angela. As far as he knew there were no dogs in the life and work of the great Italian artist and sculptor, and he certainly had no plans to make room for them in his. Plans, however, do change.

"*Daa-ad!* I can't take them *now*! Look at them, they totally *adore* you."

It was seven months later. Due to the sudden Covid outbreak in Europe, my four weeks in Italy had turned into a five-month lock-down in a small apartment in Milan where my nosophobic (irrationally terrified of disease) mother and I had tried not to kill one another. (Alone together for any length of time and we were much more lethal than any virus.) With threats, blackmail and spiritual intimidation, I'd finally got her on an airplane home and now, for the last two weeks, I'd slowly been recovering my sanity in the loft in Tribeca. I'd come up that morning from Manhattan in a rental car and the dogs, now at least forty pounds apiece and barking like banshees, had come racing out to greet me. After having had to deal with my mother, I wasn't sure if I could deal with any living thing ever again.

"I mean, *really*, Dad. (Really, really.) They're totally *yours* now."

My father grumbled for propriety's sake, but the truth was he had seen it all coming from the very beginning. Me bringing the dogs home had been the canine equivalent of my mother showing up on the doorstep with a baby in her arms. They were his now.

Over the next year and half, I came up from New York to my father's house on a semi-regular basis. When I wasn't eating Dad's cooking or writing or walking the beach and just *breathing*, I'd watch as Mick and Angela followed him around the house, from bedroom to kitchen, kitchen out to the studio, making themselves comfortable, racing back to say hello when Marisol arrived, always barking suspiciously when the mailman came to the door but invariably returning to wherever Dad might be, to plump down on the floor and wait for his attention and affection which he readily gave. True, he still had to kick them off the bed at night in order to get into it himself and yes, he now bought kibble in hundred-pound bags but they were – *are* – worth it. In fact, if my father were to think about it, he'd have to admit that in the middle of his cries in the hospital for his own self-annihilation, the future comfort and security of Mick and Angela were on his mind. He was quite aware that while suicide might not be a selfish act, leaving his dogs alone and untended for would be.

My father finds walking the dogs in the early morning a highlight of the day. The air, the light, the smell of Long Island Sound as he makes his way down Bayard Ave towards the ocean side park is soothing. It helps that his fellow dog walkers seem to be relaxed, agreeable people. Of course, having the time each day to actually walk a dog, why wouldn't they be? And it isn't as if the brief, passing conversations every get too personal. They're pleasantly redundant, mostly discussing the vagaries of their charges; their eating habits, their bowel movements, their social interactions, how they gauge one another's mood and psyche with a quick smell of the genitals and butt. It's quick and efficient and more than once Dad has conjectured that perhaps it's human beings who should be sniffing each other's assholes to figure out what's what. Oh, and how they like to play, these silly dogs. Running and rough housing and chasing thrown tennis balls, oblivious to pedigree, not caring what color or size another dog is, rarely getting aggressive with one other, those that do being quickly being reprimanded by the other dogs and just as quickly leashed and led away by their embarrassed owner. Compared to people, the wants and desires of a dog, Dad has decided, are simple. Food, affection and a bit of exercise. Of course, if they weren't so well fed, they wouldn't be nearly so affectionate, would they. If they were hungry or desperate for attention, they wouldn't be nearly so nice to one another. They'd be competing, wouldn't they. Like people. But unlike people, they'd stop all the nonsense when they'd had enough. They wouldn't be greedy, wanting more and more and more. Which makes it obvious, doesn't it, that it isn't poverty that's the bane of human existence, it's greed. Too many have more than their share and the vast majority of those that do, want even more. But not dogs. Given just the basics, dogs sleep peacefully, play happily and are unreservedly in the moment. As he walks in the morning, Mick and Angela at his side, my father has no doubt, no doubt at all, that it's so much easier to be a dog than a human being.

(And who's fault, we'd both like to know, is that?)

Week 3

Day 11 – Anxiety

It was two in the afternoon and sitting on a hard bench in the front office of the High School of Creative and Performing Arts in New Haven, Robert Boone found himself staring at a collection of garish African tribal masks mounted high on the wall. If done by American high school students, they weren't bad. If done by Africans, they were dreadful.

It was Monday, the eleventh day of COG and the morning's lecture had been on anxiety. "Anxiety," said Annie, addressing the lecture hall, "is a *medical diagnosis*. It effects our thoughts, our emotions and it effects our bodies."

(No kidding, thought Dad.)

The fact that my father was sitting in a front office anywhere at all, let alone the one in the High School of Creative and Performing Arts, was a monster McGuffin on his part and no one's fault but his own. Sunday afternoon, with a failed Social Grapes list interfering with his as yet unformed plans for dinner, Dad had come to the conclusion that if he *was* unsocial, he didn't know what to do about it. Deciding that chatting with someone, a neighbor perhaps, might get him off the hook, he meandered down the driveway, took a left and began walking. Two hundred yards on, his property line ended in a stand of trees, and someone else's began. A woman was out in front of her house raking the fallen branches in her yard. "Hi, there," called Dad, wondering if two hundred yards down the street constituted a neighbor. "Nice afternoon!" The woman promptly turned and regarded Dad as if he were a goat legged faun who had suddenly appeared out of the woods.

"Well now. To what do we owe this honor?" said the woman, stripping off her gardening gloves and walking towards him.

"I thought I'd introduce myself. Bob Boone. I live up the road?" Dad immediately knew it was the wrong thing to say.

"Mr. Boone, we've been neighbors for close to fifteen years and my husband and I have introduced ourselves to you at least half a dozen times."

"You have? Where?" The woman did look vaguely familiar, still, Dad felt certain he'd remember if they'd met before.

"Most recently at the Appleby party."

"I don't go to parties."

"It wasn't a party; it was a fundraiser."

Now he remembered. Several months ago, James Appleby, the founder of a private investment bank and a local philanthropist, had gotten in touch with Carter explaining that Robert Boone would be a wonderful draw at a local, bigwig charity event and would he perhaps consider doing a quick sketch as a prize in the silent auction? Carter, thinking it a nice idea (and possibly because Appleby was an art buyer), had gotten in touch.

"How much is a quick sketch by me worth," Dad had asked, uncomfortable at the prospect of meeting people.

"That's beside the point," replied Carter. "The point is it's for a worthy cause."

"Which is?"

"Children with cancer," said Carter.

Dad had felt so annoyed at the thought of children getting cancer, he'd had no choice but to say okay, yes. He'd gone, making sure he'd arrived late and underdressed. He was given a glass of expensive champagne and was then introduced to people, whose names he immediately forgot. He was told that someone had bid five grand for a sketch drawing which meant he felt obligated to do a decent job of it, doing not just a continuous, single line drawing of the women who had placed the winning bid but also doing a *second* detailed sketch of the woman and her husband, thrilling them by signing both. Exhausted, he'd then left and gone home. (And after informing Carter, that in the future he would be donating to such causes but not attending, had gone straight to bed.)

"I've also introduced myself to you any number of times when I brought my children by your house at Halloween," continued the woman. "They always insisted on it because you passed out money instead of treats."

"I'm not good with names," replied Dad, wincing at the thought of Halloween where he always forgot to buy candy, was not able to *not* answer the door and then felt beholden to give something to the adorable, costumed children.

"People who aren't good with names, just don't *care enough* to remember them," said the woman who my father now thought was being unneighborly if not rude. He was on the verge of turning away when the woman suddenly smiled. "I'm glad you've dropped by. I've been wanting to ask you something."

It turned out the woman, whose name was Marjorie Jo Rosello and whose husband was Ed (which *did* sound sort of familiar), was the principal of The High School of Creative and Dramatic Arts in New Haven and the something she had been wanting to ask was "would you ever consider speaking to the students in our visual arts program about your work?" Dad had blanched at the idea and had felt duty bound to say yes.

"When?"

"Monday?"

"That's tomorrow."

"Why, it is, isn't it?"

"That's not much time."

"It's my opinion," said Marjorie Jo Rosello, "that when you have a fish on the line you land him." Marjorie Jo obviously had no problem asserting herself and though my father felt she was a little bit short in the empathy department, he said that he'd be there.

"*Be aware!*"

Turning, Annie wrote the words on the whiteboard. "*Accept* the anxiety. Say hello to it. *Be one* with the experience."

(Hello, visual art kids! No, Dad didn't think so.)

"At the same time, be detached from it. *You* are *not* your anxiety."

(It had never occurred to Dad that he was. It was all these *outside the house* things.)

"Fake it to make it. *Running* from your anxiety makes it worse. *Facing it* makes it better."

(Annie seemed to be looking at *a certain someone* as she said this and that *someone* had the sudden urge to run home and face his anxiety, sitting on the toilet with a book.)

"And finally, be *in the moment*," said Annie, smiling with reassurance. "What you fear the most *rarely happens*."

Easy to say if you weren't on the verge of facing down a classroom of teenage gunfighters armed with paint brushes. And now, here was his neighbor, Marjorie Jo Rosello, marching out of her office, looking very professional in a skirt, jacket and leather shoes, smiling warmly and holding out her hand.

"You made it!"

"Looks like it!"

"Right this way," said Marjorie Jo and off she went, leaving Dad no choice but to follow. Perhaps, he thought, the masks on the wall were something he could talk about. The influence of African art on the development of modern art, the School of Paris, Matisse and Picasso and...no, if the subject of influence bored the hell out of him, what was it going to mean to a bunch of juveniles who thought pink was a primary color. He was up poop creek without a paint can, and he knew it.

The morning's group meeting had been business as usual. Dour Paul F. was doing better. The dancing with his husband had been successful enough that they'd decided to do it on a weekly basis. Paul F. was now looking to move to another department at Home Depot. "Bathroom fixtures and... *décor*?"

(Yes, if anyone could decor a bathroom, it was a ballroom dancing Paul F., thought Dad.)

Walt O. talked of having been turned down in the job interviews but said he was still optimistic. His wife was off visiting her mother and he was "*enthusiastically awaiting her return.*"

(Walt O.'s positive state of mind made Dad wonder if there was a store where one could buy a never-give-up attitude. Probably not. And even if there was such a thing, it would probably be exorbitantly priced and wouldn't have a guarantee.)

Beverly had then said that she was feeling responsible for *her* mother who lived alone in St. Louis. She was trying to engage with Zoom calls.

(Which made my father wonder if either of them had ever heard of a plane ticket. Oh, but perhaps they didn't have the money, a thought he found troubling. Perhaps he could find a way to zoom several hundred dollars into Beverly's Cog notebook, so as not to be troubled anymore.)

Stolid William G. was feeling a bit better because, he said, glancing at Dad, he was working out a little bit, Megan J. said with some enthusiasm that she *was* getting out of the apartment tonight because "*my boys are on a winnin' team!*" and Colin was looking to enroll in a web design program at Gateway Community College in New Haven.

Sara was absent.

"How have *you* been doing, Bob?" asked Heidi.

"Good. All this mindful thinking is really helping."

(Really, really.)

It was quickly determined that Dad was still not being particularly social ("I've been too busy to be social," replied Dad), had *not* finished any thought records ("They're still a work in progress," offered Dad), and had *not* made a list of his distorted, automatic thoughts. ("I'm not sure I have any," said Dad). Heidi cluck-clucked with disapproval, told my father he was letting down both himself and the group and then made a point of ignoring him for the rest of the session which allowed him to fixate on the horrors of the coming afternoon.

Twenty-five solemn looking young people, sitting at desks and tables, looked up and stared as Dad and Marjorie Joe entered the brightly lit classroom. There were drawings and paintings pinned to the walls and art supplies in cubbies and on shelves. (A Botteghe? Not quite.) A buoyant man in his mid to late thirties jumped up from his desk and hurried towards them. "Mr. Boone," said Marjorie Jo, "this is Mr. James Murphy, one of our instructors. James, this is Robert Boone."

"Mr. Calhoun, it is an *absolute* and *total* pleasure to meet you," said Mr. John Murphy, vigorously shaking Dad's hand. "We are all *tremendous* fans of your work, and we are *completely* beside ourselves with excitement to have you here." Mr. John Murphy, who obviously had a flare for hyperbole was, as Carter proudly liked to say, as gay as a gwiff.

"It's Bob, thanks. Are you an artist, John?"

"Oh, my, no. Just a teacher."

"There is no such thing as *just* a teacher," said Marjorie Jo Rosello, and with that, she was out the door and gone.

"Ladies and gentlemen," said John Murphy, turning to the class, "without further ado, the *esteemed* artist (that word again), Robert Boone." He smiled at Dad as if to say, you're on.

My father turned. The gaggle of solemn, multicultural, young faces stared at him expectantly. He didn't recognize the clothes. He didn't recognize the hairstyles. It was like discovering aliens in your closet.

The esteemed artist, Robert Boone, cleared his throat. The esteemed artist, Robert Boone, heard whispers and a soft giggle. The esteemed artist, Robert Boone, had no idea what to say. (So *this* was what his daughter (me!) had once described as the actor's nightmare – lost and naked with no lines, in front of a live audience.)

Thankfully, there was a stage manager. "We were thinking we might start by talking about this," said John Murphy and bringing out a stiff-backed poster of Angels in the Darkness #3 from behind his desk, he set it on an easel. (My father hadn't seen it in a while and was unprepared for it. It seemed like something done by a stranger a long, long time ago.) "Now. Who has some questions, for Mr. Boone? Come on, people, we discussed this earlier. Zach, let's start with you."

"Are they floating or are they flying?" asked a blonde, young man sitting at a front table.

"I don't know, what do you think?" replied Dad.

"I think they're flying," said the young man.

John Murphy pointed. "Anna, what about you?"

"Why is it so dark?" asked a young woman sitting at a desk. "If they're angels, aren't they supposed to live in heaven where it's light?"

(Dad had never considered this.) "I don't know. What do you think?"

"Maybe they're on their *way* to heaven," said another young man.

"Yeah, they have to fly through the dark to get there," said a red headed girl. "It's like a test to see if they can make it."

"They definitely make it," said a Hispanic young woman.

The room was beginning to buzz with voices and my father felt himself relaxing slightly. "Do they look afraid?" (He'd always wondered.) All the young people seemed to agree they did not.

"I like the way the woman is holding on to the children," said a dark-haired girl. "She's protecting them."

"Yeah, but from what?" asked another girl.

"From the *unknown*, silly."

"How come it's just babes," said a boy in a baseball cap. "Where are the dudes?"

"They're the ones going to hell," said an African American girl, broadly smiling. The class laughed.

"I think the figures are idealized," said a serious young woman wearing a Habib. "In their physical perfection, they don't seem quite human. Was that your intention?"

"I have no idea. What do you think?"

"I think it was. That's why you called them angels."

"Did you know these people?" asked another girl.

"Does that matter?"

"I think you did."

Dad said nothing.

"Why don't we take a look at this one," said John Murphy and he put a poster of *Aura #6* on the easel. My father groaned inside. It was the Pollock rip-off.

A young woman raised her hand. "Why do you call it Aura?"

"Because it gave me a headache," replied Dad.

The class laughed again.

"What were you thinking when you painted it?" asked a young man.

"I wasn't."

"What were you feeling?"

"I really don't remember."

"I think you were angry," the Habib wearing girl suddenly said. "I think this is the angriest painting I've ever seen. It's like someone's head is exploding."

The class murmured in agreement.

Turning, my father looked at the painting. (Possibly for the very first time, really *looked* at it.) This girl, these kids, these *teenagers*... they were right. The painting was an expression of anger. He must have been *angry* when he'd created it. But angry about what? The state of the world, the state of art, the state of *his life*? He didn't know and it put the painting in a whole new light.

It came from the back of the room, a soft, shy voice. "Mr. Boone, what is it you like about art?"

(Talk about questions.)

"Jesus, I don't know, I just *do* it." More giggles and grins and Dad smiled in return. He pondered a moment. What *did* he like about art? He hadn't so much as thought about it in who knows how long. "Okay, what is there these days? What's out there? You guys know better than I do. There's video games and music and movies and all this, what, streaming stuff? There's social media and computer web sites and everybody's on their cell phones all the time and there are... *pod* things and *bit* things. What else, what am I missing?"

"Art!" cried the voice from the back.

"Yes. There is art. What there *is*, what there has always *been*—" Dad pointed at his eyes "—is what you *see*. And when you stand in front of a statue or a painting, a mural, a photo, any work of art – what you see stands alone. There's no soundtrack, no voice over, no commercials telling you what to do or an announcer telling you how to feel. Hopefully you're not taking pictures of yourself in front of it and sending them to friends. It's a singular experience, all yours. You might like what you see, you might not like it, but if it's true and honest, you react to it. You take it in, and you hang it on a wall inside your head and it stays there because it's real and it means something to you." (Dad hesitated, wondering if he should go on. Why not.) "And I wonder if it's happening anymore. I think art today has become meaningless in the lives of most people. Yeah, they might go to a museum, but they go as tourists. It's no different than the Empire State Building or The Eiffel Tower, you check it out when you pass through town. You walk from gallery to gallery, trying to take in hundreds and hundreds of years in a single afternoon. Do you really see anything? I don't know how you can. Art can survive anything but not indifference." The room was very quiet. My father could feel all eyes upon him. "Indifference. I've been guilty of it myself. But you people haven't. You looked at my work today and you told me that it means something to you." Bob glanced at Mr. John Murphy. "I get the feeling you do that a lot in this class. I think you'll continue to do it. And if you can do it, how can I not do it as well?" Dad looked back at the young, attentive faces. "I want to thank you for reminding me today what it is I like about art."

There was applause from John Murphy and the class joined in. It was nice but my father didn't need it. He thanked the students again and told them he'd come back again soon to see what everyone was working on.

Uncertainty felt very far away.

Mona Lisa Smile

"Anyone for bran muffins?"

The wait had been interminable, but Thursday morning had finally arrived. My father was at the kitchen counter, Marisol was already attacking the previous evening's collection of dirty dishes and Kristina was pulling the vacuum from the utilities closet. Her hair was pulled back and she was wearing jeans and the sweatshirt again. Marisol looked up from the sink. She never accepted food, except to take it home.

Putting the vacuum down, Kristina crossed the kitchen. "No but I'll take some coffee."

Dad poured. "What do you like in it?" He had milk, cream and sugar at the ready.

"Just cream, thanks."

He added the cream and handed Kristina the cup. Across the kitchen, Marisol was at the dishwasher, frowning. Dad filled his own cup. "You know, I was thinking the studio actually could use a good cleaning."

"You're the boss," said Kristina, sipping her coffee.

"I'll be out there but you can work around me."

"Fine by me."

He was sitting at the easel when she entered. She carried a broom, a dustpan and a rubbish bin.

"Where shall I begin?"

Dad looked around the room. He hadn't actually considered what he wanted or needed to be cleaned. It had been an excuse to get her out there, that's all.

"You could sweep the floor. And pick up a little bit."

Kristina nodded. Her eyes settled on the wooden roll top desk in the corner. Both tambour and drawers were open and overflowing with discarded brushes, half emptied tubes of paint and junk. (In my experience, artists are not neat.) "Why don't I start over here, that way I won't disturb you."

"Disturb away."

Dad watched out of the corner of his eye as she moved across the studio, put down the bin and dustpan and began to sweep. It occurred to him he should put on some music. Except he didn't have any. His favorite melody was silence.

"You really are an accomplished artist."

"Hmm?"

Kristina swept, eyes on the floor, not looking in my father's direction. "I was reading about you. Marisol has magazines you're in."

"She *does*?" Dad was surprised.

"She does. You're well known."

"Being a well-known artist is like being a well-known ornithologist. Nobody's heard of you except the other bird lovers."

"No birds I've ever heard of go for five or six figures." Kristina turned her attention to the roll top desk. "I don't know what you want to keep and what you want to throw out."

"I don't either."

"I guess we're done here then."

"We could clean over there." Dad gestured vaguely towards the other side of the studio.

Picking up the trash bin, Kristina started across the room. Passing Dad's easel, she stopped. She stared at the canvas. Dad knew what she was looking at. Taking the sketch from the previous Tuesday, he had resized it on the blank canvas. Paint now filled the top left corner of the canvas, lines the rest. The opaque fall light from the windows would highlight the turned face of a dark-haired woman.

"Do I get a modeling fee?"

Dad grinned (unusual for him; especially in the studio). "Yes. If you stand over by the desk for me again."

Putting the broom aside, Kristina moved back to the desk. Dad reached for his sketchpad. "Better if you sit."

Pushing some things aside, Kristina sat on the edge of the desk. "How's this?"

"Look down."

Kristina looked down.

"Close your eyes."

"You ask a lot." Kristina closed her eyes.

Wishing again he had music to play, Dad reached for charcoal. "Tell me about yourself."

A small smile played across Kristina's downturned face. "I can tell you I'm not well known, that's for sure." She hesitated a moment, then became serious. "In a past life, I was a paralegal."

My father had begun to sketch. "And where'd you do this... paralegal work?"

"Now you're getting personal. Los Angeles."

"And now you're traveling?"

"Visiting friends. Family. Marisol's my father's second cousin. One of many."

"You have a big family."

"Strength in numbers."

Dad's hand glided across the pad. "... how long you here for?"

"That depends how long I can stand sleeping on the couch with six to twenty loud vaqueros coming and going at all hours."

"You could get your own place."

"No, that would mean getting a real job. I'm not ready for that yet." Kristina glanced up. "Unless modeling fees are substantial."

Putting the charcoal down, Dad smiled. "Too late. All done." He tore the sheet of sketch paper from the pad. "Here."

Kristina hesitated, then took it and looked at it. Long, dark hair, downturned face, closed eyes. A serene Mona Lisa. She handed it back. "I'm nothing like that."

"No. Keep it."

Kristina looked amused. "You're not going to paint me again?"

"It's up here," said Dad, touching his temple.

Kristina turned, made her way to the door, then stopped and looked back. "I'm going to sell this for a ton of money."

"You can't. It's not signed."

"Paralegals are good at forging signatures."

Kristina was smiling as she left the studio.

(So was Dad.)

Day 12 – Schemas

"Was I any good in bed?" asked Dad, his café latte untouched.

"That question," said Annie, "is totally inappropriate."

"Just asking."

"*Bob*…" Annie had been the one who was early today, it had been Dad who'd been late. "These meetings have already broken down all rules of professional and personal protocol."

"Whose fault is that?"

"Yes, all right, yes, it's totally *my* fault. It was my fault to begin with and it *is* my fault and yes, you were good in bed. Are you happy now?"

"No. On a scale of 1 to 10, how did I compare to all the other nameless dicks in your world."

"Now you're just being hurtful."

It was Tuesday afternoon, the twelfth day of COG and my poor father, though he was loathe to admit it, was in a complete dither.

"I took that stupid test last night."

"Which test is that?"

"The one about schemes."

"You mean schem*as*."

"Whatever."

The morning's lecture had been Core Beliefs II and having done his best to ignore Core Beliefs I, Dad had thought part II might be a little more bearable if he prepared for it by taking what was called the Jeffrey Young *Schema Questionnaire*, a test designed to identify distorted behaviors and dysfunctional beliefs. (How do you prepare for *that?*) He had ended up taking it twice.

The first time, using a pencil, he quickly went through the twelve pages, rating, on a scale of one to six, simplistic statements that supposedly addressed one's patterns of thought and behavior. When he added up the numbers and put them in the proper's boxes, he was aghast to find that he was withdrawn, had abandonment issues, was vulnerable, hyper-critical, had unrelenting standards and that he *subjugated* his emotions. (Wasn't that a sex thing?)

He obviously hadn't done it right.

Erasing all the answers, Dad went through the test again making sure he was completely aware of the ramifications of each statement before rating it accordingly. For the second time, Dad added up the numbers and put them in the proper boxes. Only to find he was pessimistic, alienated, overly vigilant, inhibited and that he thought of himself as a complete and total failure.

"Dysfunctional core beliefs," said glasses-wearing Gwyneth – she was at the lecture hall whiteboard, scribbling madly away – "are most often based on early traumatic experiences. These experiences can then lead to later negative experiences that reinforce these beliefs. We respond to these beliefs by compensating, avoiding or engaging in behaviors that confirm these early beliefs to be true."

(Talk about feeling schema-ed against!)

"I didn't test well," said Dad, pushing his coffee cup aside.

"In what way?" asked Annie.

"In every way." Dad looked around the bustling shop. How was it everyone here seemed so *normal?*

In morning group, Angry Megan J., who no longer seemed nearly so angry, had said she was feeling better—*I think the meds are finally kicking in*—but she was also sad because today was her last day.

As to the future—

"I'm gonna stop blaming myself, I'm gonna be positive." Megan J's voice tightened with resolve. "And I'm getting involved. There's people meet down to the community center twice a week. I'm starting there. Maybe I can't do nothing to help nobody else but I'm gonna try." Everyone congratulated her and wished her well and when the Indian woman in the sari came for her, Dad had the feeling he was going to miss Megan J.

Congratulations went by the wayside when it was wheel chair Sara's turn to speak. Sara's anxiety was at a sixty, her depression level was at a ninety. She was, she said, having trouble sleeping, was listless, wasn't eating and was prone to jagged crying attacks. "Oh, and my mother recommended I try wheelchair ballroom dancing. Wow, I can't wait." Sara stared down at the floor. "I miss dancing. I miss my life. I'm dead and nobody has the heart to tell me."

(Talk about dither inducing! Stuff like this was hard to ignore.)

"Did you ever take the test?"

"It's not a test, it's a list of statements—"

"Did you?"

"…And by rating the statements, you become more aware of your dysfunctional beliefs. You can then set a course of action."

Dad said nothing.

"All right," Annie said with a sigh. "Yes, I *did* take the test, Bob, and it was helpful. For example, perhaps a person has feelings of worthlessness. Perhaps they feel they're not worthy of love."

"Why would they feel that?"

"Perhaps there was loss or abandonment early in their lives. Those experiences have stayed with them. They blame themselves for those experiences, they think it was their fault. To compensate, they try to be perfect. Then, as they grow older, they avoid situations where they can't be perfect. They're afraid to trust."

"Are we talking about you now?

"We not going there. Tell me something, Bob, do you think of yourself as a good person?"

"I try to be."

"I think you are. Do you worry that things could fall apart?"

"Occasionally." (Uh… hello?)

"Why is that?"

"Because they have."

"Can you talk about that with me? As a friend?"

"No."

Annie regarded my father a moment. "Bob. Do you trust people?"

"A few. Do you?

Annie hesitated. "I try to, but sometimes no."

"Why do you think that is?"

Again, Annie hesitated. "All right, honest answer. I told you, I was adopted when I was four. I don't remember a lot of what came before, but I don't think it was very good. Growing up, I worried about a lot of things. I still do."

"I'm sorry."

"I am too."

"If I trust you," said Dad, "will you trust me?"

"I just *did*, Bob, now it's your turn."

My father excused himself to go the men's room and then, returning to the table and telling Annie that he wasn't feeling well, went home.

(So much for trust, you silly, silly man!)

Shadow in Sunlight

"I must talk to you, Mister Bob."

It was the end of the cleaning day two weeks later. Marisol was putting her on coat and Kristina was waiting in the car. Marisol seemed – what, thought Dad? – not nervous but uncomfortable. Picking up her purse and lunch bag, she turned to him, a severe expression on her round face.

"I must tell you. Kristina. She has the cancer."

Dad felt frozen in place. "...what kind of cancer?"

"It is of the blood."

"...is she in remission?"

"I no know what that means."

"Is she still sick? Or is she okay?"

"Ah. Yes. She say she is good for now. But the doctors, they do not know if the cancer comes back or not. That is why she travels. She does not wish to be where the bad news stays."

"Thank you for telling me, Marisol."

"I see the way you look at each other, Mister Bob. It is something you should know. I will not be here next week. I am going for the hip."

"I'll be checking in."

Marisol nodded and left.

The following Monday, as expected, Kristina came by herself. She had done the kitchen, the bedroom and now she was here in the studio again, sitting on a stool by the window, sipping juice from a thermos as my father worked.

"Marisol told me you had cancer."

There was silence. Dad glanced up from the canvas. Kristina was staring into her thermos bottle.

"I wish she hadn't told you that."

"Were you going to?"

"Probably not."

154

"Tell me now." Dad was working on her face; the head slightly turned, half of it in shadow, half of it in sunlight; the cascade of dark hair over one shoulder.

Kristina rose to her feet and moved away from the window. She put her thermos down on the worktable. "You start feeling bad. Tired all the time. You lose your appetite. What little you get down comes back up. Or out. You get these bruises."

"Can you look at me while you tell me this?"

Kristina did. "Anyway, you go the doctor, and he draws your blood. Then he sends you to another doctor who takes your bone marrow. Then you go to another doctor who takes fluid from your spine. They check all this stuff out, then they check out your lymph nodes and your spleen even though they're already sure what's going on. They finally sit you down and tell you that you have acute leukemia. You ask what your chances are. They tell you that because of your age, they're pretty good. But then they tell you that you have a high white blood cell count and that's not good. They tell you that a lot of it will depend on how you respond to the chemo." Kristina picked up the thermos and swirled the contents, staring down at it. She suddenly looked very tired. "So we did that. Some other stuff as well."

Dad felt relief sweep through him. "You're okay then."

Kristina shrugged. "I have what they call minimum residual disease. It means there are still cancer cells in there."

"And what does that mean?"

"That it'll probably come back." Kristina returned the thermos to the table. Reaching up, she lifted the long, dark hair up and off her head. "I decided not to wait around for it."

She wasn't bald, not quite. A layer of soft, dark stubble shaded her finely shaped skull. Kristina stroked the wig. "The funny thing is this is my real hair. When I knew I was going to lose it, I cut it off."

"It must have been long."

"It was. I loved my hair."

"I think you should move in," said Dad.

"I think so too."

She arrived mid-morning the next day, wearing her usual jeans and sweatshirt, carrying a jacket and leather satchel and pulling a suitcase on rollers. The dogs barked and skittered, happily greeting her. "Marisol's doing fine," she said, scratching their ears. "The surgery was a success."

155

Dad took the suitcase from her and together, they climbed the stairs. He started towards the guest room.

"No," said Kristina. "Your room."

They moved wordlessly down the hall and into the master bedroom. Kristina tossed her satchel towards the chair. "Be right out," she said, and she went into the bathroom and closed the door behind her. My father put the suitcase down. He looked around the bedroom. It was bright. It was comfortable.

Why was his heart beating so fast?

There was a painting on the wall. It was of me, I was four years old, and I was thoughtfully regarding a stuffed toy. Dad turned it so it faced the wall, and then, feeling like an idiot, turned it back. "Can I get you anything?" he called to the closed bathroom door.

"Not a thing," said the voice behind it.

Dad turned towards the open doorway where the dogs were looking in as if curious. He closed his eyes, wondering if he'd made a horrible mistake. The bathroom door opened behind him, and he turned.

"What do you think?"

Kristina was wigless.

Kristina was naked.

Kristina was slim bordering on frail.

Her clavicle and ribs showed. Her breasts were shriveled teardrops, slim at the top, full at the bottom. Her pubic hair was dark and heavy.

"I think you're lovely."

"Liar." Moving to the bed, Kristina pulled back the comforter and sheets and slipped under them. She shivered. "Come on, take off your clothes and get in. I'm freezing."

My father kicked off his shoes and socks. He pulled his shirt over his head and dropped it. He unbuckled his belt and pushed his jeans to the floor. There were no longer any doubts as he moved to the other side of the bed and got beneath the covers.

Kristina rolled into him. "You have a good body," she said. "I'm all skin and bone."

"Feels pretty good to me."

"No. Once I had boobs. An ass." Her hand went down Dad's stomach to lightly touch him and he gasped. "I could never have done this before. There were rules. What good are rules if they don't allow you to live?" Kristina rolled back, pulling my father with her. "If you want me to do something, tell me. Anything I want you to do, I'll tell you." Her legs went around him and as if offering him her lifeblood, she gently drew his head down to her throat. Years later, he would think of it as the beginning of a journey. Intimacy turned to passion, possession led to being possessed. With lips and hands, with body and words, Kristina loved him and my captive father, set free, loved in return.

Day 13 – Motivation

It was Wednesday, the thirteenth day of COG and William G. was clean shaven. The artist, Robert Calhoun, was shocked. He had walked through the door into group and there William sat, his hair trimmed, his face as clean and smooth as a whistle.

Click went Dad's brain. *Click.*

Perhaps it was his imagination, but William G. looked less pale and hollow-eyed. He nodded as my father sat down.

"It's my last day," said William G. said quietly.

Dad wished it was his. The morning lecture, given by Julio, had been on motivation and it had yet again thrown any sense of equanimity he might have brought to the proceedings, right out the window.

"*Motivation*," said Julio, "is the inspiration to enact positive *change*."

(Dad's inability to enact anything was the last thing he wanted to think about which meant he had no choice now but to listen.)

"Uncertainty is normal," said Julio. "It motivates us to decide and once a decision is made, we take action. We go one way or the other. Agreed?"

(No, Dad didn't agree. Better the devil you knew than the devil you might meet going one way or the other.)

"When we are *stuck*, we go nowhere. We are *frozen*, people, dealing with the same issues, day after day, over and over again."

(Was it Dad's imagination or was his breath turning to vapor in front of him?)

Turning to the whiteboard, Julio picked up a chalk and began to draw a seesaw. It was clumsy, lacked scale and my artist father wondered if he should get up and draw it for him. Too late. Julio was now sketching a large circle under each end of the sea saw.

"*Action!*" said Julio, writing the word in the circle on the left. "*Avoidance*," he said, writing the word in the circle on the right.

"Commitment! – Procrastination!"

"Confidence! Fear!"

"Alive! Frozen!"

Julio turned back to the assembly. "Which side do you want to be sitting on, people? The left or the right?" The room reverberated. *Left – left – left – left –!* Julio tossed the chalk aside. "To try is to begin. Let's talk about how we try."

No.

Dad didn't want to. He saw it so clearly now. All these words, these insights and good intentions imparted on a daily basis? They were band aids. The adhesive was temporary. In the protected environment of a three-and-a-half-week psycho-support-fest, it was easy to say I'll be okay, life will be better but outside in the world, woeful reality still waited, ready to deal another crushing blow to the weak. Motivate *that*. Dad ignored the rest of the lecture.

But now, here in group, William G. had *changed* in front of his eyes. As the other group members began to file in, they too took in the new and improved version.

"Whoa!" said a surprised Paul F.

"You're so handsome," said Beverly, hands aflutter.

"Something's different," Sara half-whispered from her wheelchair.

Something was. William G.'s anxiety was at a nineteen. His depression was at an all-time low of twenty-three.

"What do you think made the difference?" asked Heidi.

William G. quietly shrugged. "I don't know. Maybe 'cause this last weekend I went to a veteran's support group. Guys who are kinda working through the same things I am. It helps knowing other guys are having the same problems as me. I'm not so alone."

"You never told us you were a veteran," said Heidi, going to her notes. She looked surprised.

"I didn't want to talk about it."

"Why don't you talk about it now then."

William G. looked around the circle. Dad could see his throat working. There was no way William G. was going to talk about anything.

William G. talked.

"I enlisted in the Marines when I was twenty. I had nothing else to do and it seemed like a cool thing. I ended up doing two tours in Afghanistan. I saw a

159

lot of stuff. You'd have breakfast in the morning and in the afternoon, you collected body parts."

Beverly moaned.

William shook his head. "No. I did bad things too. One time we were in a village, and I saw someone move in a doorway. I fired on them. It turned out to be a little kid. My son looks like him."

"Oh, my God," murmured Walt O.

"My second tour I was stationed at an outpost in the Koregal Valley. We'd go out on missions, we'd shoot at people, they'd shoot at us. The big guys kept telling us how important it was but when they pulled what was left of us out, they blew the outpost up. And then, you know, we *all* finally left. Everybody. It was worth nothing what we'd done. The people we'd tried to help were worth nothing. It had all been a joke." William stopped talking.

How to paint silence, thought the artist, Robert Boone. How to paint heart pins dropping. The history of art was littered with paintings of scholarly looking generals and prideful kings who ordered their subjects into battle, who ruled by divine right. Lies. The image of war was a desolate, young man sitting in a chair.

William began to speak again, his voice still a soft monotone. "You get out. You come home. You try to go back to your life. But it stays with you. And you can't tell anyone about it. When you're a Marine you don't want to seem weak. I could never tell my wife.... my mom. Still... I think about it every day."

Paul F. stared at the floor. There were tears in Beverly's eyes and Sara's eyes were shut tight.

"Do you feel the things that happened were your fault?" Heidi asked quietly.

"Yes," said William G.

"C'mon," Paul F growled. "What were you supposed to do?"

"I signed up for it," said William G.

"But they sent you," said Beverly.

"I think what Paul and Beverly are trying to say," said Heidi, "is that given the circumstances, anything that happened was out of your control."

"It doesn't feel that way."

(My father wondered what he would have done. He had no idea. He'd never been in a position to so much as even think about it.)

160

"William?" It was Sara. "Are there any good memories of that time in your life?"

"My buddies. We looked out for one another. We all were in it together."

"What would they say to you now?"

"Move on. Live. Take care of yourself and your family. Do it for us."

Sara nodded.

"With that in mind, what is it you want to accomplish now?" asked Heidi. "What's most important to you?"

"I want to stop feeling guilty. I want to stop feeling afraid and sad. I want to be there for people."

"We all want that for you too. But it still might take a while."

"That's okay. I'm not going anywhere."

The Indian woman in the sari poked her head in and told William it was time for his last meeting with Dr. Giancarlo. Nodding, he gathered his things and in a matter of moments, was gone.

Reality, thought Dad? The real world? William G. was the one dealing with reality. William was the one living in the real world. He was living in a comfortable house in Branford where the world wasn't allowed to intrude. He spent his time making elaborate meals and contemplating the images in his head. It was he, who was making excuses. He couldn't seem to help it.

Things brightened a bit when Beverly said that her granddaughter had asked for an elephant for Christmas. Things darkened again when Colin recounted how he had called his sister the previous evening and she had quickly hung up on him. Things brightened again when Walt O. said he'd been asked to interview again on a really good job.

When it was Sara's turn to speak, she shook her head and said nothing.

Something had to be done.

Oh

"I want to buy you things," said Robert Boone. "Beautiful, new things."

It was a late afternoon in mid-November and Kristina had come out to the studio bearing a cheese plate and two glasses of white wine. After six weeks together, it had become a ritual between them, a signal that it was time for Dad to stop working and rejoin the real world, rejoin her. Glass in hand, Kristina was sitting near the window in what had become *her chair* in her usual jeans and sweatshirt.

"I don't need anything," said Kristina.

"Okay, then I want to take you places. London, Paris, Madrid. Where would you like to go?"

"For a walk," said Kristina, and putting down her glass, she stood.

They walked down Waterside Road. At the end, they went out onto the hard packed sand, stopped and looked towards the sound. The Thimble Islands were up and to the left. To the east, straight across the calm, grey water, my father could make out Long Island. Warm and comfortable in one of his heavy jackets, Kristina breathed in, then breathed out, smelling and tasting the air. She sighed with pleasure.

"What," said my father.

Kristina smiled softly. "Nothing. It's just.... there are times in your life all you do is run. You forget to stop and look. You forget what it's like to love."

"You love me, huh?"

"Don't let it go to your head."

Both of them tried not to smile.

"Too late," said my father and turning, he took Kristina into his arms. They kissed, then kissed again. Years later, he would remember those kisses. Like children, he would think. Like innocent children doing drawings in a safe and guarded room.

162

It was early January when the now fifteen years old yours truly (me!) came up from New York to celebrate my traditional second Christmas. Dad picked me up at the train station (I had insisted on taking the train myself – first time) and we drove out to Branford. The moment we got in the house, the very first thing he did was introduce me this *woman* (Kristina *who?*). We nodded, we smiled, we shook hands, we were cordial with one another, but I think Dad sensed an immediate coolness on my part. (To say I was interested in sharing Christmas with a complete and total stranger... well, you get the picture.)

Later that afternoon, Kristina was napping, and Dad and I were in the living room decorating the newly bought tree with ornaments that had belonged to Mary, my grandmother. Every year we brought them down from the attic and it was an unspoken tradition now. Of course, the subject of *the woman* came up. (I wonder how?)

"You enjoy her company then."

"You might say," replied Dad.

"And... where's she from again?" (So politely curious, as I hung a silver angel on a branch.) "Cuba? Mexico?"

"Los Angeles."

"I was talking about her *heritage*, Dad."

"I've never asked."

"Oh." (The look on my father's face said he wasn't sure what "oh" meant.) "Well, it's okay to have her here if that's what you want. Pass the Santa Claus."

After various stages of ongoing alienation, the next afternoon we all sat down at the dinner table. My father had brined, stuffed and roasted a turkey and had prepared mashed potatoes, green beans, cranberry sauce and pan whisked gravy. Both an apple and a pecan pie would follow. The cheese tamales and Christmas salad with apples, raisins and pecans that Kristina had contributed, were also on the table. (So far, I hadn't so much as looked at either of them and had contributed nothing.)

"What is it you do again, Kristina?" I asked, ever so mature, as I reached for the mashed potatoes.

"She was sort of a lawyer," Dad said quickly.

"I *was* sort of a paralegal," said Kristina, frowning at him.

"My mistake," muttered Dad.

"Why not a *real* lawyer?" I asked.

Oh, the young and naive, Kristina's smile seemed to say. (Which *really* got my goat.) "I'm afraid I couldn't afford law school."

"Yes, well, it can be like that for some people," I said, all smiles as I reached for the stuffing.

Okay, I have to admit, the morning tree ceremony had *not* gone well. Every gift I'd opened (and almost all of them were for *me*) had been met with a frown and a comment on my part.

"This is much too expensive. I'd feel guilty wearing it."

"*Dad.* I know you're an artist, but this color is, well… no."

"I don't think this size is right and I have the exact thing already."

And now, at the dinner table, I was pouring gravy on potatoes and still being a little bitch. "What exactly does a paralegal *do*?" I asked, picking up my knife and fork. "Is it important?"

"Research. Filing. Putting together whatever an attorney needs for a trial or a hearing."

"You work behind the scenes?"

"Pretty much. At least I did."

"So do too many women," I said with a sigh.

Kristina glanced at my father. (Neither were eating. Dad, frankly, now looked nervous.)

Reaching for the bowl, I served myself cranberry. "Did your firm include services for the working poor? Because in my opinion everyone is entitled to proper judicial representation, even if they can't afford it."

"The firm I worked for mostly specialized in class actions suits for great gobs of money."

"Oh."

(Dad now knew what "*oh*" meant. It wasn't good.)

Patting my mouth with napkin, I cleared my fifteen-year-old throat. "Yes, well, I just want to say that I approve of the fact that my father is having *an affair* with a strong and independent Latina woman. I have no doubt he's going to get a better sense of our country's diverse culture because of you." I glanced dismissively at the tamales. "Especially at Christmas."

There was a moment of silence. Dad was staring straight ahead.

"Sweetheart, no offense," said Kristina, "but please don't grow up into an overeducated, liberal cliché, putting down anyone who *isn't* without first knowing them. Don't spout what other people tell you without having experienced it. And by the way, when someone gives you a gift, open it, say thank you, I love it and if you don't love it, take it back later and have the pleasure of picking out something else."

No one had ever spoken to me like that before. I stared at Kristina, slack jawed and eyes blinking. I think I might have started to cry. "I'm sorry. Thank you so much. I've *so* been waiting for someone to tell me that. It's been so confusing having to say the right thing all the time and not being sure what it even is. Mom and Dad are no help at all."

"*Oh,*" said Kristina.

It was during the tamales and Christmas salad that Carter called and in a trembling voice told my father that the previous evening a homeless man had gone into DeVeaux's and begun screaming about terrorists and scheming Muslim immigrants. Striding out from the kitchen, Francoise/Sayid had in no uncertain terms told the man to leave. The man had pulled a pistol out of his coat and shot Francoise/Sayid in the chest, killing him on the spot.

The first real friend my father had ever made was gone.

The Magic of Wands

"Tell me something, what exactly are you hoping to accomplish in the COG program?"

The Wednesday afternoon had turned warm, and my father and Annie had decided to take their coffee and tea outside and sit at a sidewalk table. Annie had seemed distracted and tense since the first sip of tea and Dad, his latte untouched, didn't feel all that relaxed either.

"I don't know. What do *you* think I should be accomplishing?"

"That's not my decision, it's yours."

"I guess I'm undecided," said Dad.

(How about a long nap?)

"Okay, let me put it another way. What's the primary issue you're attempting to address right now? How would you define it?"

"How would *you* define it?"

"Again, it's not for me to say. But if you refuse to be honest with yourself, Bob, you're not going to accomplish anything." Annie looked around, restless. "I don't feel like sitting here. May we take a walk?"

Group had finally ended that morning with the arrival of a first day participant, Lauren D., and sadly, there had been just enough time left for her to open her mouth. Lauren D., late thirties, attractive and far too expensively dressed, was, by her own admission, *a very successful* corporate lawyer. Relationship issues had begun when her husband discovered she was having an affair with a junior associate—*not the first time, I'm afraid*—and asked her to move out of the house. The junior associate had subsequently left the firm *"unfairly"* asserting sexual harassment and because of the *"current social environment,"* Lauren D was fired. With her life now *"in pieces,"* Lauren D. took a handful of prescription sleeping pills, staggered out of the hotel hospitality suite where she was staying and asked a passing stranger to call her husband and tell him *"I beg forgiveness."* Instead, the man called 911, Lauren

D. was taken to the hospital and her husband filed for divorce. The COG program had been recommended to Lauren D. by the psychiatrist she had begun seeing—*one of the best in the field*—after her thirty-day stay in the hospital in-patient psychiatric ward. She was currently living in an "*upscale rental community*" and was looking for a new job position "*which is my number one priority.*"

"Do you have children?" asked Heidi.

"Two," said Lauren D., with an oblivious smile. "A girl, twelve, and a boy, ten. I see them on the weekends."

Lauren D. recounted all this in such an aw-shucks, no big deal, tone of voice, everyone in the room immediately disliked her. Obviously, they were letting anyone into COG these days.

"Heidi tells me she keeps asking you to do thought records and you refuse." Dad and Annie were walking along Chapel Street, the New Haven Green up and to the right.

"I'm not so good at writing."

"It's not about good or bad, it's about getting it down."

"I don't know what to write about."

"Are there people in your life causing you problems? You could write about that."

"You," said Dad.

"What?"

"You're causing me problems. I keep asking you out to dinner and you say no."

"We've been over this."

"I'm not satisfied with the answer."

Annie's face tensed and she looked away. "You want to know something, Bob? At this particular moment in time the person causing me the most problems is walking next to me. What are you hiding from? You're talented, you're successful in your field, you're attractive."

"You think so?"

Abruptly stopping, Annie turned to face Dad (the current cause of her problems). "Stop being *sarcastic*! Why won't you talk about anything real? Because a person in your circumstances not being honest with himself pisses me off!"

Two passing pedestrians were staring. Annie ignored them. "How would you describe your personality?"

"How would you?"

"Stubborn, defensive, and detached."

"Who's harassing who here?"

"Oh, for god's sake! Is there nothing and no one that's important to you?"

"You first," replied Dad.

Annie's voice went from severe to shrill. "*No! Answer the questions!* Are you an optimist or a pessimist, Bob?"

"Both."

"Do you feel sad, mad, hopeless or what?"

"Or what."

"Oh, you're fucking impossible!" shrieked Annie. "You turn self-examination into a charade. I'm trying to help you, you stupid bastard!"

And now a lot of pedestrians were looking.

"Calm down," Dad said, quietly alarmed.

"No." Annie suddenly looked pained. "No, this is pointless. I can't do it anymore, Bob, I just can't." Turning, Annie hurried away.

(And my father?)

Dad stood there, eyes blinking, mouth half open, quietly stunned. *Okay, fine. Enough already. Time to turn it around, time to go get in the truck and head on home. Time to forget all this, time to quit and move on, time to...*

"Annie!"

Dad broke into a run. Racing down the sidewalk, he dodged pedestrians. He sidestepped a car as he ran across an intersection. The heels of his Aussie-boots went clop-clop-clop in his ears. He caught up to Annie as she approached Temple Street.

"Annie? Annie, please!"

Annie slowed, stopped and turned back. There was a forlorn look on her face as Dad came to a breathless halt in front of her. They stood a moment, barely looking at one another. "Annie... I don't know what happened back there, I just... I'm so sorry."

Annie shook her head. "No. It's not your fault. I'm having a bad day, that's all."

"Because of me?"

"Yeah, sure, Bob, you're the only thing that's happening in my life right now." Annie took a breath, then let it go. "I want to ask you a last question and I want you to answer me honestly. This is important."

"Anything."

"If you could wave a magic wand, what would you make happen in your life?"

"I would go back in time," said my father. "I would change things. But there are no magic wands. Life's a bitch and then you die."

"And *that*," said Annie, touching Dad's cheek, "is what you should be writing about."

Petechiae

Kristina's nose was bleeding.

"You okay?" asked my father, trying not to sound alarmed. They were in the kitchen. He had come in from the studio to make some coffee and Kristina had been standing by the sink, looking out the window. There were bright, wet, drips of red on the counter.

"Oh, not really," said Kristina.

"What's wrong?"

"I've been tired lately. My face keeps going numb. And this." Kristina held out her arms. There were small red spots on the skin. "It's petechia. It's caused by blood vessels breaking beneath the skin."

"What's it mean?" asked Dad, knowing exactly what it meant.

"It means – probably – that the leukemia is back."

Even in the moment, my father wondered how she could be so calm about it. Was it resignation? Perhaps she had known all along it would return and now it had. "Okay. We're going to find a doctor. We're going to find twenty doctors. We're going to beat this once and for all."

"No," Kristina said gently. "I'm going home. I know what's coming. I'm not going to put you through it."

"What if I want to go through it?"

"It's not your decision."

"I'll move to LA. You can't stop me."

"No, I can't. But I won't see you. I'll get a restraining order if I have to."

Dad felt as if the room was spiraling. He felt as if he were falling down a steep hill. "Why?"

"I want you to remember me the way I am now."

"I think you're selfish."

"Oh, definitely." Kristina moved close and looked up into my father's eyes. "Let's go upstairs to bed now. I need you to hold me."

They did and for too brief a moment my father forgot that he was feeling as sick inside just as she was.

"Will you come back?" he asked the day he took her to the airport for her flight west.

"I left my suitcase with my good clothes in the guest room closet." Kristina half smiled. "I have to."

They hugged tight. And then, Kristina pushed Dad away. She kissed her fingertips, touched them to his chest and then she was gone, not looking back as she went through security.

Dad stood at the floor to ceiling windows to watch the plane rise off the runway. He waited until it had disappeared into the sky and then he went out, got into the truck and went home.

The first month alone, the artist, Robert Boone, painted as if in a frenzy, hardly eating, every day running mile after mile so as to fall into an exhausted, restless sleep at night. On the last day of the month, he took a razor-edged utility knife from a toolbox and going into the studio, shredded everything he'd done.

The second month, he drank. Bloody Mary's in the early morning led to shots of vodka by noon. Wine accompanied him into the studio and his work took on the smudged and blotted patterns of a color-numb alcoholic. Dinner became a champagne appetizer followed by a red wine entrée with cognac for dessert. By the end of the third week, Marisol had enough. "I am ashamed of you Mister Bob. Kristina, she would be ashamed. You are turning yourself into *un borracho*. If you do not stop, I will not work for you no more because I cannot see you like this."

Utility knife in hand, my father went out to the studio, shredded the past three week's work into strips and stopped the excessive drinking on the spot.

It just so happened that I came over from Wallingford to visit the following Saturday. "We broke up," said Dad, when I asked where Kristina was. "My fault completely."

"But, Dad, I totally liked her. *You* did."

"Yeah, well. No big deal."

The weekend didn't go well, and I went back to school early. (I mean, really, he acted as if nothing had happened.)

My father spent the third month driving on consecutive weeks to Washington, Philadelphia and Boston where he wandered the halls of the

National Gallery, the Philadelphia Museum of Art, and the Isabella Stuart Gardener Museum respectively. Each trip left him listless and bored and the last week of the month, with nothing to shred, he went out into the studio and broke all his brushes and frames into kindling.

And then – on the first Monday of the fourth month, Dad was sitting at the kitchen table sipping coffee when Marisol arrived for work. She didn't look at him as she took off her coat and put her things in the closet. Subdued, she finally turned to him. She slowly approached and she put down a sealed envelope. "Mister Bob, I must give you the news. Our Kristina. She is gone. She sends me this to give to you," Marisol turned and left the room. Dad stared at the envelope in front of him. He finally opened it. He read.

"Dearest Bob. My artist. My gifted bruised knight. Love of my life. You were right, I was selfish. Hoping to hold on to memories unsullied by illness, I made a terrible mistake. I denied us closure. Stupid, silly me. Not a day goes by that I haven't thought of you, dreamed of you. I have missed your touch, your voice, your smile. I was a drowning sailor, my artist, and you were a beautiful tropical island that took me ashore and filled my world with colors. Please be good to yourself. Live. Take chances. Trust. And remember. *Ningún destino es peor que una vida sin amor.* No fate is worse than a life without love. Eternally yours, Kristina."

Dad put down the letter.

Dad rose from the table.

Dad went out to the studio, locked the door behind him and taking the utility knife, he slashed the fingers and the top of his painting hand to the bone.

Day 14 – Bountiful

"I've been asked to choreograph a dance for the New Haven High School of Creative and Performing Arts this next fall."

It was Thursday, the fourteenth day of COG, and Sara sat, huddled in her wheelchair. Her depression levels were at a sixty-five. Her anxiety level was one hundred and ten. Sara, it would seem, had not been paying attention to the morning's lecture.

"Life! Is what happens in the *present tense!*"

Dr. Giancarlo had smiled his usual toothy smile as he said it. The good doctor was in a chair at the front of the lecture hall, as always, in his ski jacket, looking pleased as a pumpkin elf to be giving the morning's lecture. "The past is past. Nothing we can do about it. The future? Who knows? No, what we have, folks, *all* we have, is *right now*. And the question is, folks, what are you going to *do with it?*"

"You don't seem happy about this opportunity," Heidi said, looking at Sara. "I'd have thought you would be."

"I've never done it before." Sara stared at the floor. "And now, like this, I don't think I can."

(Oh, no, thought Dad.)

"Being in the present," intoned Dr. Giancarlo, "means we don't *react* to a given moment, we *respond* to it in a rational, mindful way."

(Oh, but wait! Having reacted, responded and *dealt* with his daughter (me) and her insecurities as a young novelist on occasion. "I suck at male characters, Daddy, I absolutely suck! I can't get into their stupid heads!" My father had a sudden, *rational* inkling of how he might respond to the crisis at hand.)

"Ahem… Sara?" Dad cleared his throat. "Excuse me for saying so but I think you're right. No way you can choreograph anything if you can't get out of your wheelchair. Never, you're setting yourself up to fail."

"Remember, folks," continued Dr. Giancarlo, "our thoughts and feelings are not *facts*. It is how we *connect* to those thoughts and feelings that's important, not the thoughts themselves."

("What do you mean I shouldn't even *attempt* to write male characters, Daddy? How can I do that when half the *world* is stupid men." Actually, you outnumber us, replied my father, which was beside the point.)

The room was still. Sara stared across the circle, her expression saying that Robert Boone was treading on fragile ground. "A dance piece is choreographed using specific terms. I could probably *tell* the dancers what I wanted them to do."

"Focusing on the past and worrying about the future," said good doctor Giancarlo, "means you're missing out on the *present*. You're missing out on honest to goodness *life*."

"Yeah but wouldn't that take a special kind of imagination?" asked Dad. "Do you even have that? I'd hate to see you blow it. You've gone through so much already."

(You're talking gibberish, Daddy. That's the problem with men, they spout gibberish, if and when they attempt to communicate at all, which means I've got to stop trying to make my little boys *think* and just let them gibber-spout and believe me, *that* I can do.)

Sara's face was grim. "I think the music would inspire me. As it does any dancer."

"Okay, but what if it doesn't? And these are kids you'd be working with. What if you screw it up completely?"

(Da-*aad!* I won't!)

Sara's eyes narrowed. She was angry. "Then I screw it up. I screw it up and I do better the next time."

"Oh," said Dad. "I don't see it as any kind of problem then."

(It wasn't.)

Paul F. snorted. Beverly tittered. Colin lightly applauded. "Is it always like this?" asked a skeptical sounding Lauren D.

"You set me up, didn't you," Sara said softly.

"He set you up beautifully," said Heidi, looking pleased.

Dad shrugged. "I have no idea what either of you are talking about."

"Being mindful," concluded Dr. Giancarlo, "is focusing on one challenge at a time as effectively as possible. Doing so can only lead to success."

(Sounds easy, doesn't it. Well, it ain't. Next scenario.)

"I don't think my husband finds me attractive anymore," said Beverly. It was nearing the end of group and she was the last one up. Never a clothes horse, today she was wearing jeans and what looked like a man's baggy, denim work shirt, untucked at the waist. Her dark, curly hair was all over the place. "I mean, we don't…." Beverly's hands fluttered with embarrassment. "He doesn't seem interested."

"Welcome to the club," said Paul F. "I'm lucky if my husband gets it on me with me twice a week."

(Hmmm. Paul F. didn't quite seem to be getting the point.)

"It's my experience that a man's libido begins to decrease around the age of forty," said Lauren D. "Perhaps that's the problem."

(Hmm. Perhaps Lauren D. was the problem.)

"You have three children in the house, "suggested Heidi. "Perhaps circumstances are getting in the way of intimacy?"

"No, I don't think that's it. I think he feels I'm just…" Beverly searched for the word and found it, in fact, found two. "Fat and unattractive."

Everyone assured Beverly that she wasn't, but my father could see she didn't look remotely convinced and it pained him.

Bountiful

"Rubenesque."

"What?" said Beverly, her mouth half full of turkey sandwich.

It was half an hour after group and she and my father were now sitting at a table in the hospital cafeteria. Dad, despite the prospect of cafeteria food, had approached Beverly in the hall and having grabbed two tickets from Heidi, asked her to lunch. Beverly had quivered with delight.

"Peter Paul Rubens was a Flemish painter, famous for his nudes. Women with stomachs and hips and thighs. Today it's all beanpoles and models and fitness instructors but that's a modern thing. For a long time, abundant was considered better. It was a tough world and people were eager for something bountiful to love."

(Now more than ever!)

Beverly couldn't have been more rapt if Dad had been giving a church sermon. She took a small bite of sandwich, chewed a moment and swallowed. "Bob? Are you saying you'd like to paint me in the nude?"

If there had been food in his mouth Dad might have choked on it. "Uh, no, *no*, I was just... I mean, we couldn't. It's against the rules."

"We're adults. We could break the rules." It was a question as much as a statement. "I would love, just once in my life, to be bountiful."

Dad watched as Beverly settled back in her chair, his silence seemingly an affirmation that she was fat and unattractive. (Oh, what to do, what to do...)

"Beverly? Nothing would give me greater pleasure."

Ten minutes later, with Dad in his pick-up and Beverly following in her Ford Focus, they were motoring from New Haven out to the house in Branford.

Explaining that what he'd attempt was a series of preliminary sketches, Dad opened a bottle of white wine in the kitchen and the two of them, accompanied by the dogs, went out to the studio.

"Just one glass," said Beverly. She looked around the chaotic workspace. She took in the brushes, the pencils and pens, the cluttered benches and table and the storage cabinets. Dad handed her the glass of wine and it trembled in her hand as she sipped, then sipped again. "Is there a bathroom?"

Dad pointed towards a closed door. "There."

While Beverly went into the bathroom, he arranged pillows on the worn, silk covered settee. He'd found it in a Guilford antique store, and it had a long seat and one inclined end. He refilled Beverly's wine glass and put it down on the floor. He got a box of sketch sticks from the supply cabinet. The dogs stared at him, tongues lolling. Putting a large pad on his easel, my father sat down. He poured himself a glass of wine and he waited.

He waited some more.

The doorknob turned and Beverly came out of the bathroom. She wore just the denim work shirt. Her legs were bare, she wasn't wearing shoes and her hair was brushed back off her face. She looked around the studio as if someone might be hiding. "Where do you want me?"

"Over there," said my father, pointing at the settee. He watched as she moved across the room, sat, quickly pulled her shirt up and over her head and placed it down and across her pelvis. Beverly's breasts were pear shaped. Her stomach was pooched, her hips were wide, and her legs were strong and surprisingly graceful.

Dad pointed. "Your wine's right there."

"Ohhhh… I really shouldn't." Beverly reached down and picked up her glass. She sipped, sipped again, put the glass down on the floor and then, wavering slightly, lay back on the pillow. Dad opened his pad and adjusted the angle of his easel.

"Bob?"

He looked up. Beverly's arms covered her breasts. "Does this mean we're going to….?"

(Whoo, boy! My father had wondered if this might raise its head. The relationship between an artist and his naked model was a notoriously intimate one. Renoir, Degas, Modigliani, Picasso; all had obtained the ongoing services of their models by making them their mistresses. My father knew that all these relationships had ended badly (hello?) and he had his answer ready.)

"Beverly, I think if we were to do that, we'd have no choice but to fall in love with each other and we both know that's not the best thing for either of us."

Beverly sagged with relief. Closing her eyes, she happily hummed. Reaching down, she picked up her glass, finished the wine in a long gulp and put the glass back down on the floor. Raising her arms up and over her head, she arched her back. "Oooh…. I think I like being naked in front of strange men."

Dad laughed. "I think you should tell your husband that."

Giggling, Beverly lay back on the settee and grew still. The dogs, as if sensing an opportunity, padded across the studio and settled quietly to the floor, Mick at her head and Angela near her feet.

Rubenesque? What a useless word.

Click.

The artist, Robert Boone, saw virtue, fertility, and desire.

Click.

He saw faith and vitality made flesh.

There were no mistakes.

My father began to sketch.

(And though this interlude might not have happened this exact way, or perhaps never even happened at all, I hope it did.

Commodities

"Bob, we haven't had a face to face in far too long."

It was the spring of my father didn't know what and Carter was on the phone. (Far too long was an understatement. Though they spoke on the phone on a regular basis, they hadn't seen one another in almost a year.)

"I've been busy," said Dad.

"Working I hope."

"Mostly jerking my lily."

"The poor thing. I'd like to come up."

"When?"

"How about this weekend?"

Dad hesitated. It had been a while since anyone but Marisol had been in the house.

(I was now a sophomore at Brown University, firmly enmeshed in the lit and theatre programs. Though I'd always come and stay over for my annual second Christmas, other than the occasional weekend, any free time was now spent racing down to New York to attend lectures and plays and poetry readings and summers were spent interning and going to writer's workshops. On my father's dime, lucky me.)

"Thanks for the advance notice," Dad said to Carter.

"Why, are you doing anything?"

"Friday or Saturday?"

"Saturday, I think."

"Train or car?"

"I'll drive," said Carter. "And I'll bring bagels and wine."

"I suppose that means you'll be spending the night."

"See you Saturday around noon, Bob."

Carter arrived around 3. Dad's impatience was assuaged by the two bottles of Lewis Napa Valley Cabernet and the bottle of Hennessy Privilège VSOP

Cognac that Carter presented as he got out of the station wagon. They went out into the back yard. It was a beautiful April day, light sweater weather, and my father had brought out the cushions to put on the old teak lawn chairs.

Carter closed his eyes and murmured, savoring the afternoon light that touched his face. He looked towards the carefully tended garden beds. They were covered with a smooth layer of mulch. The canes of rose bushes, bristling with thorns, stood waiting for new blossoms. "My compliments to your gardener."

"I'll tell me you said so."

"Really?" Carter seemed surprised.

"It's a pain in the ass but if you want something done right, do it yourself," said Dad, who secretly liked the job.

"You never cease to surprise me, Bob."

"Well, that's weird. I try and make it a point never to surprise anybody, especially myself."

Carter closed his eyes again. "Theo and I have split up." (Just like that.)

Dad faltered. "Jesus... when did this happen?" (How long had the two of them been together? Dad had wondered when they were going to get married.)

"Oh, five months ago."

"Why didn't you tell me?"

"I wasn't ready to and now I am."

"You doing okay?" Dad prayed that Carter was. He didn't know what he'd do if he wasn't.

"There's still the occasional bad day. But I choose to focus on what was positive about the relationship, not that it ended badly."

"It's always pissed me off that you're so smart, Carter."

"I count on pissing you off, Bob. It gives me great satisfaction."

They both laughed.

"I hope you're hungry."

"Famished," said Carter. They rose, went in the house, opened the wine and my father cooked.

"I don't suppose you have anything to share," said Carter. It was after dinner. They were now sipping the cognac, both more than slightly buzzed. Dad had known this moment was coming. He had known it when he hung up the phone the previous day and he'd known it when he saw Carter drive up in a station wagon. He'd thought long and hard about it. If a tree falls in a forest and no one is around to hear it, does it make a sound? Does a work of art exist if no one, not even one person, ever sees it?

(Or in my case, ever reads it?)

"Come on," said Dad and carrying the bottle of cognac, he led Carter out to the studio.

Carter said nothing.

They leaned haphazardly against the walls where my father had placed them. The oldest ones were the first to catch the eye as you came through the door. The rest were on the other two sides of the room.

Carter said nothing.

The New York City Street scenes were related to The Sound paintings. The color palate was limited to black, reds, greys and white. The paintings were heavily glazed, creating in the dark backgrounds luminosity and depth. Indistinguishable pedestrians strode to and from, all seemingly going somewhere and nowhere, hailing cabs, racing for buses and trains, loitering on street corners and in front of bodegas. In all the paintings, the present seemed ground under the gritty footprint of the past. Dad had found a use for the dust of 9-11.

Carter turned in place.

The paintings and sketches that my father had done of Kristina formed an orchestra. Nudes. Portraits. Abstracts. A dark-haired woman in jeans and sweatshirt. A bald woman with pustules on her face and shoulders. A nude Madonna with averted eyes and an abstract, brassy Latina in a pointillist dress and cubist heels.

Carter sighed. He looked for a place to sit. The closest thing was a backless stool. Carter sat and pointed at the bottle of cognac. Dad handed it to him. Carter took a sip, swallowed and handed the bottle back. When he spoke, his voice was quiet.

"Well, obviously I want to show them."

My father said nothing.

"I think they very well might be the best work you've ever done." My father raised the bottle and took a gulp of cognac. "They should be seen, Bob. They *must* be seen."

"They have been. By you."

"What the hell do you think you're doing?" Carter suddenly sounded angry. "When are you going to get it through your head that you've been given a gift? You might not like it or appreciate but other people do."

Dad drank more cognac. A sip this time. "I've been reading about warehouses in Switzerland. Climate controlled. Confidential. Filled with crates of artwork bought by rich people, by hedge funds. And then just stuck away. As investments."

Carter hesitated, then answered. "I'm afraid that's true."

"What's the point then? Books. Movies. Broadway plays. Paintings. What's the point when they're all just a commodity and the only thing that matters is how much you can sell them for." Dad stared at a portrait. Kristina's head was held high. The long hair of her wig fell down across her naked shoulders and breasts. Her eyes were fixed on something that was making her happy. (Him?) "I can't bear to think of this as a commodity."

As if contemplating the smells of oil paint, charcoal and turpentine, Carter was silent for a moment, and then he finally nodded. "I understand. I don't agree but I understand."

They went back into the house. They finished the brandy. They solved the problems of the world. Carter was a lightweight and Dad had to help him up the stairs to the guest room where he collapsed, fully clothed onto the bed.

"You're a great friend, Bob," said Carter. "Everything else is crapola."

"See you in the morning," said Dad and turning off the guest room light, he closed the door, made his way down the hall and went to bed.

They both woke up early, each with varying degrees of a hangover. "Remind me not to do this more often," said Carter, ignoring his bagel and sipping his third cup of coffee.

"You're the one who brought the brandy."

"Guilty as charged."

Around one, they went out to the car. "Next time, it's your turn to come see me," said Carter. "You're always welcome, you know that."

"I do."

Carter got in the station wagon and rolled down the window. He glanced back in the direction of the studio. "I still say they should be seen and I'm going to keep after you until we make it happen."

"You wouldn't be you otherwise."

Dad stood watching as Carter the car backed down the driveway and drove away.

The subject became moot. Late the next afternoon, my father called Carter to tell him that while he'd been out running, an electrical fire had burned the studio and everything in it to the ground.

"Tal es el destino," whispered Dad.

Such is fate.

Day 15 – Problem Solving II

"My wife and I are splitting up."

It was Friday, the fifteenth day of COG and in group it was announced that it was both Walt O. and Colin's last day. The fact took Robert Boone by surprise. Despite the departure of Megan J., his fellow group members had all started to feel like fixtures; Dad was supposed to be the one passing through. Both Walt O. and Colin had been asked by Heidi where they were mentally and emotionally and Walt O., whose depression and anxiety were at three-week highs, was going first. "She's moving out as we speak. She says everything has gotten to be too much for her."

All were very quiet.

"How do you feel about that?" asked Heidi.

"How do you think I feel?" replied Walt O., his voice rising. The group flinched. No one had ever heard Walt O. express anything close to anger before. He sagged in his chair.

The group session had started with the introduction of yet another new member. Suzy Q. (could that possibly be her real name?) was an overweight, young woman with lavender streaked hair and blue sparkled fingernails. Suzy Q. had on a sleeveless, ruffled, little girl party dress with a mocked waist and wore ankle socks and saddle shoes.

"Since, like, the eighth grade, I've loved drugs," said a matter-of-fact Suzie Q. "Pot, ecstasy, coke and meth. I loved'm all."

Beverly stifled a small cry and put her hand to her mouth.

"Is there a problem?" asked Suzie Q., looking at her.

"Why?" Beverly asked softly.

"Why what?" said Suzy Q.

"Why do you feel the need to use drugs? Isn't there anything else in your life to love?"

Suzie Q. shrugged. "Not really. When you're high, you not a fat slut. It doesn't matter that you don't pass your classes and can't hold a job. You don't care that people hate you."

"I'm so sorry," said Beverly.

"Whatever." Suzie Q. sighed as if bored. "Anyway, ten months ago, my parents got me into rehab. It was either that or they were going to throw me out of the house. Now they're telling me it's time to face my problems and get it together."

"And what are those problems?" asked Heidi.

"I just told you. I'm a slut, I'm stupid and people hate me. When I'm not doing drugs, I get really depressed."

"Ahem." Lauren D. cleared her throat. "Can I ask a question?"

Suzie Q. nodded. "Go ahead."

"Why are you dressed like a clown at a children's birthday party?" Dad felt the circle silently and collectively go *ouch*. "I'm just asking," said Lauren D., picking up on the vibe.

Suzie Q. smiled wickedly. "'Cause I like the attention, cutie-pie. What's the hitch in your little giddyap?" – causing Lauren D. to nervously look away.

It was suggested that Suzie Q. read the workbook chapter on thoughts, behavior and depression, Suzi agreeably said that she would and then it was time for her to go see Dr. Garibaldi. She rose and started for the door.

"Wait," said Beverly. Blinking back tears, she smiled at Suzie Q. "I want you to know that my daughter had the same issues that you do. I want you to know that trying is moving forward. She didn't do that but you are and only good will come of it. Bless you." Suzie Q. left the room with a curious expression on her face.

The morning lecture, given by Meredith, had been Problem Solving II and Dad had opened his notebook and tried to be attentive this time around.

"The cognitive model of problem solving," said Meredith, "is a process. One. *Identify* the specific problem."

(I can't paint anymore, scribbled Dad. It didn't get more specific than that.)

"Come up with at least four options that could be solutions to your problem."

(Realism, Impressionism, Cubism and Abstract Expressionism, wrote Dad.)

"List the pros and cons of each option."

(Not necessary, thought Dad. Any of the above would do, although Abstract Expressionism brought back the memory of applying paint to a canvas with his head.)

"Evaluate the results and if necessary, revise the options list."

(Lyrical abstraction. Surrealism. Pointillism. No, it all seemed hopeless. The only solution was not to care anymore. Which wasn't any kind of solution at all.)

And now, cheerful Walt O. sat hunched in his chair, his bald head bowed, not looking very cheerful at all. Which was another problem.

"You know," Walt O. said quietly, not looking at anyone in the circle, "I don't talk much about why I really quit teaching. In 2012, I was working at an elementary school in Western Connecticut. Maybe you've heard of it. Sandy Hook."

Oh, God, yes, Dad had heard of it. How could he have not. Twenty children between the ages of six and seven years old, plus half a dozen school faculty shot to death by a lunatic. By the looks on their faces, everyone in the circle knew of it as well.

"I wasn't there that day. I was under the weather, and I had a substitute. But when I heard that it had happened, I could see it all in my head. I can still see it. The children. People I'd worked with. Some of them hiding in a bathroom when they were shot and killed. And I wasn't there. I should have been."

How could it ever have happened, thought Dad? What could make human beings do such a thing? What could make them continue to do it. Was it crazy piled upon crazier, then piled on some more? My father wasn't sure he wanted to know, he just wanted it to stop. (Don't we all?) He turned his attention back to Walt O. who was speaking again. Any so-called problems he had were flies that had fled out the window and were forgotten and gone.

"I tried to keep working but I couldn't. I eventually got another teaching job near here. But it follows you, you know? And then, what with everything that was happening, I finally had to quit." Walt O. looked around the circle. "It's actually a good thing for my wife that she's leaving me. I've been impossible to live with for a long, long time." Walt O. forced a smile but all Dad saw now was a man veiled in sadness.

"What are you going to try to do now Walt?" asked Heidi, in a quiet but supportive tone of voice.

Walt O. shrugged. "No idea. I have some bites on the job interviews. We'll have to see."

"Jesus loves you, Walt," said Beverly. "He truly does."

"I'm Jewish," said Walt O. He rose his feet and began to gather his things. "I'm going to leave now. I have to check in with Dr. Giancarlo and then, well…" Walt nodded at everyone, then turned and left the room.

"I'm not sure I can follow that," Colin said quietly.

(What *could* follow that?)

"I think all of us wish you would," said Heidi. "I feel we've all seen some very positive changes." Everyone murmured in agreement.

Colin hesitated. He stared down at the floor. And then, he smiled to himself and looked back up. "You're right, I am better. I'm doing a whole lot better."

"Better in what way?" asked Heidi.

"Well…" Colin glanced across the circle at Sara, then quickly looked away. "Right now, I feel good just sitting here. I mean, I *like* sitting. I think I look *normal* when I'm sitting. People passing – another glance at Sara – all of *you*, for instance, would probably say, there's a normal, twenty-seven-year-old millennial. But then, when I try to get up…" Colin tried to get up. Colin failed to get up.

"Damn! What's his problem?" There was a sympathetic whimper from Beverly. The room tensed. Colin didn't. He looked eagerly in Beverly's direction. "Where'd that come from? Was that pity? I was hoping for a laugh." Beverly promptly giggled and the entire group (except for Dad) relaxed. "Thank you, very nice." Colin glanced at Sara again. "See, I've decided I don't want anyone's pity. I don't want anyone's help anymore. Frankly I just want to get laid." The circle rippled with laughter. "I mean, I can't do all the positions. I can't do doggy-style. I fall over."

"Ooh," squealed Beverly. "My husband and I did that last night!" The circle again rippled with laughter (and this time Dad couldn't help but join in) as Beverly blushed and covered her mouth in excited embarrassment.

"I'm not good at missionary either," said Colin grinning at her. "I can't go fast enough." Everyone laughed again. "Actually, I'm at my best when the girl's on top. I'm very good at offering encouragement."

"That's better than a lot of men," Sara said softly. Her eyes rose from the floor to look at Colin.

"All right," said Heidi, "now that we have *that* settled."

"Wait, said Colin. "I want to say, Heidi, that you and all the other therapists here have been great. The fact that therapists exist and are needed at all, reminds a person that they're not the only human being with issues. There's strength in numbers." Colin looked around the circle. "In fact, I want to thank all you guys. I want to tell you, these things we're working on are what you'd call first world problems. I mean, how do you equate having relationship issues or job issues or depression issues or anger issues or even having cerebral palsy, with drought, famine, or being bombed out of an apartment building in Eastern Europe? Really, we should count our blessings while we can. We've been given the opportunity to work on what troubles us. Most of you have people who care about you. You have the time, no, the *obligation*, to love and to laugh. And believe me, some of you, not me, of course, will get laid tonight."

The entire group, including Lauren D., spontaneously applauded.

Click.

The artist, Robert Boone, saw a young man in a chair, his body hunched and limp, but his face radiant as if he'd been given a gift.

Click.

The artist, Robert Boone, saw hope.

"I never got to see your work."

Fifteen minutes after group, my father and Colin were standing on the second floor of the hospital's parking garage. Finding Colin in the hallway, Dad had offered to give him one last ride home, but Colin had declined, saying it was time to get used to public transportation again. They had walked to the garage together.

"Hey, but we can still do it," said my father. "Go down to New York. Check out some museums together. I'd like to."

"Nah. Art isn't really my thing." Colin looked away. He suddenly seemed quiet.

Feeling a pang of something, my father tried to be casual. "What's next for you? A job? Computers? School?"

"Who knows." Colin half-shrugged. "I'll think of something."

"You still have the number of the lawyer?"

"Oh, yeah."

"And you have mine."

"Unless you change it."

"I won't. Any reason, any reason at all, you call me."

"I will."

Dad wondered if he should ask for Colin's number. He decided against it. Better the young man didn't expect too much. Colin abruptly thrust out his elbow. "Hey. Thanks again for everything you did, man, it meant a lot to me."

Dad raised his own arm and their elbows touched. "It meant a lot to me too, kid."

As Colin turned away and began his foot-dragging shuffle across the parking lot, my father felt the wordless pang again. He watched as at the elevator, Colin pressed the call button, turned and looked back.

"Your number!" Dad shouted.

"What?"

"Give me your phone number so I can call you!"

"It's on your Verizon bill, asshole!"

Grinning, Colin waved, then turned and entered the elevator. The doors closed. My father turned and hurried to the pickup, got in and headed down the curving exit ramp to the street. Colin was nowhere to be seen.

Absolution

It was a mid-morning, the early spring of 2021, and my father was in the kitchen making a second cup of coffee when the phone rang. Thinking it might be his daughter (me), he picked up.

"Hello?"

"Is this Robert Boone?"

"Yes."

"Mr. Boone, this is Dr. Christopher Knight. I'm calling from Broward Health Medical Center in Fort Lauderdale, Florida. I'm sorry to tell you your father is here in the hospital. He's quite sick and he's given us your name as next of kin."

Dad cringed inside. "Is it Covid?"

"No. Chronic obstructive pulmonary disease is a progressive disease that, like the Covid virus, makes it hard to breathe. Progressive means the disease gets worse over time. Your father is stage 4."

"Which means what?"

"I'm afraid he's dying."

Dad said nothing.

"He says he'd like to see you."

Dad said nothing.

"Are you there?"

"Please tell him I'm coming."

"Because of our continuing circumstances here, I'm afraid you won't be able to visit him in person."

"We'll figure it out."

Dad, who hadn't been out of Branford in almost a year and a half, hung up the phone and went to pack a bag. He was masked and on a half-full plane by two.

My grandfather had divorced the junior associate, second wife, retired to Florida and taken up fishing and golf. He remembered Christmas and birthdays and sent cards and sometimes handwritten letters that had the tone and precision of lawyer's briefs. He occasionally called but the calls were short as he and Dad had little to say to one another. They hadn't seen each other in six years and before that only intermittently.

While the Broward Health Medical Center in Fort Lauderdale suggested a large Holiday Inn with pillars and palm trees, the inside lobby of the hospital was the inside of hospitals everywhere, reception desks, elevators and sterile halls. Dad was told his father was in the ICU but was well enough to do a video call. He was taken to a disinfected, first floor waiting room and was given an Android tablet. When it was turned on for him, he saw his father reclining in a hospital bed, eyes closed with sheets pulled up past his waist. Ben was wearing a loose-fitting hospital gown and a clear, plastic mask covered his mouth and nose and even on video, Dad could see that his skin was mottled and grey and that he looked exhausted. My father pulled down the hospital mask he was wearing.

"Dad? Can you hear me? Dad?"

At the sound of my father's voice, Ben's eyes opened. His head weakly turned as if he was looking towards a camera. The eyes widened when he saw who was there. Slowly reaching up, Ben pulled the oxygen mask down to his chin. "I don't suppose you thought to bring me cigarettes?"

"I'll put it on my to do list," said my father.

Ben chuckled. The chuckle quickly turned into a rasping cough and he pulled the oxygen mask back over his nose and mouth. The coughing didn't stop and my father grew alarmed. "Dad! You okay?" The coughing got even worse. Suddenly a nurse was there, the camera was abruptly turned away and Dad found himself staring at a wall. A moment later there was no image at all. Was this death?

"I was always a heavy smoker."

"You're kidding."

Two hours later, Dad, having never left the waiting room, was back on a video call with his father. "Don't make me laugh again." Ben stifled a quick cough. "I thought the shortness of breath and hacking up crap every morning, came with the territory."

"You see a doctor?"

"Of course, I did."

"And?"

"The stupid son of a bitch told me to quit smoking." My grandfather closed his eyes. He looked more exhausted than ever. Ben coughed and then opened his eyes. "I'll be fine."

"The doctor says you're stage four."

My grandfather took a moment, then he nodded. "It's stupid and insulting. Taking up space here. I should give this damn bed to someone who can really use it. You can go now."

Dad left. He walked back to his hotel and lay awake all-night staring at the ceiling.

"For I don't know how long I've been looking for something," said Ben. It was the next morning and Dad was again sitting in the empty waiting room with the tablet in front of him. The image in it was such it had started to feel as if he was sitting at his father's bedside. "I didn't know what I was looking for, but I was looking. I think I know what it is now."

"What's that?" Dad asked.

"Forgiveness."

Dad took a moment to swallow whatever it was he was feeling. "For what?"

"Your mother. Karen and Melissa. Them dying." Dad now felt as if he was the one suffering from shortness of breath. "Your mother was such a terrible driver. Distracted by everything. Taking in the scenery as it were. I've always thought that if I'd been the one behind the wheel…"

"You weren't though."

Ben sighed, then coughed once. "Then you forgive me, Bob, for failing you. Not being there when you needed me. I wanted to be, but I couldn't. I was so angry… bitter… being with you made me miss them so. I miss them now." Ben Boone turned bleary eyes to the camera and to his son. "Can you do that? Forgive me? Can we be friends?" Reaching out, Ben's fingers touched the screen.

As if feeling those fingers on his cheek, Dad touched the pad in front of him as well. "We are."

My father and grandfather spent the next two days chatting, playing cards at a distance and watching the same television offerings on different screens in different, empty rooms. Both agreed it was god-awful. Looking at the monitor,

Dad sketched his father while he napped. He watched a nurse feed him from a tray because he was too weak to raise an arm. Ben coughed a lot. He complained a lot. "If I can't have a cigarette, at least they could give me a good martini." Ben asked about my father's love life and Dad told him about Kristina. Ben wept when he told him that she had died. Ben asked about his granddaughter (okay, yes, me). He was pleased and proud to hear I was an aspiring writer, but again, he felt remorse. "I was a worse grandfather than I was a father. I wish I'd done better. Twenty-twenty hindsight." They talked about Dad's work. "How's the painting going?" Ben asked.

"It's not. I haven't done anything original in a long time."

"I'm sorry to hear that." Ben put the oxygen mask over his mouth and nose, took a deep breath and lowered it. He pondered the ceiling a moment. "Did I ever tell you I was in a contest once? I was eighteen. First prize was a career as a high school custodian. Last prize, you became a lawyer. I came in last."

Dad laughed. Ben laughed with him. Neither could remember the last time they'd laughed with one another. It made them laugh even more.

"There were three robins in a tree outside the house the day after your mother and sisters died." It was early evening and Ben's eyes were half closed. He had spent the day drifting on memories and telling old stories. "They shouldn't have been there. It wasn't the time of year. But there they were. They were quiet. They didn't act like robins at all."

"What are you saying, Dad?"

"It was just nice to see them there. They were pretty birds."

"I regret the time wasted," Ben said the morning of the fourth day. His voice was a rasp and air burbled in his chest. The doctors had administered morphine with the hopes of it improving his shortness of breath. It wasn't working.

That evening my grandfather, the lawyer, Benjamin Boone, died in his sleep.

My father settled the estate. There were retirement accounts, there were investments, there was a condominium filled with overflowing ashtrays and ugly furniture and albums full of old, family photographs. There was a framed painting. It was Angels in the Darkness #3, a woman and two girls flying towards the light. Dad called Carter in New York who told him that his father had been among the very first buyers, that he had paid top dollar and that he had insisted Dad not know.

My father locked the door to the condo, got on another near-empty airplane and went home. He saw Ben's ashes put into the ground next to his wife and daughters. He drove the painting down to the loft in New York City and I watched as he hung it on the wall. My grandfather had left it to me. After telling me how much he loved me, my father drove back to Connecticut pondering the fact that an individual could die of regret as much as shortness of breath.

Week 4

Day 16 – The Unwanted Guest

On the fourth Monday of COG – Dad's second to last day – Dad almost never got there. The traffic on the I-95 was heavy and a BMW sedan abruptly changed lanes, cutting him off and forcing the pick-up onto the shoulder of road. As Dad hit the brakes, the back wheels skidded, and the front of the truck slammed into the guard rail knocking him into the steering wheel. The BMW drove on as if nothing had happened (par for the course) and wincing, Dad settled back in his seat to sit a moment.

Arriving home last Friday afternoon, my father had felt unsettled. About what, he wasn't sure. It had been a positive day. That's what he told Marisol as she was leaving.

"It was a positive day."

"Bueno, Mr. Bob. You deserve it."

He had then gone for a run, and after showering, he tried to relax by preparing himself an elaborate dinner of veal, prosciutto, and sage with an unnecessary side of spaghetti. As usual, he made enough for three people (imaginary dinner guests?) and then sat down and as if in a trance, methodically ate all of it, hardly tasting a single bite. With nothing else to do, he then went out into the studio and – call it problem solving – tried to work. There were images in his head absorbed over the last three weeks and they demanded attention. It was hopeless. It was as if there was no connection between his brain and his brush and Dad finally blotted out the shapes and colors he'd spent the last fifty minutes putting to canvas and sat and stared into space. Two more days of this cognitive nonsense and it would be over. Two more days of intrusion and uncertainty and things would finally get back to normal, whatever normal was. It was then, out of nowhere, that the memory of *the day* edged its way into his conscious. The breathless run, the burning and pounding in his chest, the call for the ambulance, the all-enveloping panic. Well, at least that wouldn't happen again.

And then it did.

As if called to attendance, nameless fear gushed into my father's brain and surged down through his body.

Dad gasped.

He trembled.

He shook his head like a dog trying to clear its ears.

He got to his feet and paced the room, trying to quell the tide. He tried to be logical. He had nothing to worry about. He had nothing to be afraid of. (Or did he?)

Okay, now *this* was crazy!

Dad left the studio, hurried into the house, pulled a fifth of Silver Patron from the back of a pantry shelf and took two big gulps straight from the bottle. He sighed with relief as the ocean calmed and his breathing returned to normal. He took one more hit to be sure, then another quick one. He fell asleep that night promising himself that he wouldn't let *that* happen again.

Saturday morning, worried that it might, my father decided to practice meditation. There were visualization scripts in his COG workbook and sitting down in a living room chair and opening to the first one, Dad tried to think of himself as a mountain, his breath rising from beneath the earth, his gaze looking down over rocks, crags, slopes and green forests to a distant sea.

Mountains were calm.

Mountains were impervious to rain, wind and snow.

Mountains just were.

My father was not. Impatiently turning the page, he went to the next script which told him how to access his safe place. (Exactly where would *that* be?) He closed his eyes and breathed in through his nose and out through his mouth. He tightened and relaxed different muscle groups. He thought of pine meadows filled with wildflowers. He visualized grazing, golden unicorns with flowing white tails and manes. Seeing him, they approached, nickering softly, asking for their noses to be rubbed.

"Oh, get the hell out of here," said Dad and he got up out of his chair, strode out of the living room and went to the kitchen pantry where he picked up the bottle of El Patron and with Mick and Angela staring at him with what seemed like disapproval, finished it. Better mindlessness than mindfulness.

"Something is wrong with me."

It was later that evening and my father had Annie on the phone.

"We know that, but would you care to elaborate a bit?" said Annie.

"I can't take two steps without just about pissing my pants."

"Are you talking about a urinary tract infection?"

"No! I'm talking about panic attacks! What do I do?"

"All right. Let's start by talking about what's causing it."

"No! It's all this *talking* that's causing it. I'm sick of talking!"

"In that case," said Annie, "You can call Dr. Giancarlo. He'll get a prescription for an anti-anxiety medication to your local pharmacy. You can pick it up tonight."

"I don't like taking pills."

"Well, then, I guess we're going to have to talk then, aren't we?" My father sensed Annie settling back in a chair. Oh, help, this was going to be a lecture. "The causes of panic disorder," said Annie, "are unclear. Some studies point to genetics. Has anyone else in your family experienced this?"

"I never asked."

"I'll take that as a negative. Extreme anxiety can also be caused by brain abnormalities. But seeing as you haven't experienced these episodes in the past – have you, Bob?"

"No!"

"Then I doubt that's the case. And you don't abuse drugs or alcohol, am I right?"

"If this continues, I might seriously start," said Dad.

"Let's not let that happen," said Annie. "The answer, Bob, is *stress*. Uncertainty, loss, disappointment. Unresolved issues finally coming to a head. This is what you need to be talking about, Bob. Not history, not yoga, not me. *This*. It's been building in you for who knows how long, and you refuse to face it. It can be addressed but only if you'll honestly talk about it with someone."

"Give me Garibaldi's number. I'll have him write me a prescription," said Dad. Annie did and not having written it down, my father hung up the phone. He hurried to bed where he spent most of the night staring at the ceiling. Panic was an uninvited guest that was going to crawl up through the plumbing or down through the chimney at any moment.

It was Sunday afternoon, in the middle of stalking the isles at Brigham's Fine Wines, when the uninvited guest made a surprise appearance. One moment Dad was focused on a Chablis, the next, it was as if someone were blowing smoke into his brain, turning his thoughts to cold clam chowder. Dad didn't waste any time but went right to the spirits section and the El Patron. He threw twenties at the cashier and not waiting for change, hurried outside to the parking lot, got in his truck and was about to take a serious hit when, to his surprise, he saw the formerly cheerful Walt O. go into the store. Dad considered the facts. He hadn't bought any wine, if he downed a bottle of tequila he wouldn't be fit to drive, and it might be a good thing to talk to somebody he knew and who knew him.

He found Walt in the champagne section. "Well, hey," said my father, feigning surprise.

"Bob!" said Walt, not feigning a thing. "What are you doing here?"

"A little shopping."

"Mmm. I'm looking for a bottle of good champagne myself."

"Celebration?"

"You might say. I'm a free man, right? My whole life ahead of me? I think that's worth celebrating." Formerly cheerful Walt sounded a touch bitter. "You know anything about champagne, Bob? All I know is it has bubbles."

"How much do you want to spend?"

"Around thirty?" Walt O. looked hopeful.

"Let's see…" My father began to search the shelves. He tried to keep his voice casual. "Hey, Walt, let me ask you something. You ever get, y'know… anxious?"

"What? Oh, God, yes. All the time. I've been on an anxiety meds for over a year. You add the anti-depressants and the sleep medications and I'm a walking drug cabinet." Walt O. shook his head. "Why do you ask?"

"No reason," said Dad. "Here you'll like this," and he handed Walt a bottle of Nicolas Feuillatte Brut. "Twenty-five bucks."

Bottle of champagne in hand, Walt O. hesitated a moment. "Bob…I don't suppose you want to come over tonight. Help me drink this." Walt looked quietly hopeful.

"You know, Walt, I have a few things going on, I better take a rain check."

"Oh." Walt now looked quietly disappointed. "Okay, no problem. Another time."

As Walt turned and walked to the register, Dad left the store, went out to the truck and carefully drove home. For the rest of the day, he sat in the chair in the living room, unopened bottle of tequila in hand, waiting for the unwanted guest to again crash the party. Around 5:30 the guest began knocking on the door and my father leapt to his feet. Two minutes later he had Marisol on the phone.

"Mister Bob, what is it? You are all right?"

"I'm fine… fine. Just… may I come over?"

"Why, of course, always. You will have *la cena* with us. Emiliano is here with his wife and my grandchildren. Neighbors, they are coming. You will join us, I insist."

Thirty minutes later, he was in East Haven. Adults filled the living room and kitchen, children played in the backyard. Dad was greeted by name and was introduced to the people he didn't know. Marisol instructed her son, Emiliano, to bring him sangria. Marisol ordered her eldest grandchild to serve him chalupas. When dinner was ready, Marisol directed everyone to the table and told them where to sit. (My father next to her.) Dad started to relax. There was no way the unwanted guest was going crash a dinner at Marisol's house. She would never in a million years let it happen. She would blockade the door. She would stare him into submission. She would tell him in no uncertain terms to *hacer una caminata* – take a hike!

Dad was sure of it.

Emotional Repercussions

Arriving thirty-five minutes late, my father entered the COG lecture hall to find a quiet pall in the room. Several people, Paul F. and Beverly among them, glanced in his direction and then looked away. Dad made his way to an empty chair and sat. The subject of the day was on Thoughts and Behavior, but no one seemed to be listening or taking notes. Even the lecturer, Ron, he of the hideous tie and the hipster beard, seem bored and uninterested.

A battle between avoidance and positive action *blah-blah-blah* decatastrophization of the situation and dilation of the positive *blah-de-blah-blah-blah-blah*, resulting in enhanced self-image and the power to take the next step *blahhhhhh...*

The lecture over, Ron put down his chalk and looked out at the assembly. "I'll do a relaxation exercise now but if any of you wish to skip it today, you have permission to leave." About a third of the room rose from their chairs and filed solemnly towards the door. Dad followed.

He was on his way to the outside kiosk to buy a cup of bad coffee when he saw Sara in the hallway, huddled in her wheelchair, the back of it pressed tight against a wall.

"Sara? Hey, is something going on?"

Sara looked up, bleakly regarded him and then mumbled something. Dad lost the first part of it but got the second. "*...hung himself.*"

In a flash, he knew.

Walt O. whose wife who was leaving him. Walt O. who had asked him to get together for a simple glass of champagne. And he had said no. Selfish. Unforgivable. What could he have been thinking? "Walt... it was Walt, wasn't it?"

Sara looked up, confused. "No... *Colin*. I said *Colin*."

The floor shifted under my father's feet, and he struggled to keep his balance. Some grief-stricken girl in a wheelchair was looking at him, her lips

202

were moving, and her voice was coming from someplace far away. "He asked me out Friday… I said *no*." Dad turned and sprinted down the hall. He slipped and fell as he took the corner. He scrambled up and hurried on.

Wacko John was with Dr. Giancarlo when Dad pushed opened the door and barged into the office. "I have to talk to you."

"I think you can see I'm busy, Bob."

"I have to talk to you *now*."

Dr. Giancarlo stared a moment then turned in his chair. "Do you mind, John?"

"No problem."

Wacko John rose from his chair. Disregarding or oblivious to the rules, he patted Dad on the shoulder as he passed. (Not such a wacko at all.)

My father fell into the empty chair. "Was it Colin?"

Dr. Giancarlo was very still. He didn't look away. He nodded.

"But why? He was doing so *well!*"

"No, Bob, he wasn't."

"He was. He was upbeat. Positive. He said so."

"It was a mask, Bob. He was in in-patient four times. Once because he admitted himself, three times because he called for help. This time he didn't."

My father felt so angry he wanted to scream. "Why didn't you *do* something. Why didn't you *help* him?"

"We tried. We can only try. Like we're trying with you."

"Oh, yeah? Well, it's not working."

Dr. Giancarlo sighed. "Bob, I've been doing this over forty years and I don't think I've ever seen so many depressed, stressed-out people. The world has always been a tough place but we're all so more aware of it now. It is also my belief that on a vast, unconscious level we are all connected. There is a zeitgeist, a singular spirit if you will, that binds us all together. When vast numbers of us are hurt, frightened and confused, we all are."

"What you're saying is the entire human race is mentally ill."

"No. What I'm saying is that it is more important than ever for human beings to be self-aware, attentive and generous in spirit with one another."

"You don't ask for much, do you," said Dad.

"Only everything. Go to group now," said Dr. Giancarlo.

"And do what?"

"Listen. Reflect. And talk about what you're feeling."

My father did. No one said a thing at first. Beverly kept blowing her nose into a Kleenex. Sara sat in her wheelchair, her face blank. Suzi Q. stared at her fingernails. Lauren D. looked pensive. Paul F. kept rubbing his chin.

How to paint sorrow, thought the sterile artist, Robert Boone. How to paint something palpable that has no form and no shape.

Heidi brought out a folded piece of paper. "Colin left a letter. He asked that it to be read to the group. It's not usual procedure but nothing is today. Would anyone like to read it for us?"

No one said a thing.

God. If a person was going to kill themselves, they should at least be done with it. "I will." My father reached out a hand. Heidi handed the letter to him, and he opened it. It wasn't long.

"To my group. First of all, I want to thank you guys again and I want to say you've all been wonderful friends to someone who's never had any."

Dad stopped for a moment. He gathered himself and continued reading.

"Please don't feel sad. Don't think there's anything you could have done. This was my decision, one I've been thinking about for a long time. I'm tired of all this and I look forward to seeing what's next, I really do. Take care of yourselves. Be positive. Stay well. I'll be watching. Colin."

My father handed the note back to Heidi. It only weighed a thousand pounds.

"Is anyone feeling suicidal or as if they'd like to hurt themselves?" asked Heidi. "Paul?"

Paul F. blankly shook his head. "I'm just glad I have my husband to talk to about this."

"Suzie?"

"I didn't know him," said Suzie Q. "But it puts things in perspective. I know I'm not going there."

"Sara?"

"I feel frightened I *could* go there."

(No. Oh, please, no, thought Dad.)

After assuring Sara that she would be given numbers to call and saying now might be a good time to go talk to Dr. Giancarlo, Heidi turned to Lauren D.

"I find it interesting that he went through with it," said Lauren D., as if talking about an unpleasant port of entry. "Maybe because I didn't do so myself."

It was too much. This myopic, self-centered female had undoubtedly been placed in group just so he, Dad, could feel furious at someone other than himself. Trying to keep his voice down only constricted the rage. "Interesting? You find it *interesting?* This wasn't somebody asking for attention – poor me, poor little me. This was the *real thing.*"

Lauren D. stared a moment and then turned to Heidi. "Are you going to let him talk to me like that?"

"I think," Heidi said carefully, "we're all very upset." She hesitated a moment. "Beverly? Would you like add anything?"

"Yes," said Beverly. "I want you to know I'm going to church when I leave today. I'm going to pray for Colin. I'm going to pray for all of us." Beverly wiped her eyes and looked at my father. "God doesn't ignore the tragedies we struggle with, Bob. He uses them to make us stronger."

My father sat a moment as if stricken. He tried to speak but couldn't find anything to say. He got up out of his chair and left the room.

Sisyphus

"May I come in?"

Annie arrived around seven. My father had spent the afternoon pacing the house, sitting down, getting up, pacing some more, trying not to think but at the same time trying to figure out what to do, feeling – yes, he finally had to admit it (about time) –*crazy*. Annie standing on his doorstep should have helped but it didn't, it frightened him.

"How did you know where I live?"

"It's in your medical record."

"It's a little late."

"I won't stay long."

They went into the kitchen. "You want coffee or tea?"

"Thank you, no, I'm fine."

"I'll have some."

Annie sat at the kitchen table, quietly watching as Bob filled the kettle. Mick and Angela came over to be petted and Annie did so. "Sweet dogs."

"What's up?" said Dad, putting the kettle on the stove.

"I thought we were getting together this afternoon."

"I didn't think we were."

"I hoped we were."

My father said nothing.

"Dr. Giancarlo told me you seemed particularly disturbed by the morning's news."

"I'm over it."

"Heidi said you left group at a run."

"Yeah, well, I'm fine now."

The coffee beans were in the grinder. Dad pressed down and it whined.

"You're all right with what happened then," said Annie.

"I didn't really know the guy."

"It didn't frighten you?"

"No."

"It should have," said Annie.

My father dumped the ground coffee into the French press. Annie was still quietly looking at him. "What?"

"People care about you, Bob. You know that, don't you?"

"What people are we talking about?"

"Your daughter. The friends you do have. The people in your group. We've talked with them. We know what you've done for them. We know how you've tried to help them. We know how you tried to help Colin."

"I didn't do a damn thing."

"Bob. He told us."

Trembling, Dad poured hot water, inserted the top and pushed down the plunger.

"I want you to know," said Annie, "that I applaud what you were trying to do. But at the same time, I can't help but wonder if you did it because you feel overly responsible for people and are compelled to try and fix things for them."

"Since when is that a bad thing."

"It's not always. But sometimes taking responsibility for other people's problems can come at the expense of taking care your own."

"I take pretty good care of myself."

"Do you? Do you really?"

Dad poured coffee into a mug.

"I think you feel guilty," said Annie. "The money and success. The accolades. You don't enjoy it. You don't feel you deserve it. To make up for it, you try to help people but at the same time you resent them for needing help and when you can't fix things and Bob, often people can't, you step back, put a lid on your own feelings and you isolate yourself."

"What makes you think you're so goddamn smart?" Stung, my father spit the words. "What makes you think you know the first thing about me?"

Annie stared a moment. "Maybe I don't. But I know why people commit suicide. Loss. Sadness. Sometimes just feeling all alone."

"Thank you for coming by," said Dad.

Annie rose from the table. "People care about you, Bob. I do. Thank you for being my friend."

Dad walked Annie to the door and then, returning to the kitchen, threw the dregs of coffee into the sink. He went into the living room and stared into the empty fireplace, listening for voices in the house that were no longer there. He knew now, they never would be.

Click.

Robert Boone found himself thinking of the Renaissance painting of Sisyphus who, in Greek mythology, was sentenced for all eternity to push a boulder up a steep hill, only to watch it come tumbling back down. Up and down in fruitless labor.

Click.

He pictured The Death of Seneca, a naked man preparing to bleed his life out into a tub of water.

Dad went into the pantry, opened a drawer and reached for a utility knife. Releasing the pointed razor, he stared at it a moment, then, holding the knife in his right hand, he slowly lowered the blade towards his left wrist. The edge touched the skin. A tiny jewel of blood blossomed.

Dad's hand froze.

His brain somersaulted and landed hard.

Dropping the knife, my father bolted out of the pantry. He staggered through the kitchen and down the hall, stripping off his clothes as he went. Naked, he stumbled into the foyer, pulled open the front door and with Van and Gogh following, went out into the night.

Dad ran.

His legs felt like they were made of lead.

His breath came in painful gasps and his heart felt as if it was about to burst out of his chest.

Shards of blacktop cut at his feet and the night air felt like it was blistering his eyes and skin.

It had come to this.

Robert Boone didn't want to die but had no particular reason to want to live. This was a truth now fully realized and he had been hiding from it. He had spent three weeks in a program that might have helped him, going sideways, up and down, but never forward because he'd been afraid to recognize that there was anything wrong and out of place. The choice was simple now. End it all or begin again. Make a decision.

Dad stumbled.

He almost fell.

On either side of him the dogs barked and moaned.

Not knowing if was running from something or to something, my father cried out. He cried out to his mother. He cried out to his father and his sisters and to Kristina. He cried out to Marisol and Beverly. He cried out to Megan J. and William G. and Paul O. and Sara. He cried out to Carter. He cried out to Annie and to me, his daughter. He cried out to Colin. He cried out to the night.

The night answered back. As if a wand had been waved, my father's heartbeat began to slow. His brain calmed and his legs and breath found a rhythm. No longer tired, no longer feeling cold, not feeling the road beneath his bloody feet, just feeling the simple machine that was his body, Dad ran. Was this mindfulness? Was this being in the moment? Was this *God?* It didn't matter. It just *was.* It was doubtful he could go running naked and barefoot on a regular basis but that didn't mean he couldn't do it on occasion. Dad, with the dogs at his side, ran on and on and on.

Getting back to the house, the artist (whatever that word truly means anymore), Robert Boone, closed the door behind him. He gratefully petted Mick and Angela, then took a hot shower and put on some old sweats. Knowing only that he wanted to live, my father went downstairs, then out into the studio where he turned on the lights and began to work.

(And I know all this to be true because he told me so.)

Day 17 – Thought Records

On Tuesday, his seventeenth and final day of COG, Robert Boone arrived late and went straight to group. Much to his dismay Beverly wasn't there. The previous day had been her last and having fled the room, Dad had squandered it. He tried to put his disappointment aside by telling himself that Beverly had understood.

There was a new member sitting in the circle. John H., a heavy-duty looking man around sixty, was voluble and forthright, nodding hello to everyone even before being formally introduced. He was, he said when asked, an alcoholic and drug addict, clean for eight years. He lived now with a woman—*a great lady*—that he had met at Alcoholics Anonymous. He had three children from two earlier marriages, a boy who had died in an alcohol induced car crash, a second boy in jail, and a third, a girl, who refused to see or speak to him. John H. had heard about COG from people in his AA program and now, at the behest of his partner, he figured it was time to "dive in."

"And what are you looking for?" asked Heidi.

Absolution," said John H., not hesitating even for a moment. "A pardoning of sins. I was a bad father. A bad partner. A bad human being. I can't do anything about the past, but I'd like to do something with the future. Especially when it comes to my son and daughter."

(It was Dad's immediate opinion that anyone who was willing to be so nakedly honest with himself right from the beginning was already halfway there.)

Group continued with Paul F. proudly saying that things were very positive at home with his husband, Bill. "We just sat, and we talked last night. About what happened… about pretty much everything." The group nodded and smiled. Well done.

Suzie Q. then said she had already come to realize that she spent far too much time thinking negatively of herself. It seemed important to turn that

210

around. "Just because I'm fat, doesn't mean I'm unattractive. Just because I like sex doesn't make me a total slut."

"If it does, said newcomer John H., drawing laughs, "I'm the biggest slut there ever was."

Lauren D. then recounted how the psychiatrist she was seeing had suggested she might suffer from Depersonalization Disorder. This apparently was the feeling of being a detached observer of one's own thoughts and actions. "It's as you're along for the ride, looking out the window," said Lauren D. "It's probably why I have a history of making bad choices."

(Having done the same thing, Dad realized he now felt sorry for her.)

"I went to the school late yesterday afternoon. I wasn't sure I was up for it but I made myself." It was Sara's turn, and my father was relieved to see she seemed much better than she had the day before. "I met with the principal, the students and the instructors. They were really nice. They thought it was the coolest thing I was going to be working with them. I even know one of the dance teachers. He's going to help me translate." Sara hesitated. "I think it might work."

"We'll all keep our fingers crossed," said Heidi.

Sara looked down into her lap. She smoothed the blanket that covered her thighs. "I asked the principal how she heard about me." Sara looked up and then across the circle at Dad. "She said *you* told her."

My father now felt as if all eyes in the circle were upon him. He shrugged and tried to be off hand. "I knew they were looking for someone."

Sara stared solemnly into my father's face. "Thank you."

(How to answer? What to say? Suddenly Dad knew. He'd been told what to say years ago.)

"Someday do the same thing for somebody else."

"Bob?" Heidi was now looking at him as well. "Today's your last day. I wondered if you had any thoughts or feelings to share with us before you go."

My father glanced around the circle, taking in the faces. "I'd like to start by saying that my anxiety level this morning is at a thirty-eight and my depression level is eighteen."

"That's higher than in the past," said Heidi, sounding concerned.

"No. It's lower. I haven't been telling the truth these last three weeks. To myself or to you." Reaching down, my father picked up the backpack he'd brought with him and opening it, pulled out a rolled sheaf of heavy sketch paper. "I did these last night. They're the thought records you've been asking for. As you can see, I didn't write them." Dad held up the first sheet.

"This is my depression."

Swirls of dark color cascaded down the page, becoming denser and denser. At the bottom, they pooled like poured cement around a huddled figure, trapping the figure completely. Dad tore the paper in half, threw it aside and held up a second sheet.

"This is my anxiety."

In scrawled lines, a naked man twisted in a tidal surge. The man's eyes were closed tight, and both his hands were clasped over his mouth. Dad tore the sheet up, dropped the pieces to the floor and held up the third sheet of paper.

"This is loneliness."

It was an abstract drawing of Colin. He was walking along a street, head down. Around the edges of the paper, crowds of boisterous people all walked together. Colin was alone. Dad balled the page and dropped it. He held up another.

"This is loss."

A woman with curly hair, drawn in quick, broken lines, was crying. Beneath her face, the tears, now the smudged figures of children, lay in pile.

"Guilt and shame."

Tiers of blurred, round faced stick figures were pressed against vertical cell bars. A red brick wall was behind them, trapping them and holding them tight. It went to the floor.

"Anger. This was an easy one."

A frothing dog surged against the heavy iron chain that held its neck to the ground.

"This is my panic."

A shell-shocked face peered numbly out of a surrounding storm that funneled into an open mouth.

"And this is my apathy."

My father held up the last page. It was empty. He crumpled the pages, and they joined the others at his feet.

The group was very still.

"I'm not sure what you're telling us here." It was Lauren D., and her voice was tight. "Are you saying because you tear up some drawings, you're miraculously cured?"

"No," said my father. "I'm saying that by finally accepting that these are things I deal with, I can start working on them. For your sake, I hope you'll consider doing the same."

Lauren D. blinked, then looked away.

My father reached down into his backpack and pulled out a last tubed sheet of paper. "There's one more I'd like to show you." He unrolled it and held it up. "This one's called a new day."

It was of a sunrise. Dawn light was coming up over the Thimble Islands, brightening the clouds and coloring the waters of Long Island Sound. In the foreground, a small single boat was sailing away towards the horizon. (Dad had done it early that morning using his mother's old brushes and watercolors.)

"I think," said Heidi, softly, "that a picture can be worth a thousand words."

My father again looked around the circle, taking in the faces, old and new. Did he have anything else he wanted to share? He hadn't planned on it, but now, yes, he did. "I'd just like to say in that the last three weeks, I've come to know complete strangers as well as I've known anybody in my life. They gave their truth to me and by doing so made me face my own. All they asked for was honesty and support and in return, they offered theirs completely. I'm hoping I'll do the same from now on. I hope all of you will too. That's all."

"Thank you, Bob," Heidi said quietly.

As if on cue, the door opened. The Indian woman in the sari, poked her head and smiled at Dad. He nodded and reaching down, began to carefully gather up the torn pieces of paper at his feet.

(A metaphor? I think so, yes.)

And that was that.

(Hardly.)

Fifteen minutes later, my father and Dr. Giancarlo were sitting across the cluttered desk from one another. Dr. Giancarlo's ski jacket was zipped to the top and his fingertips touched in front of him like a church steeple.

"How you feeling, Bob?"

"Better. How about you?" answered Dad.

"Not bad. Not bad at all." Dr. Giancarlo looked down and began going through the loose papers on his desk. "You've gone over your relapse prevention plans with Heidi?"

"I did."

"We also have a weekly on-going support group, if you need it. And you know about the monthly mindfulness lecture. They're free and I recommend them both."

"I'll keep them in mind."

Dr. Giancarlo stopped shuffling papers and looked up. "You've been a tough nut to crack, Bob."

"Maybe because I'm a nut clear through." (Salt free, dry roasted.)

"Any questions before you go?"

"Yeah," said Dad. "Why do you always wear that ski jacket?"

Dr. Giancarlo settled back in his chair and regarded my father a moment. "Bob, when I was nineteen years old, I was drafted out of college. Columbia in New York. It was 1967, the height of the Viet Nam war and I was part of a group that was sent to Quang Ngai Province, North of Saigon. There were tunnel networks, and I was what was called a tunnel rat, one of the men they sent in with a pistol and a flashlight to kill anybody hiding there."

(This innocuous little man? It seemed impossible.)

"The tunnels were like ovens. They were narrow and dark and I'd come up out of them and no matter how hot it was, I'd shiver even sitting in the sun. I've been cold ever since, Bob." Dr. Giancarlo leaned towards Dad, now very intent. "And when a man is *cold*, he *does something* about it."

"How?" asked my father, "did you ever stay sane?"

"I didn't." Dr. Giancarlo's eyes twinkled. "Why do you think I became a psychiatrist?"

Breaking the Silence

"Come in?"

There had been no coffee planned on this, the final day but Dad knocked on the office door, hoping Annie might be in and she was. She rose from her desk as he opened the door and they gazed at one uncertainly for a moment.

"I was concerned about you last night," said Annie.

"That made two of us." Dad stood quietly for a moment. "I just wanted to say thank you."

Annie blinked in surprise. "Oh! It's your last day, isn't it?"

"On my way out."

"Would you like to sit for a minute?" She gestured at the chairs by the window.

"If you're sure it's okay."

"Oh, I think we can chance it."

Dad entered, closing the door behind him and the two of them sat. Annie quietly adjusted her long skirt. "I understand you had a bit of a breakthrough this morning."

"Really? What did you hear?"

"That you finally discussed the issues that have been bothering you and you said you were going to start working on them. Heidi also said the drawings you did were wonderful. I wish I'd seen them."

"I'll do them again."

Annie said nothing.

Oh, what the hell, thought Dad. "May I ask you something personal?"

"You can ask."

"Is it hard dealing with messed up people all the time?"

"It can be difficult. But you don't let it become about you. You monitor your own mental health as well as theirs."

"What if it does become personal? What if you find yourself caring about someone?"

"You often do. Good therapy has been called a cure through love. But that doesn't mean you go jumping into bed with your patients. It means that love is part of healing."

"And if you already have jumped into bed with them?"

Annie's gaze didn't falter. Dad wondered if she was deciding now or if the decision had already been made.

"Bob... that's why we won't be doing this anymore."

"Not even as friends?"

"It's too confusing. If you'd like to start individual therapy, I'm happy to recommend some people."

My father shook his head. "I don't think so."

"You're sure?

"Yeah, I'm sure."

Annie looked away, eyes suddenly blinking, her face tight. "I can't say I blame you. I haven't exactly been a fountain of good advice, have I. In fact, this has been a farce from the beginning. I spent more time talking than you did." Straightening her shoulders, Annie rose to her feet and forcing a smile, offered her hand. "Take care, Bob."

"You should have said that back in New York." Ignoring the outstretched hand, my father stood. "I want you to listen. I have gone through three and a half weeks of this mindful stuff and I've learned a few things. To celebrate, I'm throwing a dinner party tonight and the recipe calls for two people.

"Bob... I can't."

Dad took a quiet step forward. "Yes, you *can*. You're not my therapist, I was never your patient. You care about *me,* and I care about you."

Annie bowed her head and said nothing.

"You can leave whenever you want. Before dinner if you'd like. Though that would be a mistake because I'm making a flourless chocolate cake for dessert."

Annie softly moaned. "That's not fair."

"It's not meant to be."

Annie exhaled and shook her head. "All right, yes, I'll stay for desert... *if* I show up at all."

"See you around six and I hope you like shellfish." Dad turned and left the office before she could change her mind.

Annie showed up at six-twenty-five.

My father had almost given up hope. She was dressed in her usual drab ensemble but her hair, instead of it being pulled back into its usual tight braid, hung in a long ponytail.

Dad led her into the living room. There was a fire in the fireplace. There were canapes on a plate. There was white wine in an ice bucket and bottles and assorted glasses on an antique liquor tray. Dad moved to the side table. "What would you like to drink?"

"I'm not sure I do."

"Suit yourself. I'm drinking vodka." He picked up his empty glass and rattled the ice cubes.

"How much have you had?" asked Annie.

"Not nearly enough." Reaching for the bottle, my father refilled the glass to the brim and slugged it down.

Annie looked alarmed.

"It's water," said Dad.

"What?"

"It's tap water. I haven't had anything to drink. But I'll have a glass of white wine if you do."

"A small one," said Annie.

"Help yourself to a canape," said Dad, as he poured. "They're cranberry and goat cheese." (They're awesome.)

After Annie acknowledged that the canapes were delicious, my father suggested a tour of the house and glasses in hand, off they went. He showed her the wall sconces, the vintage carpenter's box with the wood working tools and his modest collection of other artist's paintings.

"None of your work around the house?"

"Come on," said the decidedly non-eminent artist, Robert Boone, and he led Annie through the kitchen and outside to the studio. Entering, he turned on the lights and waited. Annie looked around. Not seeing anything, she looked around again. My father glanced up. Annie's eyes followed his gaze. Slim skylights separated the high vaulted ceiling into large, square panels. In each panel was a painting.

"These are yours?"

"I painted them but no."

The first panel painting was of a frightened man and his family. The second was of a girl wearing a red hat. The third panel was a naked man surrounded by hungry lions, the fourth was the self-portrait by Rembrandt, hat, hair and face surrounding the famous eye. The fifth was a painting was of a woman, curling ringlets of hair topping a beautiful, dark eyed face. The sixth was a child scooping food from a bowl. The seventh depicted the angel, Gabriel, giving Mary the news of the virgin birth, the eighth was a portrait of a grim looking, bearded king and the ninth was a simple painting of oysters on a plate.

Painting Techniques of the Masters. My father had created his own Sistine Chapel from the cover of a book.

"They're remarkable," said Annie.

Dad tried to keep his voice light. "If I don't do anything original ever again, I'll always have a career as a forger. Come on, dinner is served."

He had made cioppino. It was, he explained, as they sat down at the table, a tomato-based fisherman's stew with crab, clams, mussels and whitefish, seasoned with fresh herbs and copious amounts of garlic. The dish was served with warm, crusty bread on the side.

They ate in silence, shucking the shellfish, dipping the bread. Stopping for a moment, Annie patted her mouth with her napkin and reached for her glass. They had moved from the white wine to a red. "What did you mean about not doing anything original ever again?"

Dad considered.

Dad decided.

"Several years ago, I burned my studio down. I told people the fire was an accident, but it wasn't, it was me, I did it. I built a new one, but I haven't worked on anything original since. I spend my days out here pretty much doing nothing."

'I wish you'd told me this earlier."

Dad spooned broth from his bowl. "Let me know when you're ready for dessert."

It was, as promised, a flourless chocolate cake. My father brought it to the table and served. "Oh, my God," groaned Annie after the first bite "How do you make this? I'm in love."

"Seconds?" asked Dad, already reaching for the knife.

Dinner and desert finished, they moved to the kitchen and did the dishes together, my father washing, Annie drying.

"What would you have done if you hadn't come over tonight?" asked my father.

"I don't know. Called a friend and gone out. Or just had a light supper and read.

"Cosmopolitan?"

Annie smiled. "I keep meaning to cancel my subscription."

"Are you ever lonely, Annie?"

Annie looked away.

"If you were, what would you do about it?"

Annie put down the dish she was drying.

"All right," said Dad. "Let me ask you another question. When was the last time you got dressed up and went out on the town?"

"This last week," said Annie, not looking at him. "Nothing happened but it made for a very bad next day."

"Oh. You mean *that* day."

"Yes. *That* day."

"It wasn't all me then."

"No, Bob, I told you it wasn't."

"When was the last time it wasn't so horrible? Going out, I mean."

"Eight months ago, it wasn't so bad. With you."

Except for the soft pulse of the dishwasher, the kitchen seemed very quiet.

"That's a long time."

"Yes, it is."

"What are we going to do about this?"

"You asked me that once before," Annie replied softly.

"And here you are." Dad hesitated. "There are some women's clothes upstairs in the guest room closet. You could go get them, put them on, see if they fit. Your call. But please don't do it for me."

"It's for me," said Annie.

Dad was sitting in the living room in front of the fire when he heard the click of shoes on the wood floor. A moment later Annie appeared in the entryway. She was wearing a sleeveless, red cocktail dress and black high heels. Her blonde hair was loose around her shoulders and there was blush on her cheeks and shadow and liner on her eyes. Dad recognized the color of the lipstick. He rose to his feet.

"Who was she?" asked Annie.

"A woman I loved," said Dad.

"What happened?"

"She died."

"How long ago?"

"I don't count."

"Why haven't you talked about it?"

"It's hard."

"Will you?"

"I might. But not now." Dad hesitated. "You look very beautiful."

"She had very good taste," replied Annie.

"No. It's not the clothes. Clothes don't make a difference. You look like you always do. You're you."

As if pushed from behind, Annie started forward. Dad moved forward to meet her, and they embraced. Pressing her face into Dad's shoulder, Annie softly murmured.

"Annie, what, are you crying?"

Looking up at Dad, Annie softly smiled. "If I am, it's only because crying can deepen happy moments."

They kissed then, hungry for one another. "Call me kryptonite," said the artist, Robert Boone, and lifting the superhero into his arms, he carried her out of the room and up the stairs.

Plus One

"Sometimes my life feels like a series of events that just happened to me."

Dad didn't know what time it was. He'd lost track. He and Annie were in bed together. His arm was around her. Her head was on his shoulder, her hand on his chest.

"I didn't plan for them. I didn't hope for them. There was none of those two paths in the woods with one less taken stuff. There was only one path and I walked it."

"Go on," Annie said.

"I was given a talent. I have no clue as to why. The work came easily to me and I was obsessed with it. All that mattered was what I was doing. Certainly, not other people."

"Why not?"

My father hesitated. "Since my early teens, I've felt most comfortable alone. When I got successful, I used the money to retreat completely. It was a mistake. To be any kind of artist you have to reflect life, not avoid it. That's what I've done."

Annie's hand caressed Dad's neck and shoulder. "If I go and wash off the make-up and come back to bed, will you tell me more?"

"Yes."

My father told her everything.

"There are," said Annie, "five stages of grief." It was now early morning, the sun was beginning to peek through the curtains, and they were still in bed, on their sides now, facing one another. She paused as if waiting for an answer.

"Go on," said my father.

"First there's denial which is the feeling that the loss can't be true. Then comes anger. You rage at something or someone or even yourself for having allowed the loss to happen. Then there's bargaining., take me instead, take me.

Sadness comes when the loss can no longer be ignored and finally, there's acceptance which is putting the loss behind you."

Dad said nothing. It was easy now to see that he had done all these things and none of these things. He had denied, bargained and blamed. Anger and sadness had long been a stone around his neck. He had refused to accept events that were beyond his control and having never let them go, had lived with them.

"Some people avoid these feelings. They use substance abuse, isolation and compulsive behaviors to numb the loss."

Yes, Dad could admit that too. He ate too much without tasting, he drank too much without enjoying it, he ran and exercised because exhaustion allowed him not to think.

"But…there's also a sixth phase of grief," said Annie.

"What's that?"

"Reaching out. Putting your grief aside and caring for the people that are close to you."

"I've tried to do that."

"Yes, you have. But being afraid of losing someone is not the best way to love them."

"When did you get so smart?" Dad asked.

Annie smiled. "The people you've lost. Do you know what you'd say to them if you had the opportunity to talk to them again?"

"Yes," said Dad. "I do now."

"That's your first real step towards moving on."

"Do I have to make an appointment to see you again?" asked my father.

"I think," said Annie, "we are way beyond that."

An hour and a half later, Annie left to go to the hospital. Shortly after, Dad left the house behind her, got in the pick-up, and drove to the Mill Park Center Cemetery in Branford where his mother, father and sisters were buried.

He parked his truck and walked to the gravesite. It was a well-maintained plot, the grass trimmed, the stones clean and polished and Dad felt as if he were seeing it for the first time.

Sitting down, he took Kristina's letter from his pocket and placed it on the grass next to him. Reaching forward, he dug a shallow hole in the ground. When he was finished, he picked up the letter, placed it down and then covered it with soil and grass, patting it firm. He stared a moment. "I know where to find you now." My father touched his heart, then touched the ground and head bowed, sat awhile.

He looked up when he heard the call of birds. He saw them then, four robins in the branches of a nearby tree and above them, towards the top, an exotic, multi-colored kestrel. Fluttering and calling, they flew out from the tree to circle above his head. He recognized the voices resonating in their wings and knew what they were saying to him.

"No fate is worse than a life without love."

Renderings

Robert Boone began to paint again. His hands remembered as all the photographs stored in his head began to pour out. It was both exhilarating and overwhelming. Some of the images and figures were starkly realistic, some were distorted, squeezed and elongated, some were just feelings expressed in smudges, shapes and colors. How to really paint anxiety? What color was depression? How to embody contentment? How to best portray two women, one black, one white, arms around one another, feeding each other strength? How to find the essence of a pale, young man with crooked limbs smiling or a pretty girl in a wheelchair dancing, or a dour Falstaff dancing with another man. How to render a child shot dead in an open doorway that leads into the mind of a traumatized human being. What about a man with two faces, one cheerful and smiling, the other twisted in grief? It was a slow but satisfying process and with no expectations, none at all, my father embraced it.

*

Dad shopped and he cooked. He ran. He went to the gym. He attended the weekly support group and monthly lecture series at the hospital where, much to his delight, he encountered and shared phone numbers and addresses with Paul, Beverly, a cheerful Walt O. and even a revitalized Suzi Q.

For the first time ever, Dad acknowledged people. In the grocery store, at the gas station, on the street. A nod here, a quick smile there. It was a pleasant revelation to realize that people responded in kind. What was it Colin had said? "We have people who care about us. People who want to. We have the time, no, the obligation, to engage and enjoy."

He so wished the silly kid was still here.

*

Dad visited John Murphy's visual arts class at the New Haven School of Creative Arts on a weekly basis. It got him out of his routine, it solved both the social and accomplishment boxes on the Grapes list, and he found himself looking forward to it. He found the young people enthusiastic, idealistic and ambitious. He also found many of them lazy, over stimulated and woefully uninformed. Sounds like kids to me, said John Murphy. And yet my father knew there were young people in the world like the serious, Habib-wearing, young woman in the class who were aware, talented and motivated by more than money. He offered praise and encouragement to all of them, his strongest criticism usually beginning with "think about this."

(I try, Dad, I try.)

*

"That's me!"

Beverly couldn't stop giggling and blushing as she gazed at the painting Dad had brought over. Done, in heavy oils, it was of a naked woman reclining sensuously on a settee.

"That's you, all right," said Dad.

"Oooh, I'm so naked!"

That's what happens when you pose that way.

"Ohhhh... I'm fat."

"Rubenesque," said Dad. "Bountiful."

Beverly happily giggled again. "I don't know what you're going to do with it."

"Giving it to you."

"What? No!"

"It's yours."

"Ohhhh...." Beverly eyes began to filled with tears. "Oh!" She abruptly looked alarmed. "But what am I going to tell my husband?"

"That you had it commissioned just for him."

"Oooh!" Beverly shivered with delight. "He's going to love it. I'm going to put it in the kitchen."

"What?" Dad found the painting anything but kitchen sensible. "Why?"

"Because it will remind me not to eat so much!"

Turning, Beverly hugged Dad and smooched him wetly on the cheek.

225

On a pleasant Sunday morning, my father got into his pick-up, motored down the interstate towards New York and crossed the George Washington Bridge. From there he headed southeast to Elizabeth, New Jersey and The Rosemount Cemetery. To Makbarat Al-Rahma. A Muslim resting place. *He who forgives.*

By Muslim tradition Francoise/Sayid's body had been put in the ground within 24 hours of his death. Upon hearing the news from Carter, Dad had left Kristina and fourteen-year-old me in Branford and though he had broken all speed limits to get there, had missed the funeral prayer and burial. Uncertain as to what to do and unrecognized, he had stood apart, dazed and speechless.

Sayid's grave was near a heavy granite bench, beautifully engraved with what Dad could only assume were Islamic prayers. His gravestone consisted of a base, a tablet and a curved, Mosque shaped headstone. Sayid had been placed in the grave on his right-side facing Mecca. The sun was shining. A breeze rippled the surrounding grass. People wandered and stood. My father took it all in. Finally kneeling, he reached into his pocket and pulling out three small plastic bags, sprinkled Herbs de Provence, Saffron and a small, loose Bouquet Garni on the ground. They were three of the essentials in French cooking and knowing his friend had loved them, Robert Boone felt blessed.

*

"*Me gusta el marco.* I like the frame."

Dad, Marisol and Marisol's twenty-six-year-old granddaughter, Inez, were in Marisol's West Haven dining room. It was Marisol's day off. She was taking more and more of them of late and Dad, in fact, had hired Inez to keep her company and help her out around the house.

She was perhaps thirty in the painting. It was based on a drawing Dad had done at age ten. In soft lined, highlighted colors, a small, dark haired woman was hanging laundry on a line, the green of the yard and the blue of the sky behind her. The painting sat on the kitchen counter, where he had placed it. The frame was museum quality with an embossed outer edge. Dad had picked it up in an antique store for one hundred and fifty dollars. Still ignoring the painted canvas, Marisol reached out and ran her hand down the side.

"Yes, the frame, it is *bueno*."

My father had wondered if this would be Marisol's reaction. He had reminded himself before bringing it over that she had never liked her image put to paper and had often told him so. Still, he felt disappointed. It was then that Inez, probably not knowing anything about art but certainly knowing something about my father, spoke up. "*Lita.* What are you talking about? Do you know how much this is worth?"

Frowning in disapproval, Marisol spun to face her granddaughter. *"Por supuesto que lo sé! No tiene precio! Es un regalo de mi hijo!"* Lifting the painting off the counter with both hands, Marisol turned and with imperious strides, left the kitchen. *"Estoy poniendo debajo de mi cama donde estará seguro!"*

Seemingly tickled, Inez turned to Dad who gave her a questioning look. "She says, of course she knows. She says it's priceless because it's a gift from her son. She's putting it under the bed where it will be safe."

*

"Bob, this is Carter. I'm speechless."

"Then why are you talking?" asked Dad.

"The truck arrived two and a half hours ago. I have the crates unloaded and unpacked. You son of a bitch, you saved them. How?"

"You think the Swiss are the only ones who know about climate-controlled warehouses?"

"I didn't know *you* did."

"Yeah, it's called a public storage facility."

"Bob, I want you listen. You have to let me do a show. They have to be seen, they *have* to be."

"That's why you have them. But no selling to investors, no off-limit private collections. Being seen means being seen. Especially the ones of Kristina."

"I'll make sure of it."

"Oh, and listen, I need a favor."

"*You?*"

"Ha-ha. I need you talk to the guy who throws those stupid fundraisers."

"Which particular stupid fundraiser are we talking about, Bob?"

"The one where you volunteered me to do twelve drawings in twelve minutes for charity."

"I know for a fact, that's not what you were asked to do. What do you want me to say to him?"

"Tell him I want him to throw a fundraiser for a community outreach center in Bridgeport. If he does, he can count on me for anything he wants to do in the future."

"Including a deal on a painting?" said Carter, trying to sound only half serious.

"I'll do one for him and one for the center," replied Dad.

"I think that sounds like a plan."

"Have fun."

"I am already."

*

It was a weekend in May when I came up to visit and Dad led me into the downstairs hallway so I could see the newly hung, framed portraits of a girl. They were innocent. They were sweet. They were serious and self-absorbed. They were me captured in line, light and color from the ages of three to present day adult.

"Dad... where have you been keeping them?"

"In the attic."

"Why are you pulling them out now?"

"If people come over, I want them to know how much you've always meant to me."

"People are coming *over*?"

"Maybe... sometime."

I regarded the painting in front of me. It had been done recently. I was in the backyard, filling a basket with flowers. Four birds were hovering around my head. Turning and embracing my beloved father, I began to cry.

*

When I came downstairs later, Dad was in the dining room, setting the table. I took in the crystal wine glasses and the place settings. "Three?"

"Someone *is* coming over," said Dad.

As if on cue, I heard the sound of the kitchen door opening and closing and I turned towards the approaching footsteps. The woman had longish blonde hair and was wearing a skirt, white blouse, a stylish jacket, and boots. Her satchel was over one shoulder and she dropped it the hall table. She smiled. "Am I late?"

"Right on time," said Dad, ignoring my quizzical look. "Annie, this is my daughter, Isolde. Holdie, this is Anne Gilmore."

"We finally meet," said the woman, Annie, smiling and holding out her hand. "I have to say, your father does nothing but talk about you."

"Really?" I took the outstretched hand in my own. "That's funny. I haven't heard a thing from him about you." I glanced at Dad who was just standing there as if nothing was happening. "But that's pretty par for the course with this guy."

"Oh, it's terrible, isn't it?"

"It is. He keeps everything to himself."

"He does. But we're working on it."

"That is *so* nice to hear."

As if drawn together by a shared secret, Annie and I turned and already buzzing with conversation, went down the hall and into the kitchen leaving my father standing all by his puzzled self.

(Yes, Dad, women endure. Especially when they're stuck with men.)

*

It was a week in late August, the visual arts class had ended, and Dad was walking towards the school exit when he ran into Marjorie Jo Rosello who was coming out of her office. He had been hoping to see her. He wanted to know if the Fall dance rehearsals had started and if so, how were they progressing.

Yes, they had started but without Sara. "We tried to get in touch with her. We left messages. She never answered. I'm sorry."

The news accompanied my father home. It sat on his shoulders when he went out to the studio. It raced around the room as he smeared gobs of paint onto a canvas with his hands. Whatever had happened, it wasn't good. He considered calling Annie for information but decided against it. He had done what he could.

"What happened to the girl in the wheelchair? Her name is Sara." It was five minutes later, and Dad had Annie on the phone.

"Bob, you know I can't give out personal information on patients."

"She was going to choreograph a Fall dance at the High School of Performing Arts. She never showed up."

"Please…"

"Just tell me she didn't do anything crazy, that she didn't hurt herself."

"…I can't."

Dad sagged. He forced himself not to say another word.

"Bob? Would you like come over?"

Dad nodded. "Yes."

"Have you eaten?"

Had he? "No."

"I'll make you supper."

"You don't cook."

"I make good scrambled eggs."

My father arrived at Annie's apartment in New Haven with oil paint still on his arms and face and in his hair.

"You're a mess," said Annie.

"I know."

"How about a bath?"

Annie drew the bath. She helped Dad undress. Once he was in, she took soap and a cloth and kneeling next to the tub, began to wash him.

"Why do you feel it's your job to save people?"

"Let's talk about it another time." The warm water felt wearying. Or maybe it was Dad who was weary, and the bath was drawing it out of him.

"You can't save the world, Bob. You can only try to improve it."

Dad nodded, then sighed. "It's just been one of those days."

"Mmm." Annie rinsed the washcloth. "I tell my patients there are days that can be like that. Know what else I say?"

"What?"

Plush!

Holding the wet washcloth over my father's head, Annie squeezed soapy water down onto his face. "Deal with it."

(Laughter. It makes all the difference in the world.)

"Remind me again how I shouldn't be afraid to express my feelings," said Dad.

"You're officially reminded."

Robert Boone said nothing, hoping his face said it all.

"Me too," said Annie. "Me too."

The scrambled eggs were over seasoned and undercooked but, in the end, were very good.

Sort of like the day.

*

"Hey, how you doing?"

My father found her at the corner of Grove and Orchard Street in New Haven, sitting on what looked like the same soiled blankets and holding the same small sign – *I may be fat but I'm still hungry.* Pulling to the curb, he got out, walked over to her and knelt. The woman blinked at him in surprise.

"I'm okay." The voice was tranquil.

"You have people looking out for you?"

The woman gave Dad a small, mysterious smile. "They try. I like my independence." The woman peered at him. She smiled. "I remember you."

"And I remember you. What's your name?"

"Nancy."

"Nancy, I'm Bob." Dad reached into the pocket of his jeans and pulled out some folded bills. Taking the woman's hand, he put them into her palms and closed her fingers around them. "You take this." He patted her hand. "I'll be checking in."

Nancy smiled again. Her round, red cheeks glowed. "It's nice to see your real face."

"It's nice to see yours."

Rising, my father walked back to the pick-up, started it up and with a last wave, went home to paint.

It was getting easier every day. The rooms in the house were filled with voices. Voices telling Robert Boone that to be an artist, you had to love and that to love, you had to be an artist.

Robert Boone

From Wikipedia, the free encyclopedia

Robert Boone is a prolific American artist known for his range and versatility. His work is rooted in both classical and modernist traditions. Theatrical contrasts of light and color are the mark of his realistic images while other work shows the fierce influence of both fauvism and abstract expressionism.

Early life and education

Robert Boone was born in New Haven, Connecticut July 3rd, 1974. His father, Benjamin, was a successful lawyer and his mother, Mary, an illustrator of children's books. The family resided in Branford, Connecticut where Robert first attended public school and began drawing and painting at an early age. In 1986, Boone's mother, Mary and his two sisters, Melissa, 16 and Karen, 12, were killed in a car accident, victims of a drunk driver. Robert Boone has said the accident and its aftermath effected much of his early life and work.

Robert Boone attended the private Choate School in Wallingford, Connecticut from 1987 to 1991. In 1991 he was accepted at the Rhode Island School of Design. He left after one year citing "an apathy for academia." For the next three years, he commuted on a weekly basis from Connecticut to New York City where he attended classes at The Art Students League, working with different teachers. He has likened the experience to that of an apprentice's training in a renaissance workshop where young artists learned to paint by studying and copying the paintings made by other master artists. He has been a visiting instructor there since 2023.

Artistic Life

In 1995, Robert Boone was introduced to Carter Hurly who, upon seeing Boone's work, insisted on showing him at The Hurley Gallery in New York.

The now famous *ANGELS IN THE DARKNESS* are a series of paintings, based on Boone's mother and sisters; vividly realistic images of women and children, singularly and together, sometimes suggesting the idyllic and the divine, but most often in a physical state of agitation. The figures are set against a vast, fugue-like blackness. In contrast, *THE SOUND* series which debuted a year later, are depictions of the shorelines and islands of Eastern Connecticut, featuring rich color, masterful brushwork and bold contrasts of light and dark. Seven years later, the *AURA* paintings showed a complete change of technique. They were "action-paintings"—Boone has referred to them as "anger paintings"—which suggest the visual symptoms associated with pre-migraine auras. In 2022, The Hurley Gallery presented Robert Boone's esteemed *REMEMBERED* series. These were sketches and paintings of a beautiful, dark-haired woman, serenely facing the final stages of cancer. They were followed later the same year by the *DUST* paintings, highly stylized depictions of post 911 New York. In January 2023, Boone produced the *THOUGHT RECORDS* series; emotionally resonant paintings of people and subjects done in a multitude of styles ranging from realism to expressionism; "states of mind expressed in colors, figures, shape and line." A majority of these paintings were donated to individuals, museums and charitable organizations. Robert Boone is the illustrator of two acclaimed children's books, *The Boy Who Couldn't Walk Straight* and *The Wheelchair Dancer*, both written by his daughter, the novelist, Isolde Boone.

Personal Life

In 2022, Robert Boone established The Kristina Mendoza Foundation, an organization that donates art supplies and brings artists and instructors to Connecticut's inner-city schools and community centers. He is on the board of Community Art Ways, an organization that helps individuals of all ages engage with art and ideas and New Horizons, a charitable group that works to provide affordable housing and community support for families and individuals in need. He is married to the psychologist, Anne Gilmore, with whom he has a son, Benjamin Colin Boone.

References – The Hurley Gallery, New York, N.Y.

Printed in the USA
CPSIA information can be obtained
at www.ICGtesting.com
LVHW011353310723
753920LV00003B/93